Neanderthal

A HOT ROMANTIC COMEDY

A HOT ROMANTIC COMEDY

AVERY FLYNN

Entangled Publishing, LLC
10940 S Parker Rd
Suite 327
Parker, CO 80134
rights@entangledpublishing.com

Amara is an imprint of Entangled Publishing, LLC.

Edited by Liz Pelletier
Cover design by Bree Archer
Cover photography by Wander Aguiar
Ranta Images/GettyImages

Manufactured in the United States of America

First Edition October 2021

an imprint of Entangled Publishing LLC

At Entangled, we want our readers to be well-informed. If you would like to know if this book contains any elements that might be of concern for you, please check the book's webpage for details.

https://entangledpublishing.com/books/neanderthal

To Kim and Robin who, after a decade of friendship, still haven't figured out how to block my texts even though I send them pictures of creepy things I find on Etsy, pissed-off diatribes, and videos of hairless cats feeding their weird-looking kittens that they swear give them nightmares. You two are stone-cold weirdos and I love you.

Chapter One

Griff Beckett had lost the art of conversation sometime around middle school, when his legit genius dad took every opportunity to tell him how stupid he sounded every time he opened his mouth. But honestly, he'd never understood everyone's love of flapping their gums in the first place. You could solve so many more problems if you just kept your trap shut and focused on the solutions.

Which was why he was currently doing his favorite thing: juggling fifteen problems at once.

Straddling the narrow wood bench in the locker room at Vera's Gym, two phones and an iPad laid out in front of him while fellow gym rats talked loudly and gave each other shit as they changed or showered, Griff Beckett was a man dealing with ninety-nine problems and solving all of them—except one.

The holdup wasn't on the solution to the seating chart disaster for the next Beckett Cosmetics family stockholder meeting that his cousins, Nash and Dixon, were debating via group text. That one was easy: hold the damn thing via Zoom and everyone gets a front-row seat.

It wasn't the hiccups about the protective packaging measures for the new line of serums launching next year that his deputy at the Beckett Cosmetics R&D Department had just emailed about. Keeping the serums on dry ice would meet the temperature requirements and give marketing that visual pop they were always after.

Questions about the best bidding strategy to get the rare vintage Lego set off eBay (swooping in at the last moment was always the best option) or just how much to up his hops percentage for his next home brew (a solid 23 percent) or whether to add hot yoga to his workout routine (he was going to sweat his balls off, but yes) were a blip on his mental radar.

"Heads up!" someone yelled.

He barely glanced over before shooting his hand into the air and catching the half-filled water bottle in midair.

"Sorry," one of the newer guys said. "I meant for that to go into recycling."

Griff didn't answer, just adjusted the trajectory and sent it flying. It landed in the blue bin with a *thunk*.

The phone closest to him buzzed with an incoming text.

DIXON: *You're up, Griff. Don't let Nash win.*

Yeah. *That* was the problem he couldn't quite unwind.

The Last Man Standing bet. How in the hell was he supposed to get through six dates with a stranger when he barely felt comfortable talking to people he *did* know? He was going to have to make small talk and do the whole *getting to know you* chatter?

Kill him fucking now.

Another buzz.

NASH: *Don't get his hopes up. He doesn't have a chance. Anyway, my mom just did G's reading. All she would say is that love chooses you and he's been chosen.*

Great. Now Aunt Celeste was doing tarot readings about this hell bet? It just kept getting worse.

The whole bet was ridiculous. The stupidest thing he'd ever agreed to do. So why had he done it? Because Grandma Betty's death last year had sucker punched him right in the kidneys and followed up with a rusty shiv to the jugular.

Summers with his cousins and Grandma at Gable House had saved him growing up.

There was no one like Grandma Betty, and when she'd died, she'd left behind one last gift for the oldest Beckett cousins who'd spent every summer with her as kids—the only snag being that she didn't specify whether it was for Dixon, Griff, or Nash. Nash was the one who'd come up with the Last Man Standing bet. Each of them had to go out on six Bramble dates, and the last man still single at the end of the year got the present. Agreeing had been a moment of sheer lunacy at the corner of the first Christmas without Grandma and way too much whiskey to be good for his liver.

Whatever was inside the box wrapped in fat-Santa paper with a huge silver bow on it wasn't important. That wasn't what had all three of them determined to win it. The fact was, it was from Grandma Betty, and it was one last memory they'd have of her. So, bet or not, he was in it to win it. Lucky for him, he had an advantage neither of his cousins had.

Cold, hard logic. Love only caused problems; it never solved them.

GRIFF: *You're both assholes.*

DIXON: *Am I supposed to disagree with that?*

The alert dinged on his iPad. Thirty seconds to go on the auction. He updated his bid, waited, and smiled when the notification popped up that he'd won the first edition Lego Taj Mahal. It had almost six thousand pieces, was still in the sealed box, and was the perfect addition to his collection. He couldn't fucking wait to build it.

Another text made his phone buzz.

NASH: *You agreed to the bet fair and square, Griff. It's mano a mano time since Dixon went down in flames of luuuuuve.*

The jackass drew out the last word like a character in a campy movie, which was appropriate considering the ridiculousness of the bet they'd all agreed to. Of all the probability scenarios he'd run when Nash had proposed it, Dixon falling in love with the first woman to answer his Bramble bio had happened in less than a percentage of them. And yet, here they were, with Dixon acting like he'd won by losing and Nash as smug as if his winning was a given.

Well, Nash was about to find out how wrong he was.

GRIFF: *You don't stand a chance.*

He grabbed his work phone and finished the email with the packaging solution to his number two. No doubt she'd take it (yes, and make it better) and come up with something the marketing folks would get all hand-clapping giddy about.

His other phone vibrated with his cousin's reply.

NASH: *You're only saying that because you haven't seen your dating bio yet.*

After the shit Dixon had pulled when he'd tried to bend the odds of staying forever single in his favor with a shit dating bio, Nash had added an addendum to the rules. Not that

Dixon's attempt at subterfuge had worked. He was currently coupled up with Fiona Hartigan and counting the days until they were walking to the altar.

DIXON: *It's a work of fucking art.*

NASH: *Morgan helped.*

Griff ground his molars down another few millimeters. What the hell? His sister had joined in on this farce? Of course she had. As soon as she'd heard about the bet, she'd probably rubbed her hands together with absolute glee the way only a younger sibling could do.

GRIFF: *Text it.*

He waited a second, then the bio popped up.
He read it.
Then he read it again.
He had a full-body cringe all the way down to his nuts, which had all but crawled up inside his body. His cousins were such dicks, and Morgan was buying at their weekly lunch for the foreseeable future.

Strong and Silent Type No More

Want to talk for hours about everything under the sun? Looking forward to a guy who really wants to deep dive into feelings and emotions? Ready to settle back and just enjoy doing nothing but living in the moment for hours on end? Reforming Neanderthal type seeks extrovert for conversation and love.

Just when he'd thought this whole Last Man Standing bet couldn't get worse. Emotions? Feelings? Small talk? Doing nothing? LOVE?!? This was pure nightmare fuel. Were they trying to sabotage the bet in his favor? There was no way this would fly. He was not that guy. He'd *never* be that guy.

NASH: *I was ready to go another direction, but Morgan convinced me that this would be your downfall. Get ready to fall for the yin to your yang.*

GRIFF: *Not gonna happen.*

DIXON: *Morgan says this is the kind of woman you need in your life.*

Yeah. No. This was how to send him over the edge.

He liked his life. He had his job. He had his million and one hobbies. He had his family. He didn't need anything or anyone else. Additional variables would just complicate things. Griff was a simple man—not simple in the head like his father had always told him, but content. That was enough. He didn't need anything—or anyone—else.

GRIFF: *My little sister doesn't know what she's talking about.*

NASH: *Wow. More than four words at a time? You're getting chattier by the moment.*

GRIFF: *Dickheads.*

DIXON: *Back to one-word answers, huh?*

He was going to kill Dixon for putting him in the position where Nash got to write his bio as well as plan all his dates.

NASH: *Like it or not, this is your dating bio. You have to post it.*

GRIFF: *I'm at the gym.*

DIXON: *So?*

He checked the time on the digital clock above the locker room door. It never had the right time, but it was the only clock his corner man Eggsy would use—and according to it, Griff had seventy-five seconds to get out to the ring.

GRIFF: *Hard to text and box at the same time.*

NASH: *And yet you're texting right now.*

GRIFF: *eBay auction. Just won.*

He got up from the bench and opened the locker that had been his at Vera's Gym for the past ten years. It didn't have a lock or personal photos—only his name written in black Sharpie on a piece of beige masking tape stuck to the front of the door. His phone buzzed again.

NASH: *Post the Bramble bio.*

GRIFF: *Gotta go.*

He put both phones and the iPad in his locker and grabbed his boxing gloves. Avoidance was not a solution but, at the moment, it was the only one he had.

He'd figure out the answer to winning the bet without talking about his feelings for six dates; he always did. And nothing was going to change that.

Chapter Two

Kinsey Dalton was going to puke.

Not literally, but the uncomfortable rumble in her belly was definitely there.

"There is no way you can live here," her formerly-online-and-now-in-real-life-too friend Morgan said for the tenth time—not coincidentally the exact same number of apartments available to rent at outrageous prices that they'd toured so far today. "The toilet is in the kitchen!"

Kinsey's whole body clenched with revulsion as she tried to keep the sweet-as-pie smile on her face from crumbling like dry pastry crust.

She sneaked a peek at the landlord standing in the doorway to see if he'd caught Morgan's true-but-better-kept-to-herself statement. Lucky for them, his attention was fully focused on his phone screen and the soccer match playing on it. If he'd heard, he didn't seem to care—unlike his thoughts about how Manchester United was doing.

Still, the fact that he hadn't noticed didn't matter. Her home training alert system had kicked in. Meemaw had drilled manners into her with the strenuousness that could only come from a seventy-year-old who still mowed her own lawn, canned her fruits and veggies the old-fashioned way, and had taken in her wayward daughter's three kids when the law caught up to her—again. Talking shit about an apartment with the landlord *right there* definitely would have landed on the do-not-do side of the ledger.

"But look at the window. It's south facing, so the light will be great," she said, focusing on the first possible positive thing she spotted in the otherwise very questionable apartment. It only took a few steps from the toilet of infamy to look through the pane and onto the trash-strewn plot of weeds surrounded by a chain-link fence bearing a No TRESPASSING sign. "It's practically a park."

"Yeah, maybe if the light is just right and you've been hit in the head with a brick," the other woman said.

Rounding her eyes, she sent Morgan a pointed hey-shut-your-mouth look as she tilted her head toward the landlord. Morgan just pointed at the toilet, which was literally right next to the fridge without even a half wall between them. On the other side of the toilet was the glass wall of the shower. Yes. That was right. One entire wall of the studio apartment was kitchen cabinets, the sink, the world's skinniest fridge, the toilet, and finally the shower—all of which looked out onto the living room/bedroom and the window overlooking the very much not a park.

"Okay, it's not ideal," Kinsey said with a shoulder-drooping sigh, already eyeballing the space in front of the toilet and shower for a ceiling-to-floor curtain that could give a little privacy and slow down the free flow of airborne bacteria. "But I start my new job on Monday, and I want to live within walking distance, since I don't have a car and don't want to waste work time on multiple trains—which means living in Harbor City's expensive downtown area. Sadly, this is all I can afford." She spun in place, taking in the full majesty of exactly how little a dollar went in the city, and shrugged. "Besides, I'll be spending so much time at work, I'll hardly even be here."

Maybe she could make it the entire term of her lease without using the bathroom.

Probably not, but a woman had to have dreams in addition to working her way up from her current job of entry-level skin-care scientist to someday becoming head of research and development at Archambeau Cosmetics.

Morgan lifted an eyebrow and slid her gaze over to the toilet. "Honey," she said, settling her gaze on Kinsey again. "This is almost as bad as the five-floor walk-up with the mysterious goo on every window ledge."

Yeah, that place had been scary. Meemaw definitely would have pulled on her bright-yellow plastic cleaning gloves and broken out the small emergency bottle of bleach she carried in her purse—in a Ziploc bag stuffed with dryer sheets, of course, so neither the liquid nor smell would leak on the Baggie of peanuts sprinkled in Old Bay seasoning or the extra tube of watermelon-pink-colored lipstick she always had on her as well.

The kitchen-slash-bathroom was nasty as well, but Kinsey's options were limited. Finding an apartment in Harbor City was a total and complete racket.

Morgan strutted over in her mile-high heels and slung an arm across Kinsey's shoulders like she were her kid sister even though they were both twenty-five. "We can do this the long way or the short way," she said. "But either way, by the end of this conversation, you're coming to live with me until you can find something that isn't this."

One look at Morgan's face was all it took to confirm

she was sincere. The woman had the poker face of a toddler looking at a pilfered handful of Pixy Stix. It really was a sweet offer. One Kinsey shouldn't agree to.

After being a part of the same online planner group for the past year and a half, when Morgan had found out Kinsey was moving to Harbor City for a job, she'd almost lost her mind with excitement. When Kinsey spilled that she was putting her PhD in pharmaceutical sciences to work in the R&D department at Archambeau Cosmetics, Morgan had called her immediately and had sworn her to secrecy in the planner group. That's when she'd found out that the bullet-journaling fiend and corgi-butt sticker aficionado was one of the Beckett Cosmetics heiresses (sadly, Archambeau's biggest competitor)—something Morgan really wanted to keep on the down-low with their group because people always treated her differently when they found out.

Now *that* Kinsey could understand—not because she was also in line for a billion-dollar fortune but because people loved to take one look at her and put her on the shelf as big-boobed blonde with bupkis for brains.

So she'd promised to never tell, and they'd made a million plans about what they'd do as soon as Kinsey got to Harbor City, including apartment hunting and lunch—but definitely not sponging off her mega-rich friend.

"I can't impose on you like that," Kinsey said.

"What imposition?" Morgan scoffed. "My place is big enough that we might not even see each other."

"But no toilet in your kitchen?" Kinsey teased. "How would I survive?"

Morgan laughed. "I have no clue what is actually in my kitchen, but I can guarantee there isn't a toilet in it."

The offer really was the nicest, but Kinsey's brain was going a million miles an hour pulling up all the other options and tossing them out one after the other in quick succession. Morgan was right—living here wasn't an option. Toilet kitchen notwithstanding, the rent was already over her budget. The walk-up could be cleaned, and it was cheaper, but it also meant a three-train trip to get to work. Morgan's place, though, was a fifteen-minute walk from Archambeau, and it would only be until she could find a better fit. It was the logical choice.

Still, it was a big ask for someone Morgan hadn't set actual in-person eyes on until yesterday.

"You barely know me," Kinsey said. "What if I'm the kind of person who hits snooze on a super-loud alarm clock forty-five times every morning?"

Morgan planted her hands on her hips and narrowed her bright-blue eyes. "We've been a part of our online planner group for two years and snarky DMing each other the whole time. I know you wear days-of-the-week panties."

Heat exploded in Kinsey's cheeks as her head whipped around to look at the landlord, who—thankfully—was just as entranced with the soccer match as he'd been before.

"You know I can't get pedicures because people touching my feet freaks me out, and you know that I didn't lose my virginity until last summer," Morgan continued, seemingly impervious to the idea that the landlord was literally six steps away and could probably hear every word. "Anyway, we're good enough friends that if you pulled that shit with snooze, I'd just smother you during your eight minutes of extra sleep."

"And what about the work thing?" Archambeau *was* the biggest competitor to Beckett Cosmetics's spot at the top of the luxury, privately owned cosmetics companies.

"Considering I have nothing to do with the family business, if you've chosen to befriend me in order to do some corporate spying for the Evil Empire—oops, I mean for Archambeau Cosmetics—then you've made a massive mistake."

"Morgan—"

"Nope." She raised her hand. "You sound just like my brother when you say my name like that. Speaking of which, his gym is just down the block from here, and he owes me brunch. Let's go drag him out of there. I need some eggs Benedict in my belly, then we can get you moved in"—she shot Kinsey a don't-even-think-about-arguing look—"to my place."

Chapter Three

Fifteen minutes later, Kinsey had exhausted every excuse not to move in with Morgan that she could come up with. "Is there a point in arguing with you?"

"Never." Morgan grinned wide enough to make her dimples sink a mile into her cheeks. "I always win."

Kinsey had no trouble believing that, or that she'd be moving her meager belongings into Morgan's apartment after lunch with her brother.

Walking into Vera's Gym, Kinsey was assaulted by the sensory overload of the place. As if Harbor City wasn't already enough of a shock to her country-homemade-biscuits-made-with-eight-sticks-of-butter soul, she had to add in a gym that Meemaw would have labeled as not fit for polite company.

"Are you sure it's okay that we're here?" she asked, feeling more out of place than she had when she'd walked into her first college chemistry course at fifteen.

"Why wouldn't it be?" Morgan asked, strutting in as if

she owned the place and no one would even dare to say boo to her, which they probably wouldn't.

Kinsey, wide-eyed and sending every silent hey-girl signal she could with her blue eyes, gestured at the scarred-up wooden benches in front of the banged-up metal lockers, the punching bags hanging from chains hooked to the ceiling and patched up with duct tape, and the bald guy with very aggressive fire-engine-red eyebrows chomping on an unlit cigar while eyeballing them as if sizing them up for dinner—to gobble them up, not for a date. Two guys were arguing over no-carbs versus low-carb diets during training. Meanwhile, another was fighting with a mop that kept getting caught in the wringer as he stood in front of what she was really hoping wasn't a bloodstain on the cement floor.

All of this on top of the echoes of gloves thwumping against flesh and the corresponding grunts of men of all sizes sparring in the huge space, the humidity of sweaty men you couldn't miss with every breath you took, and the occasional squeak of laced-up boxing boots pivoting on rubber boxing rings.

It was noisy and smelly and an overload of the senses and, although not entirely unpleasant, holy hell it was a lot of testosterone to take in all at once. Kinsey struggled to sort out all the different compounds, break them into discrete elements. It was a habit she'd developed in that first college course as she navigated an unknown adult world as a mere teenager. If you knew what made up the confusion, it wouldn't be overwhelming. Life was just a giant chemistry set to Kinsey.

Morgan scoffed. "They're all a bunch of kittens."

Kinsey looked around at the guys working out by beating the crap out of each other and barely-keeping-it-together punching bags. Kittens? No. Feral barn cats on meth? Quite possibly.

"Which one's your brother?" she asked.

"That one." Morgan pointed at the ring in the middle of the room where two guys were going at it while a third stood, forearms resting on the top rope and yelling about keeping hands up and minding footwork.

He was a wiry guy with dark hair a little on the long side, light-brown skin, a nose that obviously had been broken a time or twelve, and more freckles than Meemaw had Thomas Kincade puzzles glued together, framed, and hung on the walls of her house.

Trying to block out the guy who was now cursing as he yanked on the mop handle and the Bickerman twins who'd moved on to who was the best lightweight boxer of all time, all while the back of her neck prickled from the cigar-chomping creeper still watching her from behind the desk, Kinsey squinted, trying to see the family resemblance between the guy pacing outside the ropes and Morgan. As far as she could tell, there wasn't even a smidgen of resemblance beyond the hair color.

"The dark-haired guy is your brother? You guys don't look much alike," she said.

"No, not Eggsy," Morgan said with a roll of her eyes. "Griff's in the blue trunks."

There was only one guy in blue shorts in the middle of the ring. He was wearing one of those padded-headgear things on his head with hair the same shade of dark brown as Morgan's sticking out from the top and a snarl that could be seen for miles. He had tats going up both arms and covering most of his muscular back, tree-trunk legs, and was definitely tall enough to reach the stuff way back on the top shelf in the grocery store without going up on his tiptoes.

She shot Morgan a questioning look, but the other woman just grinned, showing how much she was loving her big reveal. "Knowing Griff, he'll be done sparring—or more accurately his partner will be begging to stop—in about ten minutes. Then brunch!"

The sound of a punch landing jerked her attention back to the ring, specifically at the giant in the navy boxing trunks.

She winced when he landed a hard right jab followed by an equally ferocious uppercut that sent the guy he was sparring with back a few steps. There was a beauty to the violence, an elegance of movement that she'd never linked to boxing before, despite the fact that Meemaw never missed a televised fight night.

It was as if the whole world shrank down into the give and take of the two men in the ring. It was something to soak in, to study as if it were a chain of peptides—which was exactly why the continuing background racket had her ready to snap. She couldn't concentrate on dissecting the two boxers' moves with the distractions behind her. Didn't they realize she needed to focus?

Like they'd heard her, the two arguing men grew silent for a beat, and Kinsey sighed. Excellent. Blue Trunks sent another jab-jab-punch combo, weight on his left leg, pivot, dodge, jab-jab. It was almost like a ballet, and Kinsey couldn't get enough of watching.

But then Humpty and Dumpty moved on to debating the best *Great British Bake Off* hosts, the guy with the mop gave the metal bucket a loud kick, and Cigar Man rounded the front desk and started right for her, a leer on his face that he probably thought looked debonair.

And she knew she had to quiet the noise or she was going to miss the rest of the sparring match.

"You two," she said, pointing at the gym's two-person debate team. "First, carbs are necessary for your body to function, so don't skip them. Second, Roberto Durán was the best even before he beat Sugar Ray, and no one has come close since. Third, there is absolutely no doubt that Mel and

Sue get the cake stand when it comes to *GBBO* hosts."

She marched over to the mop bucket, jiggled the wringer handle. "Apply less force and the spring will adjust more easily." And then she handed the now-free mop to the man, whose eyes were as wide as his jaw agape.

Then she whirled around and glared at Cigar Man. "And you—you need to learn that women are not what's for dinner, so stop eyeballing us like perfectly cooked steak before I put a fork in you and call you done."

She glanced around at the four men with their jaws hanging open and said, "Can't you all see I'm trying to watch a boxing match?" She let out a deep breath, feeling every bit like an Instant Pot after the steam vent switch had been flipped.

"Hey, Griff!" Morgan called out, grinning at her. "I brought Kinsey by."

"She's got a lot to say," he said, his voice garbled a bit by his mouth guard as he continued to jab-jab and dance around the ring.

He was shiny with sweat and had a red mark on his right cheek that promised a bruise sometime real soon. She didn't know whether to smile or wave hi or pray the floor would open up and swallow her whole for her own safety because she could do things with that man. Bad things. Good bad things. The *best* good bad things.

"Well, I'm right. There's just no way anyone can beat Mel and Sue." The words flowed out, even as Kinsey tried to stop them—but when she was on a roll, they just didn't. "I mean, sure, change is constant, but if you look at the joke per aired minute—not to mention the quality of the preshow skits— versus the heartwarming moments that make the show, there's no comparison."

Heat flushed her cheeks because everyone but Morgan— and her brother's opponent—was staring at her as if she'd grown a second head, but the words kept coming.

"Mel and Sue were a stronger heartbeat for the show. That's just all there is. Plus, if you quantify the awkward cringe factor for the bakers when they interact with the current hosts, it's much higher until at least the fourth episode than it ever was with Mel and Sue."

Finally out of breath, Kinsey had to pause just as Morgan's brother turned his head.

His gaze paused on his sister long enough for him to lift his chin in acknowledgment before moving on and landing on her.

Ho-lee sheeeeet.

The sizzle in his blue-eyed look zinged right through her with such heat that she lost her grip on her purse strap slung over her shoulder as if she'd been burned.

Griff started to lower his gloved hands, his intense focus on her, and took a step toward the ropes.

While he was in the ring.

With another fighter.

And the bell hadn't been rung.

What would happen next all unfolded in her mind in rapid flashes of understanding. "Watch out!"

Her mouth was slower than Griff's sparring partner's right hook, though. It landed with a hard thump against Griff's jaw. The bottom half of his mouth went one direction while the rest of his head stayed still. He stumbled back on his heels, gloves still chest high instead of blocking his head from another punch. It came on the next breath. A vicious shot to the head that knocked Griff off-balance and down to the mat.

Oh. Shit.

Chapter Four

While countering Mac's hard jabs and right hooks in the ring, Griff had been unwinding the details of how he was going to rearrange his Lego room to best display the Taj Mahal when he completed it. There were pros and cons to moving the Death Star closer to the Millennium Falcon, and he had been working through them when a woman's voice cut into all the noise in his head.

All the background racket stilled.

Mac's punches shifted into slow motion.

It was just this voice, thick like honey barbecue sauce with a snap of something tart in it to balance out all that sweet.

He delivered a swift one-two combination that had Mac back on his heels just so he could listen to that voice. Thirty seconds. Tops. That's all it took for her to silence Eddie and Phil, who'd been having the same three debates every day for the past week and a half (she was correct on all three counts, even if the argument could be made for Manny Pacquiao) and put Eggsy's shithead friend Wade in his place. Hell, it probably wasn't the first time someone had threatened—or wanted—to stab Wade with a fork, but it still had probably moved the asshole back to his spot behind the front desk. Griff had planned on telling Tommy what he was doing wrong with the mop bucket as soon as his match was over, so she beat him to the punch there as well.

Whoever she was, this woman was someone special, and out of all the gyms in Harbor City, she'd chosen him—no, his gym, not him. Aunt Celeste and her tarot readings were not influencing his thinking on this. Hell, he hadn't even had a chance to turn and check out the woman the voice belonged to yet—or her ring finger. Not that he gave a shit about that, of course, because he was happily staying single.

"Hey, Griff!" his sister called out, ending the silent spell and bringing all of the noise crowding his head back into play. "I brought Kinsey by."

He muttered a few words that were practically a six-page monologue for him while his brain tried to unravel what it was about that woman that clicked with him. Then she went into a no-doubt-about-it monologue about *The Great British Bake Off* hosts, and everything clicked. Her logic was impeccable. Her defense of her position passionate. Her diatribe was lengthy but fucking fascinating.

Time seemed to stop.

Everything went silent.

He was already at the altar before he'd even seen her.

It took only as long as his inhale to have all the details about Morgan's friend fall into place. Country bumpkin who was new to town. Working for the enemy. The closest person his all-acquaintances-and-few-friends sister had to a bestie.

On the exhale, he glanced over at Morgan, and then for the first time his attention traveled over to the woman next to her. The one who had Wade looking sheepishly at her while

Eddie and Phil were in awe. The voice, it had been her.

It was like there was a blast of lightning from the heavens followed by a crack of thunder that shook him down to the soles of his boxing shoes.

It wasn't until he was on his way to the mat that Griff realized it had actually been Mac's fist crashing into his jaw with enough power to lay him out flat right in front of the woman he was going to marry.

Way to make a first impression, dumb-ass.

Chapter Five

Kinsey and Morgan sprinted to the ring. Kinsey's hands pressed to the springier-than-expected mat, her heart hammering against her ribs as she stayed on the outside of the ropes as close as possible to where Griff fell while Morgan did her damnedest to practically hurdle the three rungs and get to her brother.

Griff's long, thick eyelashes rested against his cheeks. For once, Kinsey didn't know what to do. Call 911? Flag down a cop? Scream for a medic? Shut up and stay out of the way? In the ring, Morgan was shooting daggers at the wiry guy who had gotten to Griff first.

Eggsy smacked a palm against Griff's cheek. "Stop being so dramatic, Beckett. Get up."

Kinsey glared up at the other man. Had he not heard of concussions?

Griff groaned, a sound that made it seem as if he were half dead—or wished he was, then opened his eyes and sat up. "What the fuck happened?"

"You dropped your hands like a dumb-ass." The other guy let out a disgusted snort. "If I didn't know any better, I'd think it was your first time in the ring. Rookie fucking mistake."

Griff's gaze landed on Kinsey again, and all the haziness went out of it. A zing of awareness zipped through her, settling low in her gently rounded belly. For a woman who was never at a loss for words or gonna turn down a second order of Meemaw's biscuits—thigh cellulite be damned—she couldn't put together a string of thoughts right now.

"Not a mistake," Griff said, still looking right at her.

"Oh, you meant to let Mac knock you on your ass?" the other man asked with enough sarcasm to slather on a pork chop.

The question seemed to take a second to register, but once it did, he sat up and rolled his neck. "Never doubt that I have a plan."

"Yeah, well, how about instead, you have a care for that ugly fucking mug of yours and keep your damn hands up," the man grumbled as he stood from his crouch over Griff. "Losing my biggest investor would be hell on my business."

"You know what would be worse?" Morgan asked, jabbing a finger into the other man's chest. "Imagine dealing with me on a mission to make your life hell because my brother got hurt."

There were more threats, promises, and dire warnings, but Kinsey didn't hear them because Griff turned and locked his focus back on her again. His eyes were the same violet-tinged blue color as the wild blueberries that grew on bushes in the backyard at Meemaw's place, and looking away wasn't an option even if she'd wanted to.

"Fuck me," he said in that low, rough voice of his that made her want to purr as he got up, rubbing his jaw and shaking his head. Then his gaze landed on her face again before dropping down to her hands clasped together in front of her, and his expression went from fierce to granite. "Shit. You're a fuckin' disaster."

His proclamation stopped her cold.

A disaster?

They'd just met, and he had already declared *her* a disaster?

After being the youngest person in Caldwell County to graduate high school, *she* was going to be a disaster?

After putting in the work to get a full academic ride to the University of Virginia and graduating at the top of her class while pulling overnight shifts to cover room and board, *she* was going to be a disaster?

After getting her master's in pharmaceuticals and drug delivery systems and then going straight into earning her PhD in pharmaceutical sciences while carrying a teaching course load and helping Meemaw take care of Kinsey's brother and sister, *she* was going to be a disaster?

Her?

Nope.

Not even in a month of Sundays was she gonna be that, but that didn't mean his words didn't hit like a linebacker on college football Saturday. After everything that Morgan had said about her big brother, Kinsey had pictured someone who wouldn't be like the others. Who wouldn't take one look at her, clock the blond hair, her age, her gender, and the fact that she was a woman who believed that lipstick and mascara really could make her day better, and then place her on the not-to-be-taken-seriously shelf.

Still, if there was one thing Kinsey had learned from her meemaw, killing them with kindness still meant they'd end up dead.

Kinsey batted her fake eyelashes and curled her lips

into her best sugar-I'm-gonna-poison-your-sweet-tea smile. "Well, I guess I'll just have to prove you wrong."

People just loved to underestimate her. Let them. She was about to go all Southern Fried Elle Woods on Harbor City. Griff Beckett was about to find out how *not* a disaster she could be.

Chapter Six

Griff had never been so happy to be knocked on his ass.

His jaw ached. His ears were ringing. He'd have to listen to Mac brag about this for months while Eggsy bitched about it for a millennium.

Worth it.

He'd just met the woman he was going to marry.

The realization had hit him harder than Mac's punch the second he'd heard her set everyone in the gym straight. It was an unexplainable feeling, a sense of surety so deep, so right that it had wound its way into his DNA. This was it. Bam! There might as well have been a beam of light shining down from heaven and a full-on orchestra playing the "Bridal Chorus." When he'd glanced at her and taken in the electricity in her intelligent eyes, he knew he was a total goner.

Fuck Nash's stupid Last Man Standing bet.

He was halfway through mentally rearranging his closet so she'd have more than enough room for all her clothes when he caught the murder gleaming in Kinsey's eyes.

He stopped. Rolled back a few minutes. Replayed. And... Fuck, he never wished he was a man good with his words more than right now.

But he'd already opened his mouth, fucking himself over into oblivion, judging by the look on Kinsey's face that said she'd already mapped out where his spleen was and had a rusty spoon at the ready.

That was okay. He could outthink a problem like her plotting his death.

"I didn't mean it." At least not like it came out.

"Really?" She scoffed. "Or is it that you didn't mean to say it out loud?" She crossed her arms. "I graduated at the top of my class."

"I know." He'd done a quick check on her after Morgan had mentioned Kinsey was moving to Harbor City to work for the Evil Empire. He couldn't be too careful where his baby sister was concerned.

"My doctoral adviser said mine was the most put-together defense he'd ever seen."

"I'm aware." He'd talked to Dr. Pearson himself. Okay, Pearson had talked; Griff had grunted.

"I am *not* a disaster," Kinsey said, her voice shaking by the time the last word was out.

"I agree," he said as he pulled off his boxing gloves.

Her blue eyes were the exact same color as their bestselling All Night Moisturizer serum. This was where Aunt Celeste would have told him the universe was speaking to him. He wouldn't have believed her—at least not before.

As soon as he took off his headgear, he noticed the difference again. The quiet. The absolute stillness inside his head—not emptiness, but stillness. It was like all the constant buzz of ideas and thoughts and energy that was the reason why he only slept four hours a night and kept up a million and one hobbies had mellowed into a low-level thrum instead of bouncing around his brain like balls in a plastic ball pit.

And it was all because of her.

His brain was still running ninety miles an hour—but only in one direction. Toward this woman. God, he'd fucked this up. How could he convince her he was even worth a second chance—and not use words to do it? How could he beg her to keep talking? The more she talked, the more his mind was able to block out everything else as he focused on her logic, the flow of her arguments, the swiftness of her sharp conclusions. It was the sexiest thing in the world.

Kinsey shot him a syrupy smile he didn't buy for an instant. "Glad to hear it."

But she didn't believe it. There was no missing that.

He gave a grunt of a reply because his brain was working overtime trying to find a way out of this mess he'd made of things. He'd fucked up. That was 100 percent clear. What he'd meant was that he had absolutely no clue how to get someone to fall in love with him; he was a lost cause at speaking to women, let alone charming them.

Now, in addition to his natural grunty ineptitude, he had to figure out how to get Kinsey to stop eyeballing him as if she was going to fillet him and feed him inch by inch to a hammerhead shark.

Morgan, unfortunately, chose that second to stop her usual pick-a-fight moment with Eggsy and turned her attention to him. Sandwiching his face between her two hands, she turned his head from one side to the other while looking up at him.

"How many of me are you seeing?" his sister asked.

"Too many," he grumbled, mind still working through his plan to win over Kinsey, who really was beyond out of his league, if he was being honest.

Morgan rolled her eyes and dropped her hands. "You're

being your usual super-talkative self, so you must be okay."

"I'm fine." Well, he would be as soon as he got home to his whiteboard and could start mapping out the details of his plan. He loved his little sister, but she was a giant pain in his ass, and there was no way she was done giving him shit yet.

"Kinsey, meet my oh-so-talkative brother, Griff," Morgan said as she lounged against the ropes. "Griff, meet Kinsey. She's staying with me until she finds a place she likes. Can you believe she was gonna live in an apartment with a toilet in the kitchen? I told her, real estate in Harbor City is a cutthroat game—she cannot get stuck in a situation where she has to go with the first acceptable place she finds in her price range."

He grunted, mind already spitting out ideas on how he could help her find the perfect place. That could get him in her good graces. If she liked her job—even if it was for the wrong cosmetics company—and liked the city, she'd be more open to staying here once they got married…if he could figure out how to talk to her, of course.

Was he getting too creepy?

Moving too fast?

Sure, they'd barely said two words, but as Aunt Celeste always said, when a person knew, they knew. Then she'd launch into the story of meeting Nash's dad. Five minutes of casual conversation on the train, and they hadn't separated since. Of course, five minutes of conversation with Griff was usually four minutes and thirty seconds too much, but for the first time in his life, he finally understood what his aunt had felt.

"Griiiiiiiiiiiiiiiff," Morgan said, putting every ounce of annoying little sister possible into groaning his name. "I told you she was coming. You had time to prepare actual words to say rather than your usual Neanderthal-grunting thing. I promise, she's not interested, so you don't have to worry about losing your bet with Nash and Dixon. Kinsey's engaged. So you're totally safe and single forever."

Too bad "safe" and "single" were the last things he wanted to be now that he'd met Kinsey.

It would be fine. He had this. All he had to do was get the woman who kept looking at him like she was ready to personally etch *Good Riddance* on his gravestone to fall in love with him. Probably using hand signals.

That's when his sister's words sank in, and it was like having Mac's fist connect with his jaw all over again.

He looked down at the gleaming diamond on Kinsey's left ring finger.

He. Was. Fucked.

Chapter Seven

GRIFF

Griff's hair was still wet. It stuck to the sides of his head, and a single line of water slow-dripped from his nape, ran down his neck, and snaked its way south along his spine. The feeling was almost as unnerving as sitting this close to Kinsey and not being able to say a damn word.

Not that he hadn't tried. It all came out as grunts or a handful of grumbled words. Talking around her was like trying to carry water cupped in his hand across the room—a lesson in futility.

So it was a silent movie on his side of the table while Morgan and Eggsy were yapping back and forth like the two main characters in a screwball comedy from the forties. Sure, those two were arguing per usual, but they were like that, always had been. Him? He'd always been like this, king of the mumblers. Most of the time, he was like that because he had 482 possible responses and couldn't figure out the right one to use. With Kinsey? He was just too fucking nervous that he'd say the dumbest thing and ruin any chance he had. Not that he had a chance.

Engaged.

Decent-size rock on her left ring finger.

It was a fake diamond, but still it was there, glinting in the light coming in from the big window next to their table. Outside, people were chatting away while he was sitting in the restaurant like his mouth had been glued shut.

He snuck a glance at Kinsey over the top of Wakin' Bacon's ten-page menu. Her blue eyes met his. His gaze dropped immediately back to the menu page showcasing the twenty-five types of waffles available (chocolate cherry for the win).

"How are the biscuits?" Kinsey asked, her attention still focused on the menu. "I mean, nothing can touch Meemaw's, but I've got a hankering."

It was like coming into a movie when it was three-fourths of the way through and being expected to know all the characters anyway. The challenge of it made some of the wayward strands of his thoughts thread together as he ran through the options. His closest guess was a cat, but that made no sense because cat-made biscuits were definitely not the kind served at a restaurant.

"Meemaw?" he asked.

"My grandma. She makes the best biscuits with enough butter in them to knock your heart straight outta your chest." Her eyes rounded and she winced, her face squishing up with regret. She reached out and covered his hand with hers and gave it a quick squeeze before releasing it. "Sorry, I know y'all lost your grandma recently. I shouldn't have brought it up."

"It's okay," he said, not wanting her to feel bad. He liked talking about Grandma Betty. Really, she'd be pissed if people stopped talking about her. She hadn't lived her life to be forgotten about. "You sent a pie."

It had been homemade and wrapped in a red-and-white-checked tea towel with a rooster embroidered on it.

"Mm-hmmm." Kinsey nodded as she put down her menu. "Sweet potato pecan. It fixes just about everything and, if it doesn't fix what's ailing you, at least it makes your belly feel good." She shook her head, sending her blond hair waving around her shoulders. "You do *not* want to know the fight I had with Earl at the post office about the fact that dry ice was not a liquid but that it was carbon dioxide in solid form and that it wouldn't melt, but that sublimation would take it straight from that Ziplocked chunk into a gas."

She leaned forward, her forearms on the table, the fire in her eyes snapping. "Plus, I'd met all the requirements for regulation three forty-nine in the postal code, but instead of seeing my logic, he just about threw a fit. You'd have thought I'd asked him the oxidation/reduction reagents of carbonyls and alcohols for an organic chemistry test. I was half tempted to tell him all about Carbon-13 NMR just to see the smoke come out of his ears, but then the postmaster came in, and she set him straight." She sat back, her grin big enough to show matching dimples on each side of her smile. "I know I shouldn't cause a scene, but good gravy, that was worth it."

Griff loved the way her brain worked, how it moved from one interconnected topic to another at lightning speed. There were a zillion questions he wanted to ask, details he needed to get about everything, from if she'd share the pie recipe to what regulation three forty-nine was (he'd look it up later).

Instead, all that came out was, "Thanks."

"For the pie?"

"For thinking of us." Grandma Betty had left behind a lot of people who loved her, and they'd hung together the best they could.

"Well, of course," she said, her dimples deepening a bit. "Morgan's my friend."

The light caught her ring as she tucked her blond hair behind her ear, taunting him with the realization that he was fucked. He'd met the woman he wanted to marry, and even if he could string together more than five words when talking to her, he was too late.

"You're engaged." Damn. Did he sound like Eeyore to her? Because he sure did to his own ears.

"Not exactly." Her gaze dropped, and her smile faltered just a bit. "It's a pre-engagement ring."

"Tell me more." About anything. He liked listening to her even if she could not, would not ever be his, because he was too fucking late and she was already engaged.

Her cheeks went pink as she fiddled with the napkin in her lap. "Todd lives in Canada. This cute little town in Alberta called Moose River, but someday—once our careers are settled—we'll get married."

Then she went back to looking at her menu, flipping the pages like it was a speed-reading contest. Something that felt a little bit like hope—of the fool's-gold variety, no doubt—had his mind going a million miles an hour. The woman could tell an in-depth story about mailing a pie but only a sentence or two about her almost fiancé? Griff had questions.

"How'd you meet?" Griff asked.

"Oh, you know, the regular way—online," she said, eyes glued to the menu. "We were both part of the same maple-syrup-aficionado group. Did you know most of the world's maple syrup is from Quebec?"

Now she did look up, setting her menu down next to the glass of water the server had dropped off a few minutes ago with a promise to return to take their orders. "They make nearly two-thirds of the maple syrup found across the globe. You know, people always say to cut down on syrup because it's unhealthy, but the real stuff is filled with antioxidants as well as zinc, magnesium, calcium, and potassium. When I told Meemaw, she swapped from the imitation stuff to the real thing, and I'm telling you right now, her pancakes were good before with all the butter-crisped edges, but you add on the syrup and it's like a whole new perspective on breakfast." She leaned in, and he couldn't resist leaning forward, too, as she lowered her voice. "The secret is to add a few tablespoons of real syrup to the batter. It will change your life, I'm telling you."

He was about to ask another question when the waitress stopped by and took their order. He would have sworn that Kinsey let out a relieved sigh at the interruption, and he ran through everything he'd said—mercifully few words—to see if he'd annoyed her again.

"All this chatting about syrup has me craving waffles," she said and turned her attention to the server. "I'll go with two of your extra-fluffy blueberry waffles with bacon and a side order of grits."

"Do you want a few sugar packets to go with your grits?" the waitress asked.

Kinsey gasped, her palm going up to press against her heart. "No, thank you."

Griff had no clue what that was all about. He always mixed a packet of sugar in his grits—okay, fine, he mixed in three packets.

As soon as the waitress left with their orders, he was ready to ask more about this almost fiancé of hers, but before he could say anything, she was out of her seat with an "I'll be right back" and was headed toward the door with the restrooms sign hanging above it.

"She's the best," Morgan said, shooting her brother a look that dared him to disagree. "Don't you just love her?"

Griff didn't say anything out loud, but the answer was definitely yes.

Chapter Eight

Lying was like eating a pizza roll straight out of the oven—it felt satisfying for a second, but then it was like having a mouth full of piping hot lava—and Kinsey's mouth was burning up.

Stupid Todd.

Stupid fake Todd from Moose River, Alberta.

Stupid Moose River that is actually a river in Ontario and not a town at all.

Wait a minute. Moose River was actually kinda cool with its bird sanctuary and Polar Bear Express train flag stop.

Okay, so how about stupid Kinsey Dalton for fabricating a fake almost fiancé three years ago and bringing his syrup-loving made-up butt along with her to Harbor City?

Yeah, that was definitely a yes.

Guilt at lying to Griff, who might be (totally was) a big jerk for calling her a disaster swirled around inside her. Meemaw had raised her better than that. Lying was lying, even if it was for a good reason. Most of the time, people didn't ask for details about Todd, so it felt less like lying than just letting folks believe what they wanted to—which was what they always did anyway when it came to her.

Rationalize much?

Blocking out the annoying voice of truth in her head, Kinsey made a beeline for the bathroom but came to a dead stop in front of the large standalone pastry display case.

It was opened up, and pieces and parts were everywhere. A string of curses and a few metal-on-metal bangs came from behind the behemoth. She could relate. This same model was sitting next to the counter at the diner back home. Kinsey had done her fair share of cussing out the evil thing under her breath while working as a waitress when she was home for summer break during college.

"Is it the capacitor?" she asked, naming the number one culprit that had killed the display case's ability to cool the contents back home.

There was something super sad about a key lime pie with formerly stiff peaks of cream turned into sad little white pools.

A guy not much older than her with a snarly expression looked around the case, giving her a quick up-and-down—lingering for a few seconds too long on her boobs—before dismissing her without a word and going back behind the machine. She peeked around at what he was working on. She couldn't help it. Some weird inner compulsion mixed with the you-gotta-help-even-grumpy-strangers lessons Meemaw had drilled into her—second only to no white after Labor Day—drove her forward. It would be easier to turn down fresh-made country gravy or crispy fat than to keep her mouth shut when she'd lay one-hundred-to-one odds that it was the evil capacitor.

She took a step closer, not rounding the case *exactly* but getting as close to that as possible. "We have one just like this back home, and that capacitor is worse than sweet tea made with agave syrup. My cousin tried that once. He nearly got run out of town."

"Look," the man said without even glancing up. "I don't know what you overheard your dad or brother or whoever saying, sweetheart, but you don't know anything about this. Go on back to the land of Barbie. I've got this."

Sweetheart? Land of Barbie?

Kinsey came from the home of calling everyone "sugar" or "honey" or "sweet child," but this was different. "Sweetheart" wasn't being used as an endearment. It was a dismissal. And anyway, Barbie had been an astronaut, a computer programmer, and more. Hell, she had the scientist Barbie still in the box on display in her room at Meemaw's house.

She should walk away.

She should let him spend the next forty-five minutes trying out everything but the one thing that would no doubt fix it.

She— Fuck, who was she kidding?

"Really?" Two and a half decades of home training was the only thing keeping the smile on her face as she gave it one last shot. "So the compressor runs normally after you short-circuited the display?"

The man stilled. "No."

"Then I imagine with my tiny little girl brain that you checked to see if both electricity poles are working?"

Okay, Meemaw would have shot her *the look* for that little bit about her brain, but a woman could only take so much before her sass outweighed her sugar.

"It's a defective relay," the man said, sounding way less than 100 percent sure as he looked up at her.

"So the relay electricity isn't flowing?"

He winced.

"Uh…" He looked down at the gauge in his hand, his confident expression morphing into annoyance. "Shit."

"Defective capacitor," they said at the same time.

He let out a deep sigh and stood up, a little more sheepish than he'd been a minute ago. "Thanks."

"This machine will drive you to the edge and then poke you until you jump off," she said with a genuine grin this time. "The pie will be safe—that's what matters."

"Maybe we could share a piece to make up for my being an asshole?" He rubbed the white towel in his hand against the back of his neck as his gaze moved down to her hand. "Or not."

"Yeah," Griff said from behind her, the sound of his voice making her heart speed up. "Not."

Kinsey whipped around to see Griff standing a few steps away, his arms crossed over his massive chest and a look on his face that could only be translated to I'm-gonna-floss-with-your-bones.

What in the blue blazes was that all about? He didn't know Todd and, even if Todd were real, there was no reason for Griff to go all territorial on someone else's behalf.

Ugh. Men.

"Thanks for the capacitor tip," the man said, already sinking back down behind the display case to finish the repair job. "I'll remember that next time."

Well, at least two good things had come out of this. One, the pies were saved. Two, Griff got to see how wrong he'd been about her. Did disasters fix refrigeration equipment?

"Just happy to help," she said. She kept her smile in place but let it drop from her eyes as she lowered her voice so only Griff would hear. "See, cavemen not required here."

Then she whirled around, chin held high, and walked straight into the bathroom, letting the door shut behind her without looking back at him even once.

But the temptation to see if he reacted to her calling him a caveman? Oh boy, it had her buzzing more than a shot from the jug of lightning water Meemaw put out for the grown folks during the Fourth of July fireworks.

Because as much as Griffin Beckett was sexy as sin, one disaster comment aside, what was far sexier was that he asked her questions and then *listened* to her answers. Not one time did he interrupt her or tell her she was talking too much or decide what she had to say wasn't as important as something he wanted to say. Whether she talked about syrup or complex carbon bonds, that man had listening down to an art.

For a woman who was too often ignored for her words because of her looks, it was quite literally the sexiest thing in the world. The tatted arms and intense jawline were just whipped cream on his pecan pie.

Which was why she just had to ignore him. He was her best friend and soon-to-be roommate's brother, and he thought she was an engaged disaster. So ignoring him was her only choice.

How hard would that be? It wasn't like they'd be hanging out together.

Chapter Nine

By the time Kinsey and Morgan got back home—well, Kinsey's temporary home until she could find one with an actual functioning bathroom not next to the oven—Kinsey had had all the Griff she wanted.

Liar.

The know-it-all voice in her head could just hush its mouth already.

So what if she'd enjoyed sitting across from him at brunch. It was a one-time-only meal. And he had big hands. If she would have ordered the colossal bacon, egg, and cheese bagel, she would have had to cut it in half or double fist it while Griff practically looked like he was eating those tiny little sandwiches with the crusts cut off. Okay, so that was an exaggeration, but his hands were big, with long, thick fingers.

The man could definitely palm a gallon of milk.

It was distracting.

It put thoughts she had no business thinking in her head.

It was exactly the type of information she did *not* need to have about a man who labeled her a disaster the first time he'd set eyes on her—which was exactly why she'd forgotten all about him the second they'd walked out of the restaurant. Okay, definitely during the Uber across town to Morgan's place. All right, fine, she was still thinking about him even during the tour of Morgan's amazing apartment that took up half the top floor of the Hilltop Building and had amazing views of the harbor from every window they'd passed by so far.

She followed Morgan down the hall on the opposite side of the living room from Morgan's room.

"So this," Morgan said as she opened the door and walked through, "is your room."

Okay. Now this zapped thoughts of Griff and his tattoos and his big hands and his shy grin right out of her head.

This wasn't a room. It was a suite, complete with sitting area, separate bedroom, and a bathroom with a tub that had a view of the harbor. It. Was. Stunning.

"Morgan, I can't stay here for free." Meemaw had not raised her to take advantage of her friends.

"Why not? It's just sitting empty otherwise," Morgan said with a shrug. "Anyway, when Todd gets a free weekend, you'll want to be able to have your couple space without me crowding in on you."

Kinsey's gut twisted up tighter than the thick braids Meemaw used to tie her hair into as a kid that could withstand a whole day of running around like a hoyden without a single strand coming loose. By the time she'd taken them out at the end of the day, her scalp had pulsed with relief. Eight-year-olds weren't meant to have hair pulled back so hard it looked like they'd had a face-lift—any more than friends who opened up their hearts and their homes didn't deserve to be lied to.

"Morgan, I have to tell you something."

"Oh, this sounds juicy." She clapped her hands together

with glee and sat down on the black velvet love seat. "Tell me everything."

Time to rip off the Band-Aid and just do it.

One.

Two.

Three.

"I'm not engaged."

Morgan ran her hand over the smooth velvet as she nodded in agreement. "Right, it's a pre-engagement situation."

"No." Kinsey sat down on the other end of the love seat, her guilt sparking like a live wire and making her entire body tense up with pain. "Todd doesn't exist. I made him up."

Morgan's eyes went wide, then widened up some more when she let out a gasp. "Why?"

"It seemed like a good idea at the time?" Damn, saying that out loud had her cringing. What in the fuck had she done?

Taking a deep breath, she tried to get her mind straight and to list out some of the eighty million factors that had gone into her decision to fabricate Todd. "When I walk into a lab, I'm already working at a disadvantage when it comes to being taken seriously. I'm a woman in a male-dominated field. People take one look at me and decide at first glance that I've got to be lost. I'm younger than everyone else there. I've got this whole blond-bumpkin thing going on with how I look and my accent."

She let out a shaky breath. She'd never said any of this out loud before—not only because she was ashamed but also because even though she was smart enough to graduate at the top of her college class, she hadn't been able to find a solution to changing the way other people thought about her.

"No one takes me seriously. I can't control any of that. Added to that, at my last internship, one of the guys kept hitting on me, and so I made up Todd. And just like that, not going to lie, all the men in the lab started paying more attention to what I had to say more than what I wore to work that day."

As soon as she'd put on the ring, the number of overt and covert leering glances in the lab had been cut down by at least 60 percent. Her stress levels had gone down. Her productivity had increased because she could just walk into the lab and work. Just. Work.

"How long have you been"—Morgan put air quotes around the word—"'with' Todd?"

Kinsey wanted to disappear into the dark cushions of the couch. "Only a year, but when I interviewed for the job with Archambeau, I realized that one of the R&D scientists here knew someone there. Long story short, those two started talking, and news of my fiancé made it up to Harbor City, and I can't just come out and admit that I made him up or I'll look like a total dumb-ass—which, for the record, I am."

Morgan's eyes went wide. "Oh my God, Kinsey!"

"I know," she groaned, dropping her head with embarrassment, heat eating its way up from her chest until her cheeks blazed. "I don't just bust out and tell people about him. They see the ring. They make more assumptions—this time ones I'm pointing them to. It's only if there are direct questions that I say anything about it."

Morgan scooted closer on the love seat and threw her arms around Kinsey's shoulders. "That's a long way to say you're lying because you couldn't see any other option."

"Ugh." Kinsey didn't deserve her friend's understanding. "I'm an asshole."

"News flash, a woman not being taken seriously by the patriarchy is not, well, breaking news." She gave Kinsey's shoulders a squeeze. "You aren't hurting anyone with this. It's just—"

"Weird?" Kinsey finished for her. "Lame? Ridiculous?"

"Not at all, but watching my brother glare at your ring all brunch is even funnier now," Morgan said through her giggles.

"Oh, that's not what he was glaring at," Kinsey denied. She knew exactly what had upset Griff. "We ran into each other near the bathrooms, and I called him a caveman."

Morgan's eyebrows shot into her hairline before she burst into another round of laughter. "You. Did. Not." She grabbed her side as she tried to get her laughing under control. "Oh my God, you can live here as long as you want rent-free for that. My brother is amazing, but his grunting gets on everyone's nerves after a while."

Now Kinsey felt bad. She actually liked his short answers. "It wasn't because of how little he talks. I mean, that was kind of great. It was—"

"You actually liked his powerful response to my asking whether he was interested in going to a play next month? I mean, 'intriguing'?" Morgan rolled her eyes. "I still don't know if I should buy us tickets or not. So frustrating!"

But beneath the frustration, Kinsey could see Morgan absolutely adored her brother. So she commiserated. "Yeah, I can see how that response could be a pain. But he seems like the kind of guy to know how to say no, so I took his response as an enthusiastic yes. A caveman yes, if you will."

She winked at Morgan, and they both laughed.

But Kinsey sobered then. "I think we need to find a way to lose Todd before the lie grows more here, you know? I want this to be your forever home in Harbor City, and that's hard to do when you're worried about getting caught in a lie, I'd bet."

She wasn't wrong. It was all of that and Kinsey knew it, had known it. "I just need to get established in my new job and prove to them that I belong there, and then Todd and I can break up or something."

"Sounds like a plan," Morgan said, giving her a final squeeze.

"So you don't hate me for being a giant fake?"

Morgan shook her head. "Nah."

"And you won't spill the beans?" The cosmetics industry was big, but people talked. "I mean, I'm not asking you to lie, just not to say anything. I need a few months to get settled, and then I promise, Todd and my relationship will meet an untimely demise."

"I can agree to that, but I am gonna need a favor."

Relief flooded through Kinsey, and her shoulders sank down from up by her ears. "Anything."

"Come to dinner with me tonight at my cousin Dixon's place."

"Sure." That was easy. "You don't think he'll mind?"

"I think Fiona will be thrilled to have another pair of X chromosomes there."

"But why do you want *me* there?"

"Because then Griff won't start hollering at me about Eggsy."

Kinsey cocked her head. Her brain worked pretty quickly, but she couldn't make the connection. "I don't see how I can stop that."

"He's so chatty around you that he won't have time to chew me out for yelling at his trainer." Morgan bounded up from the love seat and did a hip-shaking happy dance as she made her way toward the bedroom door. "This will be perfect. I'll owe you forever."

Then she was out the door and down the hall before Kinsey got a chance to ask a single question about dress code, what she should bring, or anything else. Truth be told, she was stuck on Griff being "chatty" around her. That had to be sarcasm, since the man basically just grunted at her with a few short sentences for variety. There was no other explanation.

A few hours and every single box she'd brought with her unpacked and broken down ready for recycling, Kinsey followed Morgan out the front door of her apartment and stopped dead. There, directly across the hall, standing in the open doorway of *his* apartment was Griff.

"You live here, too?" The no-shit-Sherlock question was out of her mouth before her brain could catch up.

"Well, technically he *owns* this whole floor," Morgan said. She crossed to the elevator. "That door at the end of the hall by your room? It connects the apartments together just in case we ever decide to sell it as one giant penthouse. Don't worry, we keep it locked on both sides."

Yeah, safety wasn't what Kinsey's brain was getting caught on about the door to Griff's place being right next to her room. Her *bed*room. Nope. That was way down the line right after about a billion dirty thoughts about Griff's tattoos, his muscles, the way his voice would sound when he told her all the things he wanted to do with her as he kissed his way—

Kinsey Anne Dalton!

A quiet beep sounded, and the elevator doors opened up. Morgan stepped inside, but meanwhile Kinsey was still standing in front of the closed door of her new temporary home and her feet were refusing to work. She took a deep breath as discreetly as possible and did her best to pull herself back together when she felt as out of place as salt in the sugar bowl.

Oh God, what had she done?

She was living next door to temptation, and that was just as bad as living in the shitty apartment with the toilet in the kitchen—well, almost. Either way, she felt like a woman who was going to be caught out in the open with her drawers down.

"You ready?" he asked, holding the door to the open elevator for her.

No. She most definitely was not ready for whatever was coming next.

Chapter Ten

Kinsey was here at Dixon's house, talking to everyone and having a grand old time, while all Griff could do was stand on the edge of the living room and scowl while scrolling through the work email on his phone.

Of course, he still clocked the way she laughed at all the right spots when Dixon told her about being chased by Grandma Betty's attack goose at Gable House. While he shot off a quick emailed response to a question about the latest test results for a new line of hydrating lipstick, he couldn't help but notice how she heaped praise on Morgan for helping her pick out the perfect bottle of wine to bring to dinner and confessed that she came from more of a moonshine and sweet tea family. Then, when she and Dixon's fiancée, Fiona, bonded over the importance of STEM education for elementary students, he ignored the incoming text from his dad and shut out everything else but Kinsey.

Normally, this would be where all the pieces clicked

together, quick and easy to create a solution. This time? Yeah, he had a better chance of getting Nash to stop talking for twenty-four hours than to make sense of the situation with Kinsey and how he'd been so fucking wrong about love.

He'd done his research. Lust was simply a chemical reaction, a twin hit of dopamine and norepinephrine, followed by a wave of serotonin and then the release of oxytocin and vasopressin to seal the deal. That's what people were talking about when they said they were in love. They were only putting a life-complicating societal construct on top of what was simply biology. At least, that's what he'd thought until Kinsey Dalton walked into his gym and he knew the second he'd heard her go general on three grown men that she was the one for him—the woman he hadn't even realized he'd been waiting for.

Caught completely unprepared, he had no plan, no ideas, and no fucking clue. What was he supposed to do when he'd finally met "the one" and not only was she engaged already, but he couldn't talk to her even if she were single and flirting her perfect ass off with him? He was an idiot.

A second text notification from his dad flashed across his screen.

Right on time to remind me what an idiot I am, Pops? His dad had won a Nobel Prize in chemistry at the age of forty-two, and to say he was self-important would be an understatement. He loved nothing better than to point out how Griff was wasting what little intelligence he'd inherited from his father on barbecue sauce and Lego sets. It was everything in Griff not to remind his father that he also managed *all* of R&D for the most innovative cosmetics company in the world.

Knowing he'd regret it, but that it was better than floundering for solutions to a problem that didn't have any, he tapped the notification.

DAD: *The state of affairs Morgan has created for herself is vexatious.*

Jesus. And to think half his DNA was from this pompous asshole. Griff looked up from the screen, his gaze catching Kinsey's. That same shock of awareness that had thrown him at the gym when he'd heard her the first time hit him again, making his jaw ache all over, as if Mac had just landed that bone breaker of a punch a second time.

She smiled at him, and everything went fucking haywire. It was like his brain sent the signal to his mouth to turn up at the corners, but instead his body said *fuck that noise* and he jerked his head down so fast, his chin almost hit his chest.

DAD: *Hello? Are you there? Is your silence because of a question about the definition of the words I used or do you disagree?*

The message had Griff grinding his teeth. Just because he chose not to use it didn't mean he didn't *have* a fucking world-class vocabulary. It was so typical of his dad when he was drinking. The insults that sliced right through any of Griff's defenses. The declarations about the stupidity of everyone who wasn't Holden Beckett. The inserting himself into everyone else's business with the intent to force people into living the way he wanted. Still, Griff and Morgan were all the bitter old man had left, so Griff pulverized his molars and maintained limited contact, mostly via text.

Shoving aside the urge to ignore what was no doubt a rye-fueled stewing session, Griff started to type out a response in hopes that all the old man needed was to vent, and then he wouldn't sling his poison at Morgan.

GRIFF: *What situation and why are you concerned?*

DAD: *This new roommate of hers. It's highly*

unusual that someone your sister just met is invited to live with her. Is this a flimflam? Have you conducted a thorough background check?

It was as if their dad had never met his daughter. Morgan was impulsive and headstrong in all caps with a soft heart for everyone and everything. She was exactly the kind of person who would share an apartment with a stranger. Kinsey, however, was no stranger.

GRIFF: *She's known Kinsey for years.*

DAD: *Online. That's not real.*

GRIFF: *Bullshit.*

The throb started behind his right eye, the one that always seemed to make an appearance whenever he talked to his dad.

DAD: *Cursing is the last resort of the intellectually lacking.*

He forced out a long breath as he counted to ten and loosened his white-knuckled grip on the phone before letting himself answer.

GRIFF: *Is there a point to this conversation?*

DAD: *You should be watching over your sister.*

He let out a pained groan as his temples got in on the throbbing in his eye. He should have known better. No good ever came from responding to his dad's texts. The only thing worse would be to visit the family home upstate in person so that he could see his dad drunk enough that he stood at such a tilt that he nearly tipped over. The man was brilliant, a stone-cold genius—even now, when his brain was pickled, he was the smartest person Griff had ever met.

He was also an asshole who wanted to control Griff and Morgan as if they were still children.

GRIFF: *Kinsey's a grown woman.*

DAD: *Exactly.*

He didn't even know how to process that level of misogyny. That was four-hundred-course level of patronizing patriarchy even for their dad, who excelled at it so much that Griff didn't even have to put any effort into hearing his dad voice a million unwelcome thoughts in that vein.

There was the time he got off an airplane because, when the pilot came over the intercom to welcome everyone aboard the flight, it was a woman's voice. Then there was the time he told Grandma Betty, his mother-in-law, that it was unseemly for his son to work in the family business because cosmetics were for women and beneath a real scientist's intellect.

Of course, all those digs and barbs lost some of their sting whenever Griff remembered that Dad had agreed to become a Beckett at the wedding and let his children carry the Beckett last name instead of his own last name because no Beckett last name meant no access to the Beckett family funds. The man was a complete prick, but he was also a greedy prick, and he wanted money to pay for his research without being beholden to a university or corporation.

Not that it mattered now. The only research Dad had conducted since their mom had died a decade ago was into the numbing effects of rye whiskey on bitter regret.

GRIFF: *Bye, Dad.*

He pocketed his phone. It vibrated, but he wasn't going to look at it again. The old man could go fuck himself right about now. Pulse pounding through his head as irritation scraped him raw, he rubbed the back of his neck, needing to feel the sharp sting of it to yank him back from the edge.

For as long as he could remember, interactions with his dad always ended with Griff needing to run off the anger or pound away on a hanging bag to get all the frustration out of his system. Some people said divorce was bad for the children. Those people hadn't grown up with Holden Beckett as a father.

Demanding.

Never satisfied.

Intense to the nth degree.

Nothing and no one was ever good enough for Dad. Divorce would have been a fucking blessing. Instead, their mom had stuck it out, thinking she was protecting them. Then there'd been the accident that hadn't been an accident, and he and Morgan had been left alone with an angry drunk who loved to carve out little pieces of them bit by bit.

Clenching his jaw to stop himself from screaming into the void, he looked over and caught Kinsey watching him. She didn't blush at being caught staring; she didn't even look away. Instead, she lifted an eyebrow in question as if to ask if he was all right, and just like that, the tension in his shoulders eased and the last echoes of his father's voice in his head faded away.

It didn't make sense, but that didn't make it any less true.

He was halfway across the room, heading straight for Kinsey before he realized it. A hand on his arm stopped him.

Nash stared at him as if Nash had been five minutes into one of his monologues and Griff hadn't grunted at the appropriate intervals. "Earth to Griff."

"What?" he asked, unable to keep the annoyance at being stopped out of his voice.

"The Bramble bio," Nash said, oblivious to or not

intimidated by Griff's perma-snarl. "Have you posted it yet?"

Figuring it was the easiest way to get out of this conversation and over to Kinsey, Griff took out his phone, ignored the fifteen new texts from his dad, opened the dating site's app, and posted the bio. "Yes."

Nash grinned. "And so it begins."

His cousin could enjoy the moment all he wanted. It didn't matter, because the woman Griff wanted was unavailable and out of the question. He was so fucked, and the bet with his cousins was the least of it.

Chapter Eleven

Dinner was controlled chaos per usual.

Dixon and Fiona sat at one end of the table, two chairs squeezed together where normally only one would go. They were practically half in each other's laps and neither seemed to mind; they'd been like that since Dixon had admitted last month that he'd lost the bet for Grandma's present.

Nash sat bracketed by his little sister and brother, Bristol and Macon. The three were doing that thing they always did when they were together, where it seemed like they were in the middle of two conversations at once—one that was spoken, because none of the trio ever stopped long enough to take in a full breath, and the other through meaningful looks and raised eyebrows, because not a single one of that line of Becketts could keep what they were thinking off their faces.

On the other side of the table, Morgan and Kinsey sat next to each other. Kinsey was telling Morgan about an artist she'd found on Etsy who would customize stickers for their planners. From his spot at the end of the table, opposite Dixon and Fiona, he had the ideal view of everyone at the table, but his gaze kept going back to Kinsey. Her hands were going a mile a minute, emphasizing certain words as she talked, even as her slow Southern drawl could barely keep up. It was mesmerizing.

"So Griff is about to go down in our bet," Nash announced to the table. "I promise to accept my win with all the humility you have grown to expect from me."

"Which is basically none," Bristol said in a stage whisper that was loud enough to be heard across the harbor in Waterbury. "And nothing is guaranteed, no matter what Mom says."

Nash shrugged. "He posted the bio. It's all over but the woman responding to his Bramble profile part."

"The bio I helped you with?" Morgan, her eyes almost as big as the bowl of pasta Bolognese in front of her, whipped her head around to look at Griff. "You didn't change it?"

"No point." He shrugged and kept eating—the Bolognese was really that good.

Plus, he knew his family. They'd do more than enough talking without his input, and it would all get them to the same point: him going out on six dates and not falling in love.

No matter who it was, he wasn't going to fall for his Bramble date. Kinsey, engaged or not, was the only woman for him. That he was too late to even have a chance with her was as painful as having a belly full of battery acid. Another guy would have ignored the ring and gone ahead and won her over with charm. But Griff? Yeah, that wasn't going to happen. He couldn't say more than four words to her, let alone sweet talk her into having second thoughts about her engagement, even if that wasn't a total dick move—which it was.

Kinsey's fiancé was probably the man of her dreams, and

he was just her friend's nearly silent older brother who had to go out on six dates with a stranger.

"Now we all just sit back," Dixon said, leaning in his chair and putting his hands behind his head, "and wait for Griff to get swept off his feet."

Morgan let out a harsh, derisive laugh. "By someone who wants to talk about their feelings and do nothing but sit around for hours and zone out? That bio was so bad because it was supposed to spur him into writing his own. Nash, we talked about this. We had a plan. You can't take a straight drive at him. You have to nudge him where you want him to go, like he's a sheep."

Griff took another bite of pasta, unsure if he should be more offended by his sister's misguided manipulation or the fact that she'd just called him a sheep.

"It doesn't matter now," Nash said. "Mom says the cards are in his favor. It's his time."

Next to Nash, his brother, Macon, let out a tortured groan. "You can't believe Mom about that stuff. She doesn't even know how to read tarot right."

"I offered to sign her up for a class," Bristol added. "She rolled her eyes and said the cards speak to her in a way that can't be taught."

"I believe her," Nash said in one of the most succinct sentences he'd ever uttered.

"Nash, you've lost it," Bristol said, shaking her head. "Do you remember the time she told me a yellow dog was carrying an important message for me and to be on the lookout for malevolent bluebirds?"

After that, everyone at the table shared their Aunt Celeste stories because before tarot, it had been crystals, and before that, it had been astrology, and the time before that, it had been a year of silent meditation that had lasted about two hours. Everyone was talking over one another, laughing and correcting each other's versions of one of Aunt Celeste's predictions. The din quieted, though, the second he locked eyes with Kinsey. Her full pink lips were curled into a small smile that he returned without even thinking about it. The fact that none of the muscles in his face cracked at the unusual arrangement should have shocked him, but he was too fascinated with the wow-they-are-a-lot-huh look on her face to have any reaction at all.

"Oh my God, we're being such assholes. Kinsey doesn't even know what's going on." Morgan turned to her. "Sorry. This is all about a bet our idiot brothers—and Dixon—made."

"We're not idiots," Dixon and Nash said at the same time.

Griff kept his mouth shut—one, because it's what he did, and two, because they *were* idiots.

"You are," all the younger siblings said at the same time.

As she refilled Kinsey's wineglass and her own, Morgan launched into an explanation. "When Grandma Betty passed away, she left one last present. All we know is that it is for one of the older cousins, but she didn't say which one."

"Of course, these three saw that as an invitation to make a bet about who would be the last man standing," Bristol said, continuing the story as she held up her glass to Morgan for a refill. "Hello, toxic masculinity and immaturity."

The women at the table ignored the guys' protests.

"The last man standing?" Kinsey asked. "Do I want to know?"

"No, but I'll tell you anyway," Morgan said. "These three decided that the last one of them who isn't in love by this Christmas gets the present."

"What is it?" Kinsey asked.

"That's the thing," Fiona chimed in with a disbelieving shake of her head. "They don't even know."

"But here they are, filling out Bramble dating app bios and going on six dates with the first woman to answer their ads to prove to one another that they can't fall in love," Bristol said, tilting her wineglass in Dixon's direction. "He went first."

Fiona snuggled in closer to Dixon. "And was the first to lose, because he couldn't resist the Hartigan family charm."

"No, your family I could resist," Dixon said with a grin. "You, however, were undeniable."

Kinsey turned to Griff, her eyes wide with shock and the corners of her mouth turned up in a teasing smile. "And you agreed to do this?"

He shrugged and swirled his fork in the pasta until he had a bite-size portion wound around the tines and took a bite.

"Six dates with the first woman to respond. And you can't scare her off by showing her your Legos," Nash said.

Griff pointed his fork at his cousin. "They are collectibles." And he had an entire room devoted to them with a special building table crafted just for him by a furniture builder in Vermont. The display shelves he'd put up himself, customizing them for the proper depth some of the bigger pieces needed. "Anyway, they relax me."

Dixon leaned forward on the table, his forearms going on either side of the pasta bowl he'd practically inhaled. "Well, they'll scare off any woman you show them to."

"Only the ones who aren't worth having," Kinsey said, drawing the attention of everyone at the table. Her cheeks turned a soft pink, but she maintained a steady gaze as she addressed his family. "Hobbies are important and have been shown to benefit people's stress levels and moods. If someone doesn't get that, then you don't want them, because mental health and being accepted for who you are is important."

For once, his entire family was silent—even Nash.

For her part, Kinsey gave him a wink and then went back to eating her pasta.

Unable to keep his lips in their usual flat line, he sat back in his chair and grinned at the shocked faces of his family. They gave one another shit pretty much all the time—it was just what they did, and they didn't mean anything by it. Hell, he gave his cousins just as much shit as they gave him. Becketts were competitive, stubborn, and never gave anyone else the last word in an argument—but Kinsey had shut them all up without even raising her voice.

What a woman.

Nash was the first to recover. "Excellent point," he said. "I'll keep that in mind when I'm planning his first date."

"*He's* planning *your* dates?" Kinsey asked, making it sound like as much of a monumental nightmare as it was.

"It's more of a group effort," Dixon said. "We each get to plan three dates, and he can't wimp out or submarine any of them."

Nash lifted his glass. "To the end of Griff Beckett's life as a single man."

Every one of the people sitting around the table—including Kinsey—lifted their wineglass. He picked up his beer bottle, not willing to ruin the toast just because Nash was wrong. There was no way he'd fall for whoever responded to his Bramble profile, because that woman was never going to be Kinsey.

Chapter Twelve

Kinsey

The Becketts were awesome. Meemaw would love them. Kinsey's sisters would be all over Nash like he were chocolate and they were full-on PMSing. And Griff? Good Lord. That man was completely wrong for thinking she was a disaster, but that didn't mean her pheromones weren't reacting to him as if he was 100 percent right.

He'd caught her staring at him about a million times during dinner. One time, he'd even winked at her, one side of his full mouth going up in a completely unexpected teasing grin. Her totally-not-a-disaster response? A whole mouthful of water that went down the wrong pipe. Her gasping coughs had everyone at the table staring at her as Morgan whacked her on the back and told her to put her arms in the air. It had not been Kinsey's most shining moment.

Neither was dropping a forkful of twirled spaghetti into her lap when she heard that he was on the hunt for a date—not that he wanted one and not that she wanted to date him. She had fake Todd and the found-at-a-flea-market pre-engagement ring. She didn't date. She had priorities—getting established at work and folks taking her seriously despite her age and outward Southern-sorority-girl exterior. Until that happened, she had her fingers, a drawer full of toys, and a significant collection of female-gaze-centric erotica on her ereader.

Still, she was just now realizing that a whole lot of those stories centered around gruff, strong, and silent types. By a whole lot, she meant pretty much all of them, and oh my God, how in the *Great British Bake Off* was she supposed to know that that type of tatted-up, burly, quiet, and really-could-fill-out-a-lab-coat guy existed in real life?

Even more, that a prime example lived just on the other side of her bedroom wall?

Good gravy. She was surely gonna burn for all the dirty thoughts she was having right now, because the flames were already licking at all her most sensitive spots.

Lucky for her, when dinner ended, everyone gathered up their dishes and took them into Dixon and Fiona's kitchen. While everyone else filtered back out into the living room, Kinsey stayed behind with Fiona.

"Don't you worry about this," Kinsey said, taking up the prime spot by the sink. "I'll get everything loaded into the dishwasher."

And if by doing so, she could have fifteen minutes of alone time to get her shit together before she made an even bigger fool of herself because her friend's older brother flipped her switch and had her glowing like a bonfire on the beach, then that was a win-win situation if she'd ever seen one.

"Are you sure?" Fiona cocked her head to the side and lifted an eyebrow in obvious disbelief. "Dishes are the worst part of a dinner party."

Kinsey whipped one of the tea towels with the bright-red flowers off the oven handle and tied it around her waist, Meemaw-style. "It's the least I can do for showing up unexpected."

Fiona shook her head, sending her dark ponytail swinging from side to side. "You brought wine, and we love having you."

"Well, next time when I have an actual invitation to join you," Kinsey said, "I'll ignore your dishes. But tonight they're mine."

"You're very stubborn. You'll fit right in." Fiona took another look around the kitchen counters that were piled high with plates, glasses, pots, pans, and utensils galore. Just then, Dixon's voice raised above the din in the other room as he shouted for Fiona to get in there now before Nash forced him to bet their house away. "Oh boy, there's no telling what Dixon will do without me there to remind him he actually likes losing. Just leave this mess and I'll take care of it in the morning."

And with that, Fiona darted out of the room in search of her man, which was fine with Kinsey, since that meant she wasn't here to stop her from doing the dishes anyway. She glanced at the massive stack of dishes and murmured, "Let's see how many of you I can get clean before Fiona comes back and stops me."

"I'll help."

Kinsey didn't have to turn around to identify who had just walked into the kitchen. She did anyway. Griff stood in the doorway, his corded arms crossed over his snug-fitting T-shirt, his gaze firmly on Kinsey. Heat and awareness sizzled across her skin as sure as a touch.

"You don't have to."

"I know." He crossed the room and took the remaining tea towel off the oven handle. He stared at it for a second before holding it to his waist.

Yeah, there was no way that was gonna happen. If he'd been a swimmer with a narrow waist to go with broad shoulders and long arms, maybe it could work. However, Griff was built like a concrete wall—hard, thick, and covered in graffiti that Kinsey just wanted to trace her fingers over.

For science.

Finally, he tossed the towel over one shoulder and joined her at the sink.

Kinsey might have responded. She wasn't sure. The nervous energy bounding around inside her had her as jumpy as Meemaw after her fifth cup of coffee.

She had no idea what to say, so she turned on the faucet and started rinsing the wineglasses and setting them on the counter. Griff fell into step with her, taking the glasses and doing the elite Tetris required to fit a dinner party's worth of dishes into the dishwasher.

They'd gotten through the glasses and the pasta bowls in silence while laughter and good-natured shit talking filtered in from the living room when Griff cleared his throat and said, "You're not a disaster. I'm sorry."

"Okay, I'll bite—tell me more about how you came to this conclusion." Okay, sure. Meemaw was probably on her front porch right now and had some kind of psychic urge to reach out and smack Kinsey upside the head, but every woman had a right to get her snippy on after someone insulted her.

"I wasn't talking about you." He grabbed a massive stack of plates she'd just rinsed off and started slotting them into the dishwasher. "I mean, I was, but I didn't mean it like it came out." He stopped in mid-motion and looked over at her, determination and sincerity shining in his eyes. "You're not a disaster. I'm sorry."

Something in her chest fluttered, and her insides went a little gooey. It took her a second to realize that she'd been rinsing the same colander for the entirety of what for Griff was likely a whole speech. Yanking herself back to the task at hand, she set it on the counter for him.

Cheeks flushed and hands a little shaky, she took to scrubbing the saucepot with more effort than it needed. "That was a lot of words."

He grunted his agreement.

That whole caveman thing should have annoyed her. It didn't. It wasn't endearing, either. What she felt each time he did that little growly voice thing wasn't anything close to the kind of word someone's great aunt would use to describe a puppy. Nope, the way her heart was hammering in her chest and her palms were all sweaty? That was definitely not because she found Griff Beckett *endearing*.

Good gravy, she was messier than Meemaw's kitchen that time her sister's dog Parsnip got into the five Fourth of July blackberry pies cooling on the not-quite-high-enough-to-stop-a-determined-mutt counter. It had taken hours to get rid of all the partial purple paw prints—not to mention the bits of fruit that had somehow ended up on the ceiling.

"Thank you," she said, putting the rinsed pot on the counter and then picking up the pan with burned pancetta and dried sun-dried tomatoes stuck to it. "I accept your apology."

He gave another grunt, and she went to work trying to get up all the bits seemingly glued to the pan.

"Can I give it a try?" he asked, taking a step closer so they were hip-to-hip at the sink.

She handed him the pan and the plastic scrubber before moving a step over. The extra space didn't seem to make a difference in her awareness of him, though. It just gave her a better vantage point to admire the bright reds, blues, and greens of the boiling-flask tattoo on his arm, the liquid inside realistic enough that it seemed to swish from side to side as the muscles on his forearm moved. Above it, designed to fit into the smoke coming up from the flask, was a chemical formula. It disappeared under his sleeve before she could get enough information to figure out what it was a formula for.

"Are you using the dishes as an excuse to hide out from your family?" Kinsey asked, needing to start the conversation again before she got lost in the high-end artwork on his body.

Griff shrugged and put the pan in the dishwasher before shutting the door and starting it.

Wringing out the water from a fresh dishcloth that she'd grabbed off the stack on a shelf above the sink, she started wiping down the counters. Griff echoed her move and went to work on the tomato-sauce-splattered stovetop. It was mesmerizing to watch. He kept his entire attention on the task at hand, each move deliberate and precise. God, what would it be like to be the center of all that focused attention? The idea had her biting the inside of her cheek as she pocketed that thought for later.

"So that bet," she said, pulling back from the edge of completely inappropriate thoughts. "It sure is something."

He let out a low, growly sound of acknowledgment.

"So what's the bio say exactly?" Sure, it wasn't her business, but she was nothing if not completely and utterly curious.

He stopped and turned away from the stovetop to face her, his expression grim. "It's awful."

That reaction she'd been expecting. What she hadn't was Griff fishing his phone out of his front pocket and pulling up his Bramble bio so she could read it.

Talk for hours? Reforming Neanderthal? Oh, good gracious. Were they trying to kill him?

Deep dive into feelings and emotions? That one even made her feel icky.

Settle back and do nothing? The man couldn't even do nothing long enough to get through this dinner party.

She took a deep breath, suddenly having flashbacks to her first year in college when she was a braces-wearing fifteen-year-old and had tried to rush a sorority in an ill-figured attempt to better fit in at college. It had gone about as well as could be expected. There was no way she could let another human being go through that level of awkwardness if she could help. But what was the best way? The answer came as quickly as they usually did and, after grabbing her phone from her pocketbook sitting on the counter, it took all of forty-five seconds to download the Bramble app.

"Now to fill out my profile."

His eyes went wide, and he leaned in close, looking over her shoulder at her screen. "What are you doing?"

She typed out a quick bio. "Helping you."

"This is probably breaking the rules."

That gave her pause, and she hesitated, her thumb hovering over the Submit Profile button. The last thing she wanted was to make him lose the bet. "Okay, when you set up the bet, what was the rule about who you had to go out on a date with?"

He shook his head. "Just that it had to be the first person to respond."

"So nothing about it being a person you already knew or who knew about the bet?"

He made a grunt that her brain translated to no.

"Well, we don't have any time to waste, then." She hit Submit on her profile and then narrowed her search for matches to a ten-block radius. Griff's profile was third in her rotation. She hit Like and sent a message with a waving emoji, then grinned up at him. "Looks like you have a date."

His face was only inches from hers. Her mouth went dry, and her heart went into overdrive as the air thickened with promise.

Oh God. What in the hell had she done?

Chapter Thirteen

GRIFF

Griff was many things—stubborn, surly, and stuck in his ways—but he was not the type of guy to kiss someone in any kind of relationship, let alone someone who was engaged. He wasn't that type of asshole, but at the moment, he sure as hell wished he was.

Kinsey was so close. Literally, all he'd have to do was dip his head down and—

Yeah, shut the fuck up, brain, because it's not happening.

Shoving his fingers through his hair, he grumbled who the fuck knows what as he took a step back and then another and another until he was in the living room. As if they'd all been waiting for him, the Becketts—and soon-to-be-Beckett Fiona—turned as one and looked at him. He sucked in a breath, prepping for whatever the hell was about to happen next, and ripped off the Band-Aid.

"Kinsey responded to my ad," he said, already bracing for the onslaught that was sure to follow. "She's my date."

There was three seconds of shocked silence, and then the living room erupted with almost everyone talking at once.

"She's engaged," Bristol said, her eyes wide.

Morgan followed up a heartbeat later with, "You know her!"

"You set the whole thing up, you devious ass." Dixon chuckled. "I gotta admire it."

Before he could even open his mouth, Kinsey squeezed past him through the doorway and walked right into the eye of the hurricane.

"One, it was my idea," she said, her chin tilted upward just enough to let everyone know what to expect if they doubted her. "Two, there's nothing in the rules as I understand them that requires the date to be a stranger; please correct me if I'm wrong. Three, I am pre-engaged, and there's nothing in the rules about that, either. In the future, I'd suggest you take a more thorough consideration of what is and is not acceptable prior to the start of your bet's time frame."

It was like the gym all over again. Everyone just stood there with their jaws scraping the floor because Kinsey had wrapped the whole thing up with a few choice words in less time than it had taken for most everyone else to process the news.

"She's not wrong," Griff said, unable to stop himself from grinning at the unique situation of being the one Beckett not at a loss for words.

Fine. It wasn't nice to rub his cousin's face in it, but she had them both by the short hairs, and he was here for it.

"There are the rules and then there is *the spirit* of the rules," Dixon grumbled.

"Like Kinsey said," Griff added with a shrug, enjoying the moment way more than he probably had a right to. "You should have thought of that beforehand."

Fiona turned to her fiancé, her hands on her hips. "And are you really going to be poking your nose in it, Dixon Beckett, when you've already lost the bet?"

For a guy who'd always compared falling in love to losing out on life, it was obvious that Dixon had never been so glad as when he'd lost the bet and it showed in his face when he looked down at Fiona. "And thank God I did."

"Good recovery." She pushed herself up on her tiptoes and gave Dixon a quick kiss. "Really, if anyone has the right to be annoyed, though, it's Nash."

But Nash was just standing there in the corner, not saying a word while watching the rest of the room with a shit-eating grin on his face.

It only took a matter of seconds for Griff to realize Nash was up to something and whatever it was, Nash wasn't the least bit pissed off about the guarantee that he was about to lose the bet for Grandma Betty's last present. The only way that was possible was if something else was at play. For the entirety of their lives, the Beckett cousins had competed against one another. No matter if it was being king of the island at their grandma's house, racing her attack goose, or even getting the first choice of desserts, half of the joy of winning was beating out the other two. It wasn't that they didn't like one another, it was just the way they were.

But Nash didn't seem to give a rat's ass that there was no way Griff could lose now—which meant only one thing. Nash was up to something, and Griff and Dixon were just pawns. The question was, what was really going on?

The only other person in the room who was quiet was Morgan. Instead of hollering with the rest of the crowd, she simply topped off her glass of wine as she watched everyone else in the room freak out. Gut swirling, Griff watched as his sister's gaze slid over to Nash, and she raised her glass. Nash returned the toast.

Those two were without a doubt up to something, and the only thing he was certain of at this moment was that it was definitely going to fuck up his life.

Chapter Fourteen

The next morning, Kinsey was holding it together by the power of caffeine—thanks to Morgan's fancy coffee machine that made a double espresso from dark beans that smelled like heaven with the push of a button—and the adrenaline rush that came with her first day on the job.

God knew, she wasn't benefitting from the kind of refreshment that came from eight hours of uninterrupted snoozing. Nope. Her brain had been going as fast as Uncle Herbert that time the police had found him at his moonshine still—at least according to family legend—and every thought had centered around Griff Beckett. Okay, a few of them had been her wondering what in the hell she'd done by agreeing to date him, but really, wasn't that about him, too? If so, then yes, every one of her two-in-the-morning, panic-dosed-with-giddy-excitement thoughts had been about the hot guy living on the other side of her bedroom wall.

She'd wondered what he wore—if anything—to bed. Her

money was on slouchy and soft sleep pants. The kind that were covered in constellations or other cosmic scenes. No socks, though. No one with that amount of body muscle got cold feet in the middle of the night.

She'd thought about how he slept. On top of the covers? With the comforter pulled up to his chin? Two hands pressed together in prayer position under his cheek? Around one a.m., she'd settled on spread-eagle with his arms and legs flung wide in total starfish mode.

And in the morning? He'd eat half a dozen eggs— scrambled—whole-grain toast, four slices of turkey bacon, and a raspberry smoothie the size of her head that he made with Greek yogurt and a dollop of honey for extra sweetness.

Yep, that was the ultra-productive way she'd spent the night before her first day at a new job—her dream job—in the research lab at Archambeau Cosmetics. So when she rushed down the hall to the elevator, she might look completely put together in what she assumed was chic city wear—hair pulled back in a low ponytail, black shirt buttoned up to the neck, tailored black slacks, and cute black kitten heels—but her insides were a jumble of ill-fitting, clashing neon clown clothes topped off with a bleached brassy mullet.

As she waited for the elevator doors to close, she glanced down at the street map on her phone, double-checking that she'd memorized the order of the rights and lefts correctly. She was reconfirming for the eight millionth time that yes, she had it right—did that uncertain, first-day-of-school feeling ever go away?—when *he* walked in.

The elevator definitely wasn't big enough for the two of them. Well, okay, fine, the physical dimensions were sufficient, but the mental ones after the night she'd had were teeny-tiny-size. So what did she do to combat that? She put on her brightest, I'm-totally-comfortable-and-everything-is-perfect smile (it was the one she had learned early on to cover her nerves) and turned to face him as the doors closed.

"Good morning!" she said, her voice booming in the small space.

Aaaaand that was a billion on the a-little-much scale, what with the fact that her volume was way too loud and the amount of sunshine in her tone diabetic-coma-inducing. What was wrong with her? She was never like this. She was the calm one. The boring one. The stands-in-the-corner-and-silently-corrects-people's-grammar one. No, it wasn't a nice thing, but she'd learned to live with herself about it, and she kept her thoughts on "your" and "you're" to herself because Meemaw had raised her better than to embarrass people or hurt their feelings on purpose.

Credit to Griff, he didn't wince at her loudness—resting grump face for the win. "You're a morning person."

"And an afternoon person and evening person and a night person," she blathered on, unable to shut up for some reason. "Basically, until my head hits the pillow and I crash, I'm your person." Heat beat her cheeks the moment the words were out of her mouth and her brain caught up. "Well, not *yours*, but you know what I mean."

One side of his mouth *almost* curled upward. "Got it."

She clamped her lips closed before she could say anything else. Really, this was just not acceptable. Sure, she was Southern—which meant she was friendly and hospitable and okay, fine, chatty—but she didn't usually do this verbal-vomit thing. The truth was, she usually couldn't because at the first "y'all" people had already started to judge—something that was going to happen anyway, but why add to it? She'd learned that lesson the hard way. There was nothing like going to college before being old enough to get a driver's license to bring that lesson home. They all went out to frat parties, road-tripped to concerts, and drunk-dined at the local diners before crawling back to their beds. She'd stayed in the attic room of her meemaw's best friend, who'd given her a ten p.m. curfew and had activated the three-sixty-five tracking app on Kinsey's phone. Miss Eunice was nice and she made a mean potato salad, but it wasn't the college experience Kinsey had dreamed about as a naive and overly optimistic fifteen-year-old.

The elevator continued downward along with her hope that her experience at Archambeau would be different from college or grad school or getting her doctorate. It stopped every few floors to let folks on until she and Griff were tucked in tight together in the corner. He glanced down at her phone, which still had the street map on it, her walking path denoted by a bright-blue line.

"You're walking?" he asked, the low pitch of his voice ruffling the feathers of those birds in her stomach that liked to take flight around him.

"That was my plan," she said, sounding more confident than she felt. Left for two blocks, then right for three, and a quick left across the street to Archambeau's famed Onyx Caramello double doors that bathed the lobby in a golden glow. "It's only about fifteen minutes."

He looked down at her shoes, his mouth scrunching up as he took in the barely there heel as if it were a six-inch stiletto. "Want a ride?"

"I don't want to put you out of the way," she said, adding some steel to her sweetness because she did not need to be taken care of.

He shifted his gaze from her face to the back of the guy's head in front of them. "It's not."

Yeah, that was a tale taller than the water tower back home. Beckett Cosmetics's offices and research laboratory were twenty blocks in the opposite direction.

"I appreciate the offer," she said, dropping her phone into her bag. She'd memorized the route. She could do this without any new-to-the-city blunders. "But Harbor City is my town now, so I have to learn to navigate it."

He nodded. "Fair enough."

They followed the stream of people walking off the elevator, their strides matching even though he was a good foot taller than she was, which meant he'd probably slowed down for her, or her imagination was just finding patterns where none existed. They walked out of the building and into the bright sunshine of a spring morning that reflected off the windows on the modern skyscrapers lining the street for blocks and blocks. Main Street back home it was not.

She fished her sunglasses out of her handbag and put them on, hoping the shades and the determined tilt of her chin helped her blend in with the throngs of locals speed-walking to work.

"Have a great day," she said before turning left and heading out on her way like the heroine in a movie about to take the city by storm alone and without help.

She made it three long—for her—strides before Griff fell into step beside her.

"I thought you were driving to work," she said.

"Changed my mind," he said, holding out his arm, bent at the elbow, so she could hold onto his forearm as she navigated the heel-destroying iron grate embedded in the sidewalk.

Had he changed his mind from her being a disaster to being a damsel in distress? He better not have. They'd come to an agreement last night. *She* was coming to *his* rescue by being his Last Man Standing date. She was the knight, and he was the princess.

Unable to let it go, she pressed him. "Why did you decide to walk?"

The only answer she got was a shrug as he matched her stride for stride for five and a half city blocks with enough iron grates in them to make the walk more of an obstacle course. It had been a short trip, but her heart was thumping against her ribs as if she'd just run a marathon, which had to be first-day jitters and definitely not because of the man standing silently next to her, because if it wasn't, then she really was in trouble.

She stopped in front of the distinctive golden stone doors and inhaled a deep breath through her nose. It didn't help. Her nerves were jangling and rattling like a handful of wrenches in a metal toolbox getting bounced around in the back of the truck going down a gravel road dotted with potholes.

"Leigh's tough but fair, and she's gathered a great team— I'd hire them all away if I could get them to agree to leave." He shoved his hands in his pockets and looked down at the sidewalk, the tips of his ears going cherry. "They're lucky to have you."

It took a second from his half-mumbled words to sink in, and then all the words in the world got clogged in her throat. She bit the inside of her cheek to buy the time for everything to sort itself out enough to find the manners Meemaw had drilled into her. "Thank you."

He glanced up, his gaze locked on hers, rock steady. "It's true."

Spirits a little lighter than they'd been the first time she'd looked at the Archambeau doors, Kinsey gave in to impulse and leaned up so she could wrap her arms around Griff in a quick hug. Well, she'd meant it to be quick. Once she got there, her cheek against his shoulder as he stood there as frozen as the bag of peas that were in the back of Meemaw's fridge in case of an emergency burn, she realized she'd made a mistake. A thank-you squeeze from her was obviously the last thing he'd wanted.

Shit on a shingle.

Embarrassment ate its way up from the base of her throat and had her blazing in the spring sun. She couldn't let go fast enough.

"So, um, I'll just go in now." She yanked the door open, no longer stressed about walking inside but instead seeing it as the escape hatch it was. "Bye. See you tonight for dinner."

The last she saw of Griff Beckett was him standing there in his perfectly tailored navy-blue suit, a bright tattoo peeking out from under the cuff of his crisp white shirt, confusion forming a deep V between his bright-blue eyes as what seemed like half of Harbor City walked around him, hurrying to get to work.

Oh God. Hadn't Nash told him their first date was tonight?

Chapter Fifteen

The lobby of Archambeau Cosmetics was decorated in glass, golds and greens, the aesthetic reflecting the company's commitment to both cutting-edge treatments and natural products. It's what had first drawn Kinsey to the company. Well, that and the woman at the helm of the company—the one heading straight toward Kinsey.

"You must be Kinsey Dalton," Leigh Shaw said. "Good to meet you. I'm Leigh."

For the second time in the same morning, Kinsey lost her Southern.

Manners? Gone. Her mouth was hanging open, and her eyes were bugging out.

Ability to talk to anyone? Might as well have never existed.

Staring at Leigh Shaw, the CEO who'd won the then-failing Archambeau Cosmetics in a nasty divorce and then had turned it into one of the most cutting-edge cosmetics companies in the world in less than five years, it was all Kinsey could do to remember that words existed. The woman was a legend. Six feet tall with perfect dark-black skin, gorgeous brown eyes, and a breathtaking presence that demanded a person's attention, there was no doubting she wasn't to be fucked with in the boardroom any more than she had been on the catwalk.

"If you don't breathe, HR will yell at me," Leigh said, tucking a strand of silver hair behind her ear and peering closer. "Blink if you're still inhaling and exhaling."

Biscuits and gravy, snap out of it, Kinsey Anne Dalton!

"Sorry." Kinsey stuck out her hand. "It's nice to meet you, Ms. Shaw."

The other woman gave her a warm smile and a firm handshake. "Excellent." She looked over at her assistant, who was in head-to-toe hot pink including the tips of her chin-length hair. "Billie, let's take Kinsey around to meet the rest of the team." Leigh cut a glance her way. "And everyone here calls me Leigh, so I expect you to do the same."

The three of them took the elevator up to the lab, Kinsey trying not to freak out that the CEO herself had come down to welcome a new lowly junior scientist to the team. Bright and airy, the lab took up most of the third floor. Something warm settled in her chest at the sight of the crisp white lab coats, the clear glass beakers, and the chem shower in the corner. Home was stainless steel and correctly calibrated scales. She should really stitch that onto a throw pillow because it was true, the lab was her happy place.

As soon as they walked through the automatic sliding doors, the handful of people in the lab looked up from their benches. An older man took off his safety goggles and came over.

"Gavin, I'd like you to meet our newest scientist, Kinsey Dalton," Leigh said. "Kinsey, Gavin Wedgewood is our head of R&D. His team developed the formula for Bonsoir Rajeunir."

BR to its legion of rabid fans, the overnight moisturizer was a must-have classic in the beauty world, the kind of product with the devoted and loyal following that every company dreamed of having.

"Team, huh?" Gavin smiled, but it didn't reach his dark eyes. "Well, I suppose that's one way to look at one man's accomplishments." He turned to Kinsey, putting his hands in the pockets of his lab coat and rocking back on his heels, his condescending gaze going over Kinsey from the top of her ponytail to the slightly pointed toes of her shoes. "So, this is your new prodigy, huh? Another one you just had a feeling about?"

He glanced over at Leigh and chuckled when he noticed her narrowed eyes.

"Gavin." Leigh's tone hardened, her annoyance as visible as Meemaw's laugh lines. "We've talked about this."

"Yes, yes, I know," he said, dismissing Leigh as if she didn't own the company and therefore control his employment. "But it's all meant in fun. You see that, don't you, Katey?"

"Kinsey," she said, correcting his obviously on purpose mispronunciation of her name.

She was all too familiar with Gavin's type, already having met people like him in every classroom, internship, and social situation. He was a furniture store apple, the kind employees plopped into the wood bowls placed just so in the middle of a dining table—all shiny and nice on the outside and nothing but stale Styrofoam on the inside.

"Oh, sorry about that," Gavin said as he tilted his face upward and looked at the ceiling as if trying to recall a minute detail. "Your last amazing find was Katey, or was that the one before that, Leigh? I always forget. At least they pretty up the place."

What. The. Fuck.

This was her direct boss? This asshole stuck in the eighties?

"Gavin," Leigh said, her voice firm. "We've discussed this. Don't make me add to the list our attorneys are discussing."

"Oh yes, can't acknowledge the obvious," Gavin said, waving his hand in the air, dismissing his chauvinism as if it were a spritz of rancid perfume. "I'm just a say-it-as-I-see-it type. I'm sure you'll get used to it for as long as you're here. As much as I hate to cut short any interaction with you, Leigh, I've got to get back to our latest project."

"Of course," Leigh said, her jaw tight and her eyes alight with barely repressed fury.

Gavin, though, was halfway across the lab before she even got those two words out.

Kinsey was a little shell-shocked, a lot pissed, and uncertain about her job choice enough at this point that her stomach acid was sloshing around like moonshine in a mason jar during a midnight four-wheeler race across an abandoned field.

"And that is the lab," Leigh said through clenched teeth. "Let's get you to HR so you can fill out all your paperwork."

Kinsey kept her mouth shut, even as a billion and one panicked thoughts were zooming around inside her head, and followed Leigh and Billie out of the lab. They made it halfway down the hall before Leigh paused outside the break room.

"Billie, when is the appointment with the attorney?" Leigh asked.

She consulted her tablet. "Next week."

"Thank fucking God." Leigh let out an emphatic exhale and led their little trio into the break room. "Sorry about that. There are"—she waved her hands in the air—"things being worked out that have made it a little tense around here.

Gavin's smart, but he's also a bully; don't let him get to you. Now, I'll leave you in Billie's capable hands. She'll take you to HR, and then you'll be all set for your first full day in the lab tomorrow. You'll do amazing."

And with that, the CEO walked out of the break room, took a look left toward the lab and grimaced, before hooking a right and disappearing down the hall. Meanwhile, Kinsey stood there next to one of the oval break tables, each of which was outfitted with freshly cut flowers in glass vases as centerpieces, trying to remember why it had seemed like a good idea to move to Harbor City, home of the apartments with open-concept bathrooms and lab drama that made her gut twist.

She glanced over at Billie. "What happened with the last few hires?"

"They quit," she said with a shrug.

Uh-huh. She wasn't buying it. "Sounds like there's more to the story."

"There is." Billie held her iPad to her chest, gripping the white Apple Pencil tight in her hand. "I'm not one to spread gossip, but this bit of knowledge sure could help you keep putting groceries in your fridge."

Kinsey nodded, relief letting her inch her shoulders down a tad. "I like to eat."

"Don't we all." Billie glanced around the deserted break room as if someone might be hiding by the coffeemaker that looked like it could send a rocket into space. "So, Gavin is a real piece of work."

Not a shocker there.

"When I transitioned, he made my life hell," Billie continued, "but he was smart enough to do it so that it was covert enough I didn't have anything to take to HR—plus under the old regime, it wasn't like much would have been done." She plucked a white daisy from the vase on the closest table. "I was ready to walk out on my five-inch heels and never look back when Leigh pulled me aside and let me know she was getting the company in the divorce and asked me if I wanted to be her right hand. Easiest yes I ever gave."

Billie took a deep inhale of the flower and then put it back in the vase. "Her attorney was a shark of the most glorious kind, but her ex was a stone-cold demon. He made a sweetheart deal with Gavin, giving him full intellectual-property licensing rights to the top-five products Archambeau had developed up until that point. If he decides to walk, Gavin takes eighty percent of the company profits with him—something he lords over the rest of us and turning the culture of that lab into a toxic waste pit."

Well, complete dirtbags did seem to attract each other so that made sense. Kinsey had read up on the divorce and how it impacted Archambeau before accepting the job, but there hadn't even been a hint of this fuckery.

"The last five hires quit within a month because of him," Billie said. "Leigh is working on a plan to change things, but it's taking time—so long story short, hang in there. Gavin's days are numbered." She cocked her head and shot Kinsey a considering look. "I know that expression. You're thinking about walking now. Trust me. You don't want to do it."

She may not *want* to—this was her dream job, well, minus the asshole boss—but quitting before she'd signed a lease, got attached to the city, or spent any more time having inappropriate thoughts about Griff Beckett seemed like the most logical plan.

"Why not?" Kinsey asked.

Billie's smile was megawatt bright. "Because once that man gets his comeuppance, everything is going to change."

Uh-huh. In Kinsey's experience, only movie villains ever got what they deserved. In real life, it was the working stiff who ended up getting the shaft. "You're quite the optimist."

"No." She shook her head. "I just hate bullies."

"That we have in common."

After a long pause, Billie asked, "Should I still walk you up to HR?"

Kinsey should say *thank you but no thank you*. It was the smart plan, but damn it, despite her IQ and her less-than-great experience with jerks in lab coats, she knew that feeling bubbling up inside her. It was hope, the best and absolute worst thing in the world. God, she was such a sucker, but there was no way she could look Billie in the eye and say *good luck with the asshole but I'm out of here*. She couldn't abandon her any more than she could leave Griff to fend for himself in his dating bet.

No one knew like an outsider how important it was to know someone had your back. Besides, women had to stick together if there was ever going to be change.

"Absolutely." She nodded more emphatically than she felt. "Let's go to HR."

Billie draped an arm around Kinsey's shoulders and gave her a quick squeeze. "I knew I was going to like you."

Kinsey followed Billie down the hall to HR, sending up a quick prayer with each click and clack of the other woman's heels.

Please Lord, don't let this blow up in my face.

Chapter Sixteen

Griff

Griff was halfway through reading the morning reports on his iPad while working through the question of what in the hell Nash was really up to with this bet when he walked into the conference room he shared with his cousins for their weekly Beckett staff meeting—also known as shit talking each other while stuffing their faces with the best bagels in the city.

Nash was at the espresso maker set up on the credenza, steaming the milk for his double espresso latte—the one thing he did in perfect and utter silence. He lifted his chin in greeting when Griff set his iPad down in front of his usual chair about midway down the ten-person conference table.

Dixon sat at the head of the table, a black coffee in front of him, and he slathered cream cheese on a toasted everything bagel. "You're late."

Griff swiped a blueberry bagel off the tray in the middle of the oak table. "I had stuff."

He carried the bagel to the toaster set up on the credenza

along with a fresh pot of coffee, orange juice, and a chilled bowl of mixed berries. Even with his back to them, he could feel the weight of their stares. The fact that he'd ignored their texts last night about the bet had only delayed the inevitable, but that was all according to plan.

He had his cousins exactly where he wanted them to figure out what was really going on. Nash was up to something, and the surest way to get him talking—not that it was that difficult—was for Griff to keep his mouth shut. So that's exactly what he did.

His bagel popped up from the toaster, and he stayed silent. He unwrapped the foil on a tab of butter and spread it over the bagel and didn't move his mouth. And when he loaded up his plate with strawberries, blackberries, and blueberries until they surrounded his bagel like a sea of fruit and then walked back to his spot at the table? Not a fucking peep, no matter how many weighty and expectant looks he got from his cousins. It wasn't hard; it was pretty much his MO for life.

As his dad loved to tell him, nothing was gained when Griff opened his mouth. Everyone figured out then that he would never be as intelligent as his father, according to said sperm donor.

"Sooooo," Nash said, dragging the word out as he crossed over to his chair opposite Griff's and sat down, coffee in hand. "The situation with Kinsey."

Situation.

Yeah, that was one way to describe it.

A solution that was eluding him was another.

Then there was the one he'd come up with last night while staring at his ceiling until the wee hours of the morning: a total and complete clusterfuck.

"It was her idea," he said around a bite of buttered bagel.

And a damn good one. If she was anyone else and if he'd given two shits anymore about winning the bet. As it was, it was going to be six dates of shoving how he really felt down in some deep, dark hole so no one—least of all Kinsey—figured out that he was in love with her like the dumb-ass his dad always said he was.

"She's engaged?" Dixon asked, having demolished his bagel in record time even for him.

Griff nodded and shoved half the bagel in his mouth, not that he needed any help not saying anything.

"And that doesn't bother you?" Nash asked, ignoring the latte in front of him that he usually drank with all the reverence of an Ice Knights fan getting to view the Stanley Cup.

That he wasn't but was instead focusing on Kinsey's engagement had Griff's hackles up. He wasn't in the mood for Nash's games. The man always thought he knew things better than anyone else.

"Why should it?" Griff said with a hefty dash of extra snarl. "Should help me win."

"No," Nash said, shit-eating grin firmly in place. "The way to win is *not* to be in love."

Griff stabbed a series of blackberries with his fork, his brain going in fourteen directions at once but his aim true as realization sank in. It was so fucking obvious—how in the hell had he missed it? Everything lined up in his head. It really was the perfect way to interpret the rules so that Nash won the bet. Clever bastard. If it hadn't been for the fact that Griff was the one stuck in the middle of Nash's trap, he would have admired the simplicity of it all.

"Just as there's nothing in the rules that says the date can't be someone who is already attached or someone you know," Dixon said, not realizing that Griff had worked it all out already. "There's nothing that says that Kinsey has to return your feelings."

Fucking A. Being willing to watch each other wallow in

the emotional gutters of heartbreak was harsh even for their brand of competitiveness. If Griff bought that bullshit Nash was slinging, he'd be pissed as hell. But he knew his cousins better. Soft touches, the both of them. This was reverse psychology at its most elementary.

Anyway, it wasn't like he wasn't already uncomfortably familiar with the sensation of caring about someone who didn't give a flying fuck about him.

Hello, daddy issues, it's Griff calling.

Loosening the tightness in his jaw—and giving his molars a break—he rolled his head from side to side like he did before stepping into the ring or sitting down in the chair at the tattoo parlor for the latest addition to his full sleeves. Battle required focus and calm. Usually, it took all his concentration to quiet the billion and one thoughts clanging around in his head—or the sound of Kinsey's voice, but he wasn't going into that now. He wasn't about to give that up to his cousins.

"It doesn't matter," he said as he started scanning the latest report on the new extreme hydration serum they were launching next year.

"Because you're not gonna catch feelings?" Nash scoffed.

"No." He already had—but his cousins didn't need to know that. No one needed to know that, because he was going to fix it. That's what he did. He found solutions to impossible problems, like falling in love at first sight with an engaged woman. Hell, he hadn't even seen Kinsey before he had fallen over the edge into this mess. Well, he had six dates to climb his way out of the chaos and fall out of love with Kinsey Dalton, because unrequited love was the last thing he needed in his life. "Kinsey Dalton is not going to be the love of my life."

"That may be the case, but let's go through the motions anyway," Dixon said. "When you wouldn't answer your texts last night, we had a great conversation with Kinsey, setting everything up for tonight."

Griff grunted an *of course*. He'd figured that was the case with what Kinsey had said this morning.

"You have reservations at Montclair's," Nash said, not even pretending that the place wasn't Griff's biggest nightmare.

He let out a groan that he felt all the way down to the jagged scar on the top of his big toe. "You're kidding."

His cousins' evil chuckles told him exactly how much they were not.

Exclusive, expensive, and exhausting—those were the three words Griff would use to describe Montclair's, the restaurant that had become the it place for dates. According to the media—because God knew he would rather have every tattoo removed than set foot voluntarily in that place. Snobby. Overpriced. Tiny little servings of food. A no-cell-phones rule so he couldn't monitor his latest eBay auction bids when the conversation with Kinsey petered out—and it would; it always did with him.

Montclair's was hell on earth, and Griff had reservations.

Chapter Seventeen

GRIFF

The sky had just opened up and rain started to pelt Griff on the shoulders when he threw open the door to Montclair's and rushed inside. It wasn't like he was gonna melt or anything, but looking like a drowned rat in front of Kinsey was not his ideal. His plan was to fall out of love with her as fast as possible, not embarrass himself.

Good luck with that.

Clenching his jaw, Griff ran his fingers through his hair, clearing the sound of his father's voice out of his head. He'd been ditching the old man's calls all day and it had him on edge—something he nearly teetered over when he spotted Kinsey chatting with the man in the tux standing behind the host station. Unlike him, she'd found the time to go home and change before dinner.

Her back was to him as she chatted with the maître d' at the host stand. She'd freed her hair from the morning's tight ponytail and let it flow down across her shoulders in golden waves and had changed from the all-black work outfit to an icy-blue dress that clung to her curves and had him ready to swallow his tongue. She looked like she'd just walked off an Alfred Hitchcock movie set, the cool blonde who was up to something—the only question was which side she was on.

She turned when the door shut behind him, her smile genuine. "Oh, good. I was afraid you weren't coming."

He went to say hi, but nothing came out. Instead, he just stood there with his mouth clamped shut and his eyes wide as his brain took a side trip to a fantasy land where he got to unzip that dress and let it fall to her feet, fill his hands with her tits, and listen to that honeyed drawl as she came on his fingers, his tongue, his dick. The number of scenarios that flooded his mind replaced all other thoughts and plans. His auction strategy, his plans for the next round of safety tests on the new CC cream formulations, his unwinding of Nash's suspect motivations for this bet, and his half-assed plots to shut down his feelings for Kinsey disappeared.

There was just her, taking up all the space in his head and the calm that settled in his chest even as the rest of him revved up, tempted beyond rational thought into wanting her to fall for him like he had for her—like a two-ton block of concrete tossed into the harbor.

The guy in the tux at the host table held out his hand, palm upward. "Just a friendly reminder that the use of phones is strictly prohibited on the premises, sir."

That brought Griff back to reality.

She was engaged to someone else.

This was a pity date.

She didn't want him or to be here.

He needed to accept all of that and fall out of love with her as fast as he'd fallen for her. He could do it—he had to do it—or he was exactly as smart as that box of rocks his dad was always comparing him to.

He tightened his grip on his lifeline to work—not to mention the eBay auction for the vintage 1994 Lego Eiffel Tower set. "No. I have an eBay bid."

That sounded even sillier out loud than it had in his head, and he gritted his jaw.

The man tapped the sign that stated communication devices were not to be used inside. "Then I'm afraid I can't let you in."

So be it. That just made things easier. If he didn't spend time with Kinsey, then it would be that much easier to ignore this pull she had on him.

Gaze still locked on Kinsey, he took in the way she watched him, with total focus, as if she was trying to unravel him. *Oh, honey, I'm already beyond unraveled for you.* Shit. That is not what he needed to be thinking about. Instead, his attention should be on winning the Eiffel Tower set that at three and a half feet high was the tallest kit Lego had ever released and came with four elevators and nearly 3,500 bricks. People didn't put the unopened kits up for sale very often, and the auction closed in half an hour.

"I'm afraid, sir," the host said, his tone just shy of snide, "there are no exceptions at Montclair's."

Griff was about to turn heel when Kinsey reached out, her fingers wrapping around his forearm and sending jolts of awareness straight to his cock, which was already a little too aware of her already.

She smiled at the host. "Can he come out here to check his bid during dinner?"

"That's, uh, w-well," the man stammered, the tips of his ears turning red, "highly unusual."

"I get that," Kinsey said, squeezing Griff's arm when he inhaled—as if he was gonna say anything. "But he's waiting on something really important, and he'd only check it once or twice." She looked over at Griff, raising her eyebrows.

"Wouldn't you, dear?"

Really, what answer could he give except the one she wanted?

"Yes," he mumbled.

The other man looked between Kinsey's apple-pie-and-ice-cream smile and Griff's scowl, obviously trying to process what was going on. "Okay, I can allow that just this once."

Griff grunted his assent but made no move to reach for his phone.

And so they all three just stood there blinking until Kinsey hooked her arm through his, tucking herself in close against him. Then she reached in the front pocket of his jeans and pulled out his phone, the feel of her fingers and the friction of the slide dissolving his brain into overcooked oatmeal—but not before he realized he wasn't the only one feeling an unexpected rush. Kinsey's cheeks went pink as she snagged her plump bottom lip between her teeth, but she brazened through and dropped his phone into her purse as if that solved everything.

"Excellent," the other man said. "Let me show you to your table."

The maître d' led them into the dining room. They got three steps beyond the pale-blue velvet curtain that shut it off from the entrance before Kinsey tugged on his arm, jerking him to a stop.

"I'm sorry about that; I shouldn't have"—her cheeks went from pink to red—"taken your phone out of your pocket like that. I don't know what came over me, I just..." She looked around the room as if the rest of her response was hidden in the soft, dim lighting of the dining room with its private circular booths, curtained off from the rest of the diners. The second she very obviously clocked how weird the setup was, she turned to him, her blue eyes wide. "What is this place?"

Hell?

A matchmaker's paradise?

The absolute worst place to go with the woman he loved who'd only agreed to go out with him because she felt bad for him?

"This," Griff said, glaring at the obnoxious movie-set romance of the dining room, "is Montclair's."

Chapter Eighteen

KINSEY

Kinsey had never seen anything like this place.

Sure, it looked and felt high-end, but "opulent" wasn't the right word. It wasn't over-the-top or showy with gold chairs and crystal chandeliers. "Cozy" didn't fit, either. Despite the comfy booth the maître d' led them to with its velvet cushions, there was no way she would even think about slipping off her shoes and sitting cross-legged in this place, and it was way too fancy for leggings and her favorite cropped hoodie.

She sat down on one side of the small semicircular booth with Griff on the opposite side. Then the maître d' left, and she realized that thanks to the curtains around the booth and the way the tables were situated in the dining room, it felt like they were the only people there. The word for this feeling was "intimate"—she just had to remember to stick with her plan. She was helping out her best friend's brother win a bet.

That was it.

Of course, it would be a lot easier to remember that if her

heart didn't beat faster every time she was in the same room with Griff, let alone sitting right across from him in a booth—one that was so small, her feet kept touching his underneath the white tablecloth.

He was still in the suit he'd been wearing this morning, but his tie was gone, and he'd unbuttoned the top buttons of his white shirt, revealing just enough of his corded throat and the hint of his chest tattoo that her mouth had gone dry. At least he was still wearing the suit jacket. That meant he couldn't roll up his shirtsleeves, which was a blessing and a curse. A blessing because Kinsey wasn't sure seeing all that arm porn wouldn't send her over the edge and she was trying to be a good person not someone who lusted after a man she couldn't have. A curse because now she was zoned in on his strong fingers and couldn't stop herself from imagining all the things Griff could do to her with those. Her nipples puckered against the smooth satin of her bra at the thought, and she bit down on the inside of her cheek to stop herself before she did something really embarrassing like say what she was thinking out loud.

Good gravy, girl. You are so much of a mess that Marie Kondo would just love you.

This was what happened when lying about a fake fiancé had led to not dating for the past year. Even at a fake date, she was struck too horny for words. Okay, that wasn't totally the truth. Not the not-dating part—her social calendar had been free pretty much for the past three eternities. No. She was all hot and bothered about Griff and his square jaw, dimpled cheek, thick thighs, and the look in his blue eyes that said he was solving eighty million problems at once. That mix of brains and brawn was turning out to be her catnip, and all she wanted to do was purr.

Before she could, a man in a winter-white sports coat with a gray shirt and a gold silk tie stopped at their table.

"We're so glad you're dining with us this evening. I'm Ganton, your guide for the experience." He sat a small deck of cards down on the table. "Is this your first time at Montclair's?"

Kinsey nodded, not trusting her voice at the moment.

"How wonderful," Ganton said with a wide smile. "These are your conversation starters." He gestured at the deck on the table. "You don't have to go through all the cards, but any card you turn over, we encourage guests to discuss. Montclair's prides itself not just on fine dining but on fine conversation as well." He paused as if waiting for questions, and when there were none, he gave each of them a serious look. "Do you any questions?"

"No," Griff said, his tone leaving no doubt that he meant it.

Ganton raised his eyebrows dramatically and put a hand to one side of his mouth as if he was about to whisper a secret, then said in a stage whisper, "He's a chatty one, isn't he?"

Kinsey bit back her chuckle. "You have no idea."

Ganton gave her a dramatic and conspiratorial wink. "Well, let me get your drink order, and then you two can get to your first card!"

They ordered their drinks—a red wine for her and a scotch for him—and their "guide" left, leaving them staring at each other and the deck of cards sitting in the middle of the table.

"Shall we?" Kinsey asked.

Griff fidgeted with the pink stone ring encircling the linen napkin, not looking up at her. "You don't have to."

If he was trying to fool her into thinking he didn't care, he was failing. There was no missing the way he was looking everywhere but at her, how red the tops of his ears had turned, or the way he was sinking lower and lower in his seat. For all of his bluff and bluster, the man was nervous. And in a heartbeat, it was like being in the kitchen with him again doing dishes. She couldn't leave him in this awkward space where he wasn't comfortable and—ridiculous bet aside—where he hadn't asked to go.

You are such a sucker.

"I know I don't *have* to, but it seems like fun." She picked a card up off the top. "Would you rather be able to control animals (but not humans) with your mind or control electronics with your mind?"

Griff's head snapped up, his eyes connecting with hers and sending a zing of anticipation down her spine. "How is that a question?"

She flipped the card around and showed him. "I'm not making it up."

He shook his head. "What I mean is that electronics is the only viable answer."

That was debatable, but she could at least listen to his hypothesis. "Go on."

"Electronics are everywhere," he said, scooting closer to her on the circular booth seat, his apparent excitement at the possibilities making the words tumble out. "Imagine if I could control the nuclear system, all the smart systems in people's homes, or a car's operating system? I could wreak havoc. Or it could be benign and simply send you a text right now from your fiancé."

A guilty heat made her body feel flush. "That couldn't happen."

"Why not?" he asked.

Well, number one because Todd from Canada wasn't real. "For reasons I'm not going to tell you," she said. "And anyway, you're wrong. Controlling animals would be better."

"Why?"

She didn't mean to, but she slid over a bit on the seat; it just seemed like she needed to be closer to Griff to make her point. "Because how much better would it be to use an ant or a fly to spy rather than to have to figure out how to plant devices? You could send out a swarm of bees or a pissed-off hippopotamus after an enemy."

He let his head fall back and laughed. It was a rusty sound that seemed to creak out of disuse, but it was a laugh, a real one that had him shaking his head. "That's more evil of you than I expected."

"Fine," she said with a dramatic sigh, playing up her Cruella de Vil attitude. "How about the absolute joy of sending out a flock of sparrows and having them form a heart in the sky to cheer up someone you love?"

He took a card off the deck. "Would you rather be covered in fur or covered in scales?"

They both stared at each other.

"Scales," they both said at the same time.

And so it went. They debated whether it would be better to be ten minutes late for everything or twenty minutes early over the grilled sea scallops appetizer. While they devoured the buttery, seared-to-perfection goodness, they debated whether they'd rather be the first person to explore a planet or be the inventor of a drug that cures a deadly disease. That led into a question about if they'd rather have whatever you are thinking appear above your head for everyone to see or have absolutely everything you do livestreamed for anyone to see.

"If either of those ever happened, I would curl up into a ball and cry," Griff said.

There was no disagreement on her part.

"Okay, enough of the cards," she said after the entree of lamb chops and fingerling potatoes with a hint of mint was delivered. "I want something real."

Griff did his best deer-in-the-headlights impression, his body tense and his jaw clenched.

Oh, this man, he thought everything was a trap, didn't he?

Okay, so she could easily throw in some deep philosophical questions here, but she didn't have it in her to pin him down that way. Instead, when her gaze fell to the swath of blue ink peeking out from underneath his shirt cuff, she took pity on him. "How many tattoos do you have?"

He let out what could only be described as a relieved breath as he sliced his lamb chop. "About twenty. You?"

"None." Needles? No thank you very much. "Are they all science-related?"

"No."

She cut a bite of potatoes and waited. Griff didn't add on anything. Not a word. And it wasn't that he was ignoring her or cutting her out, going by the way his eyes darkened with something that looked a lot like lust. Then he winked at her, and it was so damn sexy that the fingerling potato on her fork fell right off. Okay, that may have had more to do with the fact that she had a near-full-body shiver of awareness roll through her like an avalanche, but that didn't change that it was one helluva wink.

"So are you gonna tell me about them?" she inquired, because Montclair's didn't seem like the kind of place where she could ask him to strip down so she could look herself.

And touch.

And lick.

And—

Good Lord, Kinsey. Pull it together.

Griff shook his head.

She popped her dropped potato into her mouth and waited in hopes he'd change his mind just to fill the silence. No such luck.

"You're no fun," she teased.

He shrugged his broad shoulders and went back to eating.

"Why don't you talk more?" Too direct? Probably, but it was the question she was dying to know the answer to.

He stilled, the fork halfway to his mouth for half a second, then said, "Not a lot to say."

"Now that's a lie." She reached out without thinking and laid her hand on his, the jolt of attraction as soon as she did burning through her. "You, Griff Beckett, are a man of ideas and no one—not even you—can convince me otherwise."

"You're an optimist." He stroked his thumb across hers, looking down at their hands with a small smile playing at the corners of his mouth.

She nodded, everything inside her feeling a little bubbly and chaotic, as if someone had shaken up a two-liter of Mountain Dew and taken off the cap. "I believe in happily ever afters, in people finding their way, and that we're stronger together than apart."

"I like that about you."

"Oh yeah, what else do you like?"

Meemaw would have given Kinsey *the look* if she'd been around to hear such blatant compliment fishing, but Griff just grinned at her.

Finally, he looked up at her, an intensity in his gaze that nearly knocked her back against the velvet booth. "Everything."

Then he let go of her hand and reached for the next card on the deck, and they were back in the world of hypotheticals while she was desperately trying to process that one single word and understand why it had left her absolutely 100 percent hopeful.

By the time the apple crumble and vanilla bean ice cream were served and their guide had taken Griff's credit card to settle their bill, they'd somehow scooted close enough that they were hip-to-hip in the circular booth. They reached for the last card on the table at the same time, and when his fingers brushed hers, awareness of him—the way he smelled of cedar and old books, the flash of a red swirling design that showed beneath the open V of his unbuttoned collar, the frisson of something more that was just under the surface like an octave that wasn't audible to the human ear even though a person could feel the sound's vibration—swept up her arm, leaving her wanting.

Her breath caught.

Griff grumbled something she didn't catch and pulled his hand back, flexing his fingers. Sure, it had sounded like he'd said her name, a desperate, hungry rumble of consonants and vowels that had her heart beating fast against her ribs, but that interpretation had to be the wine. It couldn't be reality. This wasn't a real date. She had a fake fiancé, after all, and Griff had a bet to win.

"What's it say?" he asked.

Oh yes, there it was, hard reality with its sharp edges here to scrape her up.

Her hand shook as she read the card. "Would you rather be compelled to high-five everyone you meet or compelled to have twenty minutes of small talk with anyone in a blue dress?"

"If it's you in a blue dress, I'd talk for an hour."

Kinsey had no idea what to say to that. The words seemed to flow between them—even at brunch the other day—but around others, he was about as chatty as the stump in the middle of Meemaw's front lawn. And now? All the words in the world disappeared for her. He'd make small talk with her for an hour?

The silence stretched between them, thick with possibilities—or was it that she wanted it to be? Right now, she couldn't tell.

And just as Griff started to open his mouth, Ganton returned, rubbing his hands together with obvious glee as he set the settled bill and card on the table.

Griff closed his mouth, and Kinsey let out the breath she'd been holding. She couldn't process what that meant—or more correctly, what she could allow it to mean so she could stick to her how-to-be-successful-in-Harbor-City plan.

"There's a message for you, sir," Ganton said.

"Figures it wouldn't just be dinner," Griff grumbled as he took the paper and read it. "It's a dance class."

She grabbed Griff's arm, holding on to it to keep her steady as the world got all wobbly. "I've got to warn you, I'm about as coordinated as my cousin Amber after she's done the head-on-the-end-of-a-bat-spin-around thing between innings at a minor league baseball game. She took off for first and ended up in the catcher's lap. They dated for about a week after that, but it didn't work out. No shocker. Amber is all about keeping her options open."

He just stared at her for a second, and then the right side of his mouth curved upward. "I got you."

"No, I don't think you understand. I'm awful."

"I had five years of dance classes," he said. "My mom thought it would help me open up around people. I barely talked at all before that."

Despite her nerves at the absolute embarrassment she was about to be, she giggled. "Did you just make a joke?"

He didn't answer, just took her hand in his as they walked out onto the sidewalk and into her worst nightmares.

Chapter Nineteen

A half hour later at a hole-in-the-wall dance studio and Griff knew one absolute truth—Kinsey hadn't been lying. Grandma Betty's attack goose Maurice had more dancing skills than his fake date.

Their dance instructor had tried her best, breaking down the thirty-second TikTok dance into individual steps. Kinsey had each one of those, but putting them together? The woman froze and seemed to forget which was her right and which was her left.

It shouldn't have made him love her a little bit more.

It did anyway.

He was so fucked.

"I'm so sorry; it's not you, it's me," Kinsey said to their instructor, who looked like she was ready to hit the nearest bar. "I'm just not made for dancing."

It wasn't that—it was just that her brain moved faster than her feet. Knowing Kinsey, she was probably working out the final step combinations in her head while her feet were trying to carry out the opening move. There was only one option to cut through all of it.

"Can I try something?" he asked, scrubbing the back of his neck with his hands, trying to figure out what in the hell he was thinking because this was not going to get him any closer to his end goal of falling out of love with Kinsey.

The dance instructor let out a relieved sigh, obviously ready to give anything a shot at this point. "Sure."

He glanced over at Kinsey and raised an eyebrow in question. She nodded, lifting her chin and straightening her shoulders as if he was going to go drill sergeant on her and yell her into dance submission. Instead, he stepped into Kinsey's dance space.

They locked gazes and, even with the same thirty-second music clip playing on repeat in the background, all Griff could hear was the sound of his own blood rushing in his ears. This had to be the most foolish thing he'd ever done in his life, but there wasn't a damn thing that would stop him— not even knowing better.

He took her right hand in his, lifting it so they were holding hands at shoulder height. Clamping his jaw tight and keeping his gaze firmly planted on the wall just over her shoulder, he pushed past the awareness building at touching her, the sizzle and spark that shot straight to his balls. Then he reached around her and let his other hand rest lightly against the middle of her back.

She sucked in a sharp intake of breath, and for one brief balls-in-a-vise-grip moment, Griff thought he'd hurt her or fucked it all up. He jerked his attention to her, an apology already on the tip of his tongue. It never made it past his lips.

Kinsey, her cheeks flushed, was looking up at him, her pupils dilated with desire and her soft pink lips parted as if in anticipation for the kiss he was desperate to give her.

If she was single.

If he had a shot.

If he wasn't the single biggest fool on the face of the planet for falling like a Sub-Zero fridge over the edge of a cliff the first moment he heard her brain at work.

"So," he said, grinding out the single word without unclenching his jaw, desperate to hold on to the little bit of dignity and self-respect he had left—the effort of which turned his tone hard and mean. "The waltz is just a box step with turns."

She didn't even flinch at his harshness, just bit down on her plump bottom lip and cut her gaze to the floor. "I don't know—"

"Look at me," he interrupted.

She did, tilting her chin up and looking at him with wide, wary eyes.

"I got you."

And right at that moment, as the music looped back to the beginning of the clip, he started the waltz. He went forward with his left foot and she went back with her right. Then he went right and she stayed with him as they continued the box step. They continued several more times along with the song that had become one of the most popular TikTok dance challenges before he felt her relax in his arms.

"Get ready," he whispered, his mouth close enough to her ear that his lips nearly brushed against her soft skin. "We're gonna turn."

Before she could freeze up or he gave in to the heat and kissed her right there in the middle of the makeshift dance floor, he swung her around. He repeated it again and again as they rounded the small dance floor. Then, just as the song was ending, he dipped her and she went with it, bending back until he brought her up again, holding her so she was pressed against him. Their faces were so close, all he had to do was dip his head lower and kiss her.

There was nothing in the world he wanted more.

There was nothing in the world he could have less.

He dropped his hands abruptly and stepped back, flexing his fingers to try to ease the ache of not touching her anymore, ice the burn of wanting nothing else but the one woman he couldn't have. Frustration and desire slamming against him, banging him up with more force than Mac's fists in the ring, he dragged his attention away from Kinsey over to their dance instructor.

"We danced," he said, snarl dialed up to a hundred. "Is the date over now?"

Wide-eyed, the instructor nodded.

Great. He'd never been more fucking glad in his life to get exactly what he didn't want.

Chapter Twenty

Kinsey was going to hell in a very tiny, very scratchy, very uncomfortable handbasket, and she was taking Todd with her.

Making up a fiancé had made sense at the time.

Now, when she was in this way-too-small-for-comfort elevator with Griff, still feeling the weight of his hand on the small of her back and her lips still tingling from that shoulda-been-but-wasn't kiss?

It. Made. No. Sense. At. All.

But here she was. Standing next to a guy who growled as a form of communication, looked like he could be a tattooed Captain America body double—especially the butt, oh my God, his butt—and had Bruce Banner's brain. It was too much. She was in sensory overload. Even worse, the horny part of her brain would not keep its shit together.

She couldn't even look over at Griff as the elevator climbed its way to the penthouse level because every time she did, she imagined running her fingertips over the line of buttons on his shirt, slipping each one free. She'd like to imagine she'd have the control to go slowly, revealing his colorful, muscled chest one leisurely inch at a time. A kiss here. A flick of her tongue against his warm skin there. Spreading his shirt wide and running her palms over the broad expanse of him and kissing her way down as she went to work unbuttoning his pants.

In reality—not that this was ever going to happen—there wouldn't be any slow-mo speed at all. It would be lust tingled with desperation sending buttons flying across the elevator, pinging against the walls with the force of her need to get him naked right the fuck now.

Whew.

Okay.

Deep breaths, Kinsey. In and out. There you go. You can breathe the horny away.

Ha. Yeah right. Keep dreaming.

"Are you all right?"

"What do you mean?"

"Your breathing."

Oh. God. She was more obvious than neon at midnight. "I'm fine." He lifted an eyebrow, and she kinda melted a little at his nonverbal communication skills. Fine. A lot. She melted like the ice cubes in a glass of sweet tea left out on the porch in August. "Really. I'm perfectly okay."

"Your cheeks are pink, and you've got a splash of color right here." He reached out and touched a fingertip to that spot at the base of her throat right above the notch in her collarbone.

Kinsey couldn't breathe and, for the first time in her life, she wasn't even thinking one step ahead, let alone her usual three.

Griff's intense gaze went from her eyes to her parted lips.

He took a step forward. She didn't have anywhere to go in the elevator even if she wanted to. He slid his finger from her throat to the scoop neck of her dress, tracing the line of fabric as if he were trying to memorize every thread.

"Kinsey," he said, her name coming out all rough and hungry.

She would have answered if she could. Instead, all she could do was stand there, her entire body electrified with need and want and a building ache that only Griff could ease. His eyes lifted to hers again. Lust, hot and heady, steamed through her as he pinned her with a look that held so much dark promise, she wasn't sure she'd make it another minute.

Griff lowered his hand as he dipped his head, then took her hand—her left hand. She knew the second he touched her fake engagement ring. It was as if something snapped and the whole moment changed in a heartbeat. Guilt flashed in his eyes as he let out a harsh breath before dropping her hand and taking a step back.

He shoved his hands into his pockets and turned so he was facing the elevator doors, tension emanating from him strong enough that it could have acted like a force field.

"Sorry," he said, low and angry.

Damn it. Damn it all right to the bottom of Meemaw's nonfunctioning water well.

Meemaw had warned her the whole fake engagement would come back to bite her in the ass. Kinsey's overly confident response at the time was that she was always three steps ahead so not to worry about it. Well, she sure wasn't in front of the eight ball now, because it had just run her over and left her flatter than her hair after three days of not washing it. There was nothing she wanted more at that moment than to tell him that there was no Todd, but she couldn't. The only way she could get her last fling with a lie to work was to make sure that no one in the small-and-still-gossips-a-lot cosmetics industry let slip her secret shame.

The elevator dinged a second before the doors slid open. Without hesitating, Griff strode out, his long legs eating up the distance to his apartment door at a quick pace.

"Good night, Kinsey," he said without looking back as he unlocked his door and then disappeared inside.

She barely managed a "good night" in return before he closed the door behind him.

How in the world she made it through her front door, down the hall, and to her room without collapsing, she had no idea. However, as soon as she closed the door behind her, she flopped facedown onto the mattress and let out a tormented groan, because the one thing she hadn't planned on when she'd made up Todd was meeting Griff Beckett.

Now what in the world was she going to do?

Chapter Twenty-One

Three days of post-date second-guessing, two days of eight-hour shifts with Gavin the boss from hell patronizing her while staring at her not-exposed tits, and one painful walk home with a blister on the back of her heel because the rumors were not wrong that in Harbor City, folks walk everywhere, Kinsey needed a slice of sweet potato pie and a small glass from the it's-not-water pitcher. Unfortunately, none of that was available via Uber Eats from Virginia. So she went for the next best—or was it better?—option and FaceTimed Meemaw.

Tucked into the oversize chair in her room, the last orange rays from sunset coming in through the huge windows overlooking the park, she watched her screen go from her saved photo of Meemaw to her grandma's kitchen ceiling and then—finally—to Meemaw, at least from the eyebrows up.

"Sugar bee," Meemaw said, her eyebrows going high into her deep-lined forehead as she readjusted the angle so that her whole face was on-screen. "I was beginning to think that city had eaten you up."

"It's only been a few days," Kinsey said as she curled and uncurled her toes in the plush carpet. One too many times of watching *Die Hard* at Christmas had taught her that, plus how to say *shoot the window* in German.

"Well, can you blame an old woman for missing you?"

Ah. Grandma guilt. Sure, it was sandwiched between two Texas-toast-size slices of love, but the shiv was still buried right there in the middle like a two-shot revolver in a hollowed-out book on landscape gardening.

"You still have Lark and Beau." Kinsey's older brother and sister had stayed close to home as part of an unspoken pact to watch out for Meemaw, who was too stubborn to move into town or let them hire someone to help keep up the property.

"Believe me, neither they nor the interfering repair folks they keep sending out here are gonna let me forget it."

"Meemaw, you need the help," she said, playing her part in the never-ending argument. "Plus, you love Beau and Lark and you know it."

"More than honey on buttered biscuits." Meemaw let out a raspy cackle of a chuckle before peering close enough at her phone screen that all Kinsey could see of her was her eye and part of a nostril. "So how are you and what happened?"

Shit. How did the woman always know?

"Fine, and what makes you think something happened?"

"Like you said, it's only been a few days since we talked, and you'd rather text than use a phone for its actual purpose." Meemaw leaned back so her entire face was on the screen again and harrumphed. "Fess up."

So that's when she filled Meemaw in on her passive-aggressive jerk of a boss, the studio apartment with the toilet in the middle of the kitchen, and the great dinner she had at

Montclair's.

"Who did you go to dinner with?"

It took everything she had to keep her face neutral. There was definitely a downside to FaceTiming with Meemaw. The woman never missed a thing. "A friend. Well, sort of a friend. It was Morgan's brother. He has a bet going with his cousins, and I'm helping him out."

Meemaw grinned at her, obviously reading the novel that was between the lines. "So does this mean you've finally put all that Todd nonsense behind you?"

Telling her about Todd had happened during a moment of weakness and peach cobbler served with a giant scoop of vanilla ice cream. She didn't regret it exactly, but admitting out loud what she'd done had made her sink down in her chair and do everything but make eye contact with the one woman she knew would love her no matter what but she never wanted to disappoint. And now she had to do it again.

Great.

She sank down in her chair so now only *her* eyebrows and forehead were showing. "Not exactly."

Meemaw squashed her lips together in obvious dissatisfaction. "Kinsey Anne Dalton."

Kinsey let her head fall against the back of the chair with a thump. "I know."

"Do you? Because it seems like you should, but then you keep up with the ridiculousness."

Knowing she was a grown-ass woman but feeling like a little kid holding an uncapped Sharpie and a whole lotta unauthorized art on a previously pristine white wall, Kinsey forced herself to sit up, straighten her shoulders, and look her grandma in the eyes. Okay, kinda. She looked at the one corkscrew curly hair that had escaped Meemaw's braid to brush against her cheek.

She let out a breath and then launched into the speech

she had started to give herself when the weight of the lie got F-150 heavy. "Remember what it was like at my internship? People took one look at me and figured I was too dumb to be there on my merits. That led to the rumor that I'd slept my way into the lab, and then it just got worse. After I invented Todd, it got easier. Now I have the chance to really show people what I can do without them thinking I'm just a dumb blonde who sounds like she fell off the sweet potato truck."

An anxious energy had every muscle tensed, and she bounded out of the chair and started pacing the length of the massive window, no longer seeing the gorgeous park below. Now she saw the judgy looks of the people who with one glance at her figured her for being out of her intellectual depth.

"I just have to pay my dues at work, get them to see my brain and not this person who is so much younger than everyone else and they take me seriously—then I can kill off Todd. A month. That should do it. It'll be easy. No problem." Was she trying to convince herself or Meemaw? She had no clue. "It's the final countdown," she said, her tone firm. "Todd has got to die."

"Well," Meemaw said, her rasp coming in strong. "That seems extreme."

Despite it all, Kinsey laughed at her grandma's trademark dry sense of humor. "Okay, he'll break up with me."

Meemaw's eyes rounded, and she let out an angry huff. "Who would ever do that? You're better than melted butter on grits."

Now she was giggling like she was twelve at a slumber party hyped up on Mountain Dew and Pixy Stix. "You realize we're talking about someone who doesn't exist."

"I don't care—even fake people would love you."

The vote of confidence hit her right in the chest, warming her whole body. "Thanks, Meemaw."

"You got it, baby girl, but now I've gotta go." The phone screen went back to showing the ceiling of Meemaw's house as she walked from the kitchen to the front door. "Eunice is here to take me to bingo."

That meant nothing but trouble for Mr. Fairbanks, who had been the volunteer fire department's fundraising bingo caller for as long as Kinsey could remember—which was exactly how long Meemaw and Miss Eunice had been heckling him for calling out bad numbers.

That, sad to say, was Mr. Fairbanks's problem to deal with. Kinsey had her own. How to kill off—fine, how to *break up* with—an almost fiancé?

Chapter Twenty-Two

GRIFF

No matter what Nash was saying with that look on his face, Griff hadn't been *hiding* in his Lego room.

Before his pain-in-the-ass cousin had shown up uninvited, Griff had been *working* on collection development and rearranging completed projects on the custom-made display shelves so that once he finished the first-edition Lego Taj Mahal that had finally arrived, he'd have the perfect place to put it. And while he was doing that, he had been listening in on the staff call updating Beckett Cosmetics's progress on Us, a gender-neutral holistic line of hair care, skin care, and supplement products launching early next year.

Then there was the packaging debate going on between his number two and the head of marketing that he was mediating via emails on his phone. Oh yeah, and he was listening to the audiobook of the latest in the Lady Sherlock series. So he couldn't be hiding. He was just busy.

"You're so full of shit," Nash said from his spot leaning

against the doorjamb. "You're hiding from Kinsey."

"She's next door, dumb-ass."

Yep. Just on the other side of his bedroom wall. What? He wasn't weird; he'd seen the building blueprints and knew how everything lined up. That wasn't… Okay, it was weird.

But shit, he'd spent hours every night staring at the ceiling instead of sleeping and thinking about Kinsey. When he made breakfast in the morning, he couldn't help but wonder what she ate first thing. And that was just the beginning— thoughts about Kinsey had become the program running in the background all the time. What kind of music did she like? Would she find that movie funny? Did she toast her ham sandwiches? Did she brush her teeth in the bathroom or while she was walking around the house?

Unaffected by the silence outside of Griff's head, Nash asked, "And when was the last time you saw her?"

Griff was hit with the image of Kinsey biting down on her bottom lip and giving him one last look before disappearing into her apartment after their first date.

"Last week," he grumbled as he moved the Death Star on its customized stand to a shelf across the room.

"There is a time limit on these dates, you know." Nash walked into the room, swiping nonexistent dust off the Technic Bugatti Chiron and then moving along to trace the line of the Millennium Falcon, his gaze on Griff the whole time, obviously knowing he was giving his cousin a set of small heart attacks that he'd never mention. "You can't just put it off."

"What's with you?" He crossed his arms over his chest, trying to work out the twists and turns of his cousin's mind. "You know she's engaged. I'm obviously going to win the bet."

"Wrong." Nash grinned at him, the I-know-more-than-you-do smirk that was a permanent part of his resting smug face. "You already lost."

Griff froze. He'd been careful. He hadn't said shit to anyone. No one knew that he was in love with Kinsey. He locked all his attention on Nash. His cousin didn't blink, didn't fidget, didn't lose a single percentage of pain-in-the-ass from his obnoxious grin. The asshole had gambled and won—even worse, he knew it.

"Fuck off," Griff said.

Nash laughed and picked up the Captain America mini figure from the 2012 Toy Fair that had been a bitch to track down along with the Iron Man that had been one of 125 made. "You know I'm right," Nash said, putting Cap back on the shelf but facing the wrong direction. "You're already in too deep to swim back to shore."

"That doesn't make any sense." Pulse going a million miles an hour as he marched across the room to fix it so Steve Rogers faced straight ahead, hoping with each step that Nash would be distracted enough not to realize that Griff was lying his face off.

"How about you're in love, besotted, smitten, head over heels, you fancy her. Really, it makes perfect sense. You work out what's going on and what's going to happen eons before anyone else does, your brain moves that quick. Of course you'd fall in an instant because that's just how fast your mind works. Griff and Kinsey sitting in a tree. K.I.S.S.I.N.G."

"Immature asshole," Griff said, ignoring the fact that he was in a room completely devoted to an activity that a lot of people considered as being for kids only. "What in the fuck is this bet really about anyway?"

Nash flinched. It was small—barely perceptible—but Griff had clocked it. His cousin was almost unnaturally smooth without even a flicker of nervous energy. He was all confidence and know-it-all answers. But not now. Instead, he fidgeted with mini figurines and the key fob to his Maserati, which he usually left on the dining room table.

"You know the bet is all about winning Grandma Betty's last present," Nash said, maintaining eye contact but just barely.

Griff shook his head. "Bullshit."

"What? That's it?" Nash scoffed as he turned the key fob over in his fingers like one of the scam artists in the tourist-heavy zones with a quarter, distracting a mark's attention while their partner picked their pocket. "You have that big, scary brain and *bullshit* is all you can say?"

He shrugged. "It's all that's needed."

Better to be thought fool than to prove it. His dad was an asshole, but he'd been right about that. Plenty of people ran their mouths when they shouldn't.

"The next date is tomorrow," Nash said. "Since you dragged your feet hard enough to carve a pair of ditches into cement, Dixon and Fiona planned this one for you."

Griff paused midstep as he made his way over to the shelf with the Statue of Liberty displayed on it, complete with an Ellis Island backdrop and a ferry full of sightseers. His gut clenched and he chewed the inside of his cheek like it was a hunk of Hubba Bubba. He wasn't sure if Fiona being involved was a good or a bad thing. She was pretty great, but she'd also fallen for Dixon, so there were obviously some errors in judgment there. Not really, but he wasn't ever going to admit that out loud.

Nash went on, either not noticing Griff was processing the new information about date planning or pretending not to. "You're going to Paint and Sip in Waterbury."

Okay, he could do that. It wasn't like people talked a lot during those things. He could just sit there, paint some stupid sunset, and be done with date number two. Perfect. If he couldn't figure out soon how to fall out of love with her, the sooner he got through the six dates, the better.

"Fine." Griff picked up the Statue of Liberty, made sure it was balanced properly, and moved it over to its new home near the door.

There. Now there would be plenty of room to display his latest additions once they were built. All was right in the world. Well, at least in his Lego room. Except for Nash being in there and acting all squirrely. He'd figure out what was going on. He always did. In the meantime, he swiped his phone off the building table, flicked off the light switch, and walked out of the room.

Nash caught up to him in the kitchen, accepting the open beer Griff handed him.

"So are you going to call her and let her know?" Nash asked after he'd taken a sip and shot a meaningful look at Griff's phone on the counter. "You may not realize it, but most humans like a little notice—especially when they're doing someone a favor."

Griff didn't make a move for his phone. "I'll text her later."

"Do it now." He picked up Griff's phone and tossed it at him.

He caught it while grabbing a bag of chips from the pantry. "Why?"

"Because I think you're doing your best to pretend that you don't like her and, like the fool you are, have chosen the ostrich route."

He laid the phone down on the kitchen table and did the pinch, pinch, pull to open the bag. "Fuck off."

"So Mom was right; it's more than like." Nash reached in and grabbed a handful of barbecue-flavored chips. "You really do love her."

"Aunt Celeste needs to dial back on the woo-woo," he grumbled between handfuls of chips he shoved in his mouth while trying to figure out how she knew.

Nash snorted. "That's never gonna happen—especially not when she finds out her interpretation of the cards was right."

Fuck. There was no way this would end well. Aunt Celeste was scattered, but once she'd grabbed on to an idea, she didn't let it go. If he didn't nip this in the bud, she'd figure out a way to involve herself in this dating-bet disaster all the way up to her eyebrows. There was only one way out of this. He had to ask Nash for a favor.

"What will it take to get you to not say anything to your mom so she backs off?"

Nash's smug smile and cocky attitude were back in full force. "Text Kinsey about the date now and type exactly what I say."

"You are a bossy motherfucker." He grabbed his phone and opened up his texts. "One of these days, someone is going to fuck your shit up."

Now it was his cousin's turn to shrug as if he had no fucks left to give. "Stop trying to change the subject, Griff, and start typing."

He did. And then—fuck his life—he tapped out exactly what Nash said, cringing every letter of the way.

Chapter Twenty-Three

Kinsey stared at her phone.

Griff had been taken over by aliens. He had to have been. This was a lot of words.

> GRIFF: *Had a great time with you the other night. I really appreciate you helping me out with these dates. I owe you huge. Our next date is across the harbor at the Paint and Sip place. I know it's weird, but I'm hoping you're still game. Promise I'll make it up to you.*

So.
Many.
Words.

> KINSEY: *So many words. Are you okay? Have you been kidnapped and is this a call for help?*

GRIFF: *Nash.*

Kinsey relaxed back in the chair. That explained it. His cousin had either stolen Griff's phone or held him at gunpoint. But in just one word, she knew her man was back. Wait. No. Not her man. Her man was her fake fiancé, Todd. Griff was Morgan's older brother. That was all. Nothing more. Definitely not the guy she kept thinking about at odd hours.

GRIFF: *So this paint thing?*

KINSEY: *Sounds great!*

She hit Send and immediately regretted the exclamation point. Too young. Too enthusiastic. Too much, as if she was about to lie and say oh-my-God-I-dreamed-about-you-last-night-and-it-was-ah-mazing. That was not the look she was going for. Not even close.

The last thing she needed was to get distracted from work. That's why she'd moved to Harbor City: job of her dreams. Boss of her nightmares, yes, but the job was exactly what she'd been dreaming about since she'd mixed up her first face mask from a kit Meemaw had found at Michaels. She wasn't going to lose this opportunity because everyone thought she was too young and too country for it. And she sure as hell wasn't going to mess it up because she lost sight of her goal because she couldn't stop looking at Griff, who was a huge, muscular, tattooed genius of a distraction.

GRIFF: *Pick you up at seven?*

KINSEY: *Perfect!*

Fuck her life. There it was again. The subconscious why-don't-you-use-your-extra-key-to-let-yourself-in-and-ravishme exclamation point.

She needed help. She needed to kill off Todd. She needed to have a million orgasms, the kind that left a person breathless, mindless, and jelly-kneed. A million of those might burn her battery stash or give her carpal tunnel, but a few would do a body good.

Sadly, stress masturbation had its place, but that wasn't what she was in the mood for. First she needed a long bath, the kind with bubbles, water hot enough to turn her skin pink, and tons of steam that would make all her worries evaporate.

Taking advantage of the alone time because Morgan was at barre class and would be bringing home dinner for the both of them after, Kinsey crossed over to her bedroom door and closed it. She peeled off her top and let it drop to the floor as she walked to the en suite bathroom, then reached behind her and unsnapped the costs-a-fortune-but-still-hurts bra. She slid the straps off and let it drop, leaving only wide indentions on the tops of her shoulders as the kind of tit-deep relief that only came with setting the girls free washed over her.

Letting out a happy sigh, she turned on the faucet and poured in enough vanilla-scented bubbles to span the tub and then some. While it filled, she stripped off her pants and panties and then grabbed her phone. A quick scroll through her playlists and she found the perfect one, dimmed the lights, and lit a few candles.

Okay, was all of this a bit much? Yes. Was she still here for it? Fuck yes.

Self-care kept her sane, relatively stress-free, and the tub was her favorite place to let her brain unravel all the bullshit she'd encountered—like that asshole in line at Starbucks who'd told her she was being basic by ordering a black coffee. All she'd wanted was straight caffeine and the fact that she had to listen to that doofus before getting it had her reciting the periodic table in her head to keep from popping off on him.

Yeah, the last thing she wanted was for her overactive brain to flash to that jerk while she was flicking the bean. Bath first. Orgasms second.

Twenty minutes later, she was chin-deep in bubbles, her hair pulled up into a top knot, and halfway into the perfect sexy-times fantasy that involved a guy with a brain as big as his biceps when the perfect plan to kill off Todd hit her. Why it always worked out this way in the tub, she had no idea, but she wasn't about to question it. She had a solution and best of all, with her heart broken because she'd been dumped, people would give her space at the lab to work away her sadness. It was the best of all the worlds—no more Todd and a license to work her face off. Satisfied but a little drowsy, she answered the buzz of her phone without thinking first.

MEEMAW: *You won't believe what that snake did now.*

Kinsey giggled. There was no need to ask who the snake was, considering it was bingo night.

KINSEY: *Mr. Fairbanks is just doing his job.*

The three little chat dots popped up immediately. Oh man. Whatever had gone down in the Elks Lodge, it must have been wild. The old people took their church-sanctioned gambling seriously.

MEEMAW: *He cheats.*

All that explained it. Ashley Yeats must have won two in a row. Mr. Fairbanks had dated Miss Ashley a million years ago, and now that she was a widow, he had his eye on her. The whole town was watching and waiting to see if he'd be successful in getting a second chance. That, however, didn't mean he was throwing bingo in her favor.

KINSEY: *You can't prove that.*

GRIFF: *Can we leave at six thirty instead?*

Heart doing a little fluttery thing—obviously, she must have run the bath too hot—she stared at the new message notification from Griff a minute before clicking on it and responding.

KINSEY: *Sure.*

She'd barely hit Send when a new message notification popped up.

MEEMAW: *So I'm assuming you've figured out the Todd problem by now?*

Her plan was the perfect distraction to get Meemaw to forget about Mr. Fairbanks and his probably cheating ways.

KINSEY: *Figured out the perfect way to kill off Todd.*

GRIFF: *WHAT?!*

Kinsey sat straight up in the tub, sending water sloshing over the side. She checked the message she'd just sent and then the name of the person she was sending it to. Then, because maybe things would change if she looked again, she closed her eyes, counted to ten, and then opened them to look again. The information hadn't changed. She'd sent that last message to Griff instead of Meemaw.

Holding her phone in the air, she sank down under the water to her eyebrows.

Shit.

Shit.

Shit.

She stayed under until her lungs started sending an SOS and reemerged, wiping away the bubbles from her face before she opened her eyes. She immediately wished she'd stayed under longer.

GRIFF: *ON MY WAY OVER*

Oh shit.

Oh fuck.

Oh fold her up and make her eat stale store-bought biscuits for the rest of her life.

She scrambled out of the tub, leaving wet footprints across the tile as she hurried as fast as she could to grab her robe and wrap it around her—realizing as soon as she did that drying off with the towel first would have been far more prudent. Now it was sticking to her skin, and she was still dripping water everywhere she went.

The option of drying off disappeared, though, at that second because there was a knock on the front door.

"Kinsey," Griff called through the door. "We need to talk."

She closed her eyes and sent up a prayer. Not that it would help. Even Dolly Parton—patron saint of women, corn bread, and country music—couldn't save her now. Kinsey was well and truly screwed.

Chapter Twenty-Four

GRIFF

Griff had a set of keys to Morgan's place, and his first instinct had been to use them because whatever this Todd asshole had done to Kinsey to make her consider knocking him off, it had to be bad—really bad—and that meant he wanted to help make sure the sniveling little prick got what was coming to him.

Okay, he wasn't about to go the do-you-want-to-bury-a-body route, but he'd definitely gain a set of bloody knuckles if that's what was needed.

Who in the hell are you right now?

At the moment? The guy people assumed he was when they saw him and crossed the street to avoid meeting him head-on—and all because Kinsey was hurt enough to plot murder.

Not that he thought she'd actually kill someone, but the idea she'd been pushed to considering it—even if it was just a joke—had him about to lose it. That's why he'd grabbed the spare keys to Morgan's place, stormed out of his apartment, and then had turned around, jaw aching from hard clenching, and had put the keys back in the junk drawer next to the fridge.

Now here he was, cooling his fucking heels on the wrong side of the door.

Kinsey opened the door a whole two inches. "Griff, it's not what you think."

Yeah, and the last thing they needed was to be discussing revenge in the hall with all the security and closed-circuit TVs this building had. "Let me in."

"I'm sure it sounded serious but when I said—"

"Kinsey," he said, laying a shit-ton of shut-the-fuck-up in the one word as he cut his gaze toward the security camera by the elevator.

She let out a soft sigh. Then she opened the door.

The second he walked into Morgan's living room—Kinsey's living room, too, now—he froze. Well, his dick and his brain kept moving, but the rest of him shut the fuck down. Her hair was all in a giant blond ball of fluff on top of her head. That ball was dry, but the rest of her hair was soaked, dripping water that followed the long line of her neck and soaked the collar of her robe.

Meanwhile, the blue cotton material was soaked and clung to her every curve from the rounded mounds of her tits to the dip of her waist and back out again at her hips. Bountiful. Kinsey Dalton was fucking bountiful.

It was almost enough to melt his brain, until he realized what he was doing and how damn disrespectful it was—she was, after all, in her own home and he'd basically already barged in. So he forced his focus upward to her face, but the trajectory of his gaze traveled right over the hard points of her nipples.

Some part of his brain noticed that one was higher than

the other and the perfect so-called imperfection made her even hotter to him. Griff locked that information away to analyze and appreciate fully later. Fine, he *shouldn't* be appreciating Kinsey's nipples, but he was human and she was fucking fantastic and there was no way he'd ever forget it.

But that wasn't why he was here. He shut the door behind him, planted his feet shoulder-width apart, and crossed his arms. Was that to keep himself from reaching for her, pulling her closer so he could envelop her in his arms, hold her close, and show her that he was on her side now, tomorrow, and forever?

Yeah. It was.

It fucking sucked.

"You can't kill Todd." Pulling his attention away from the way she looked standing in the middle of the living room with the city skyline glimmering in the rush-hour sunlight behind her, he marshaled his mental activity to finding a solution that wouldn't end with a felony charge. "But we can make his life hell."

Kinsey wrapped her arms around her middle and did this grimace-smile thing that wrinkled her nose. "That's sweet, but—"

"Not sweet." He was very much not fucking sweet, or nice, or some other bullshit right now. He was pissed. No. Furious. It made his entire body tense as adrenaline surged through him. All he could think about was protecting Kinsey—not from herself. The woman was beyond capable of that. No, he wanted to do whatever it took to help her get her vengeance. "How bad do you want him to hurt?"

Her blue eyes went wide. "Griff."

He waited, but there wasn't anything after that; it was just his name. He couldn't blame her. They'd just met. To her, he was only her friend's older brother. She was pity fake dating him. He meant nothing to her even if she meant everything to him.

"No one gets to do whatever the hell he's done to you." He held up his hand when she opened her mouth to speak. "You don't have to tell me what he did. It doesn't matter. It's upset you. That can't stand." It might have been the most words he'd spoken in years. Yet they were still coming, bubbling up inside him and fighting to get out. "So we have options. We'll approach it like a boxing match. What are his weak points? How much damage do you want to inflict? How can I help?"

Kinsey's mouth was agape as she stared at him, blinking. "He's not real."

Now *that* stopped his mouth cold. Each one of the words made sense on their own, but put together in the context of her fiancé, Todd? It was a glitch in the matrix. "What?"

She closed her eyes and let out a long, deep breath through her nose. Then she opened her eyes, looked him dead in the face, and said, "I made Todd up. He's not real."

Griff's brain screeched to a halt. It was just white noise between his ears that was loud enough to almost drown out his raging pulse and the internal scream of *fuck yeah*.

After an audible gulp, she started pacing from one end of the long L-shaped couch to the other, a hand clutching her robe, no doubt so it wouldn't flutter open with the speed of her walking. "Okay, so I know it was immature and ridiculous, but it was the best solution I could come up with at the time." She turned and headed back toward him, her cheeks pink with obvious embarrassment and her eyes watery. "I—"

He held up his hand. She fell silent, her whole body tense and her gaze locked on some object over his left shoulder.

"Let me get this straight," he said, his brain catching back up and the never-ending line of possibilities, options, and opportunities speeding through his mind like cars on the Autobahn. "Todd—your fiancé—isn't real. He doesn't live in Canada. The ring is fake." He paused long enough for her to nod her confirmation that he was right. "I'm assuming you got sick of dealing with all the bullshit that goes along with being a woman in the lab and went with a rapid-acting solution."

She nodded.

It was science's dirty little not-so-secret. An old-boys'-club network that advised against hiring women, as they were often a distraction for others in the lab and the scientists whose egos couldn't take being turned down for a date so they retaliated. It had all gone public a few years ago on social media and, while the sunshine had disinfected it somewhat, the assholes lingered. The scientific cosmetic industry was insular and hard to break into. Her laser-focused self had zoned in on the fastest, simplest, most efficient solution to the problem with a fake fiancé.

"So there's no Todd in danger of being murdered?" he asked, as if he wasn't already sixty steps ahead of that point.

She shook her head and let out a sardonic chuckle. "Not by me."

No.

Todd.

The staticky sounds disappeared under a once-in-a-lifetime-size wave of *fuck yes*. Kinsey Dalton—the woman he loved—was single. He had a chance. Forget falling out of love with her, which was pretty much impossible anyway.

Now he just needed to make her fall in love with him.

Oh yeah, that should be a piece of cake, because you've got such an amazing way with words.

Pinching the bridge of his nose to keep from going further down that thought hole, Griff slammed the door on his father's voice inside his head—the one always predicting failure and fuckups in every part of his life that wasn't inside a lab.

"You're pissed," Kinsey said. "I understand if you don't

want to go on any more of the dates. I'm sorry."

The dates. That's how he could do this—but it wasn't going to happen because he'd lied about his intentions. "You might be the one to want to back out of the dates."

She rested her butt against the back of the couch and cocked her head. "Why?"

He closed the space between them, putting his hands on either side of her, his grip on the couch tight enough that the wood framing bit into his palms. "Because I fell hard for you the minute I heard you in the gym solve five problems in one breath."

The words came out of his mouth a million times more confident than he felt, the potent mix of want and need and hope powering him.

"That moment was pure super-achievement porn. I still think about it." The urge to tilt her chin upward so he could kiss her, hold her, fuck her until she came around him had his toes on the edge of somewhere dangerous, which was exactly why he couldn't let himself touch her—not yet. "You have a fucking sexy brain."

It physically hurt to move away from her, but he had to. He wasn't just some Neanderthal here to throw Kinsey over his shoulder and carry her back to his cave. He took a half step back, but her hand on his arm, her touch so light it was barely there, stopped him from taking another.

She straightened up, moving forward to fill the space he'd vacated, and lifted her face so she was looking him in the eye. "My brain?"

"Sexiest thing I've ever encountered." Five words that were the greatest truth he'd ever known.

Cupping his face with her soft hands, she raised herself up on her tiptoes. "Thank you."

She brushed her mouth across his, pressing in close and blowing his mind before pulling back, blinking as if she wasn't sure what in the hell she'd just done.

He could answer that. She'd started something—*they'd* started something—and he couldn't wait to finish it.

His gaze dropped to her lips, pink and soft and plump with wanting after that tease of a kiss. This was when he should walk away, get out of that apartment, and come up with a plan. Instead, he reached out and curled his hands around her ass and lifted her up. Her arms came around his neck as he took a half step toward the couch, setting her down on the back of it, sliding his hands to her hips to keep her steady, and stepping between her open legs.

Heart racing, he dipped his head down and crushed his lips to hers. Her fingers tugged at his hair as she opened beneath him, her tongue tasting and teasing him as he tried not to lose himself in the pleasure of how she felt against him.

This went beyond attraction, beyond wanting, beyond craving. This was Old Testament coveting. Lust and a possessive need roared through him. He'd known it the first time he'd heard her voice and this knock-you-on-your-ass kiss only confirmed it. He was meant for Kinsey Dalton, body and soul.

Now he just needed to convince her that she was meant for him—too bad that for once in his life, he didn't have even the first clue how to solve that problem. She was in lust with him, he was sure of that. But how was a guy who didn't know the first thing about using his words actually get a woman to fall in love with him? He should probably start by not making her more in lust.

He broke the kiss, setting her down on the ground and stepping back. They stared at each other, both breathing heavily.

"Tomorrow," he said, walking backward to the door because he couldn't seem to make himself look away from her. "Six thirty."

She nodded, her fingertips against her lips, her expression as shell-shocked as he felt.

He'd no more than closed the front door behind him, then he was texting Nash and Dixon.

GRIFF: *My place. SOS.*

Chapter Twenty-Five

Nash and Dixon sat on opposite sides of the counter-height kitchen table, beers in hand, and stared at Griff as if he'd grown a second and third head—and all those heads were having a full-fledged argument about middle part versus side part or some such shit. For his part, Griff kept shuffling the deck.

Rummy helped him focus. The shuffling. The dealing. The calculating of odds and options. Grandma Betty had taught them how to play during the summers they'd spent out at Gable House as a way to keep them out of trouble. Now he played whenever he really needed to think. So when his cousins had shown up at his place, he hadn't said anything until they were sitting down, cards in hand, the score pad sitting on the table next to Dixon. Griff had flipped over the card that would form the beginning of the discard pile and given them the entire situational rundown in the amount of time it took him to organize his hand—by suit in order of ace on down.

Dixon let out a low whistle as he arranged his hand while Nash slid his cards together so it looked like he was only holding one card—he always kept his hand in the same chaotic jumble they'd been dealt—and then took a long drink from his beer.

"So what's the plan?" Nash asked as he took the top card off the stack.

Griff shook his head. "Fuck if I know."

He'd spent the time since leaving Kinsey's in his Lego room trying to concoct the perfect plan and coming up empty. That meant the shower was next, where instead of figuring out how to get Kinsey to fall in love with him, he ended up imagining the way her face had looked after that kiss—her lips swollen and her eyes hazy with lust—so that he'd ended up grabbing his dick and jerking off imagining how good it would have been if he'd gone down on his knees in front of her, spread the wet fabric of her robe, and ate that pussy until she came all over his face.

He shifted in his seat, since whacking off in the shower and then again half an hour ago didn't seem to lessen his ability to get it up at the thought of Kinsey.

"Why does he need a plan?" Dixon looked from Griff to Nash and back again. "It's not like this changes anything. He's not—" He stopped mid-sentence and turned his attention to Nash. "You lucky asshole."

The bet. For Dixon, who counted winning as integral a thing for survival as breathing, of course the bet would factor high.

"When you've got it, you've got it," Nash said, flashing a know-it-all smug grin at their cousin. "But Griff never cared about the bet for Grandma Betty's last present."

"Not true." Okay, kind of true. At the time he'd agreed, really it was just about busting Dixon's balls. "I just don't give a shit about it in comparison to winning over Kinsey."

"Like I said," Dixon continued, drawing a card and then shucking it straight into the discard pile. "Lucky fucking asshole."

Time to bring everything back to the ranch or Nash would continue to gloat while Dixon took his revenge by pulling every petty opportunity possible to score shit points in rummy. "Normally, I wouldn't bring you two into this."

"Awwwww," Nash said, going all in on his innate patronizing tone—the one that always got him glared at even when he didn't mean it. "Our baby is growing up and he needs our help."

These fucking guys—if they weren't all ride or die for one another, he'd probably be the one planning the best option for getting away with murder.

Griff took a card and glanced down at his hand, which, just like his life at the moment, was one thing away from perfection. "I just need a plan."

"You have the dates, numb nuts," Dixon said, swiping up the four of spades that Griff had discarded and then laying down four of a kind. "That's your opportunity to make her fall in love with you right there."

"It's not enough." His gut was all twisted up. Usually that only happened when he was face-to-face with the old man, having to bite his tongue as his dad outlined all the many ways his children had failed to live up to his level of success. Griff could listen to the bitter asshole complain about him all day, but when he went in on Morgan, that's when shit got ugly.

This wasn't that, though. He knew the truth about himself. He might not look it anymore, but he was still the kid who'd spent most of seventh grade stuffed in one locker or another. So Griff did what he always did—he armored up with a scowl dark enough to get mistaken for midnight. "Because Kinsey's fun and I'm—"

"About as joyous as dandruff on a black shirt?" Dixon asked, completely immune to Griff's growly attitude.

"Children," Nash said, rolling his eyes. "We don't have time for all this. Griff here is in love, and he needs our help because he's a loser with women."

Griff would have argued the point if he could, but it was true.

"The next date is Paint and Sip, right?" Nash asked as he played a straight ace to queen of hearts.

"You picked it," Griff said before taking a pull of his IPA.

"So not a lot of talking, that's to your advantage." Dixon picked up the entire discard pile and started to lay down several sets of three of a kind, knowing full well that limited his opponents' ability to rummy off his cards and therefore would limit their points. "You need a list of talking points so you don't clam up."

"Perfect start," Nash said, scowling at the four sets of three of a kind laid out in front of Dixon. "We also need to work on presentation."

Griff glanced down at his Lego Master T-shirt and cargo shorts. "The fuck?"

Dixon nodded in agreement. "You can't wear that on a date."

"It's just clothes." Was there a dress code to go paint pictures of sunsets and—God forbid—*Live, Laugh, Love* signs?

"You need a Henley," Dixon said. "Women love Henleys."

He plucked the nine of diamonds off the discard pile and used it to lay down a four-card run and throw his cousins off his scent, because he was about to go out on their asses on the next turn. "What is that?"

Nash shrugged. "No fucking clue."

"And you need a haircut," Dixon continued, ignoring them per usual.

Griff ran his hands through his longish dark hair. He liked his hair. "Hell no."

Nash smirked. "And a shave."

He looked at his cousins, who were both grinning at him like the clowns they were. "Assholes."

Nash and Dixon didn't even bother pretending they hadn't been giving him shit.

"Seriously, though, the talking points is a solid start," Nash said, throwing away the ace of hearts—a clear sign he was about to go out. "But if that kiss was as good as you think—"

Griff broke in. "I didn't mention a kiss."

"You didn't have to." Dixon scoffed, picking up and throwing away the same card. "We know you."

"Pricks," he grumbled, taking a card from the deck that would serve as his throwaway.

"Anyway," Nash said. "What you have there is a tool in your arsenal—sex sells, and you want Kinsey to buy."

Griff paused mid-motion as he was about to lay down the three-card straight, discard, and win the hand. "That's regressive."

Nash smirked. "That's realistic. Attraction leads to more."

"So your great suggestion is I use talking points you two are going to give me and then hypnotize her with my dick?" he asked, turning the idea around in his head.

"If you can," Dixon said with a good-natured chuckle.

And there it was. The solution was so simple and so stupid that it just might work. Mutual attraction and desire were the basis for connections between people and chemicals. Keeping the right balance, conducting the dance with the right amount of give and take, and being in the right place at the right time all factored into a lasting bond.

When he laid down the straight and discarded his last

card, winning the hand, his cousins groaned and tossed their cards on the table, but Griff barely heard them. He was already weighing the options and coming up with a plan of action to follow through on that promise he made himself— that she was going to fall as hard for him as he had for her.

Chapter Twenty-Six

KINSEY

Kinsey was dragging ass into work the next morning, wishing to God she was even close to awake when she stepped into the elevator. The doors were just starting to slide closed when Billie quick-walked in five-inch heels between them, looking chic and utterly pulled together.

"Rough night?" Billie asked, cocking her head and giving Kinsey an appraising once-over, her eyes going wide when she got to Kinsey's ring finger. "Oh, honey. Bad news?"

"Not really." And the less said about it, the better.

Simplicity was at the heart of her plan. No ring. Let people make their own assumptions. A lie of omission? Okay, fine, yes it was. But it was better than having to go through and figure out a straight-up lie of a story to throw folks off the scent of the original tall tale.

Billie gave her a sympathetic head shake. "So it's like that?"

Kinsey nodded. "It is."

"Good for you." She leaned in close. "Word to the wise, you probably want to avoid Gavin today. He's in full asshole mode."

"So it's a day that ends in Y?" In the past week, he'd been curt to everyone and had even made one person hustle out to the stairwell to have a quick cry.

Billie chuckled. "Well, that and there's been—"

The elevator door opened, revealing Leigh and Gavin practically nose to nose and not in the sexy about-to-kiss way but in the about-to-go-down-on-a-felony-and-totally-cool-with-it way. Realizing they weren't alone in the hall anymore, both turned to face the elevator. Leigh's cheeks were flushed and her eyes were practically sparking. For his part, Gavin looked more than the usual level of smug self-satisfaction.

"There she is," he said.

A frigid blast of *oh-fuck* went straight down Kinsey's spine.

"Gavin," Leigh said, her tone full of warning.

He shrugged. "If she's done nothing wrong, then she has nothing to worry about."

Leigh let out a huff of frustration. "You have no right—"

"No right to what?" he asked, the words ice pick sharp and just as vicious as he turned on Leigh. "Question the employees I directly supervise? Mentor new scientists into our company culture? Find out why someone declined to disclose they were in tight with Archambeau's biggest rival?"

Oh shit. Oh shit. Oh shit. It wasn't like Kinsey had been hiding her situation, but she hadn't exactly been out in the open, either.

Boy, wasn't that starting to sound like the story of her life.

"Gavin," Leigh said, obviously exasperated. "This isn't the place."

Kinsey's palms were slick with sweat, and the everything

bagel with cream cheese, lox, and capers she'd had for breakfast was definitely thinking of making a return appearance. She'd been wary on Morgan's behalf but hadn't even given a single thought to how her boss might view their newest research and development scientist rooming with a Beckett. Oh God, if anyone found out she hadn't been able to stop thinking about *that kiss* with Griff—the head of Beckett's R&D department—she'd be screwed. Corporate spying was a huge concern in the cosmetics industry. Everyone would assume she was a double agent.

"You're right, Leigh." Gavin turned his attention back on Kinsey. "Why don't you join me in my office? We can have a cup of coffee and discuss your failures."

Leigh sucked in a quick hiss of breath, but before she could say anything, Gavin snapped at her.

"Leigh, I insist that you allow me to run my department in the way of my choosing—within the bounds of human resource approval, of course—or I will walk, and the licensing agreement for Archambeau's biggest money makers will go with me." He gave Leigh a smile that reminded Kinsey of the look Scar gave Mufasa before that awful wildebeest scene. "Who knows, I might even march my way down to Beckett Cosmetics before heading home and have them make their best offer. It is on the way, after all."

The vein in Leigh's temple pulsed in a steady *fuck-you* rhythm. "You can't do anything while our lawyers are in mediation."

"Keep telling yourself that. Unlike some people here"— his gaze slid over to Kinsey—"I've done nothing to materially harm the company, and therefore the agreement stands. I leave and the company fails. Do you really want to push me?"

Leigh stood there and worked her jaw back and forth as she flexed her fingers. She wasn't a woman on the edge. She was someone who had enough of other people's shit and was *this* close to saying *fuck the licensing agreements, the company could survive without them.*

That was no doubt possible, but Kinsey had done her research on the company, and it would be harder than the rounded toes of Uncle Earl's steel-toed boots to make happen.

Bonsoir Rajeunir and Toujours accounted for about 80 percent of Archambeau's market share. Leigh's ex-husband, Luca, had well and truly set the company up for failure after it became clear she'd get full ownership of it in the divorce settlement. By selling Gavin the licensing rights—no doubt knowing full well what a power-hungry misogynist he was— Luca had to have sliced a knife right through the aortic artery of the woman who'd helped found the company.

"I'm sending HR up," Leigh said.

"That will save me from having to send the email with my documentation. Thank you," Gavin said, not sounding the least bit sincere. "My office, Kinsey. Now."

He turned and walked through the clear glass doors of the lab. He didn't look back, but if he had, he would have realized that Kinsey was still in the hall, the bottom of her chin just about rubbing the floor.

"Billie," Leigh said. "We need HR up here as quickly as possible so he doesn't try to pull any of his shit."

The other woman didn't pause typing out a message on her iPad. "Already on it."

Leigh took Kinsey by the shoulders. "Gavin's an ass. I'm sorry. I promise I'm working on it. I just have to get through this mediation process and then…" She glanced over at the lab door, her jaw tensing. "Well, then things will be different. He'll be gone. I promise."

Kinsey's gut was somewhere around her knees—despite the fact that she wasn't a confrontational person. That was part of the reason why she'd come up with Todd in the first place. Having a fake fiancé killed a lot of conversations before they could even start. All she wanted was to go to work, do the job, and go home to... Well, lately that had been to have inappropriate fantasies about her best friend's older brother.

"It's okay," Kinsey said. "I'm sure everything will work out."

Was she offering assurance or trying to convince herself? A bit of both? Yeah, totally a bit of both. Taking in a deep breath before exhaling it slow and steady, Kinsey straightened her spine, squared her shoulders, and shot Leigh and Billie a smile she hoped looked more determined than shaky, then headed into the lab.

Gavin was waiting for her in his office, which meant he hollered "come in" when she knocked and then ignored her for a full three minutes while he typed on his keyboard. Several of the other folks in the lab had a pool going about this move of his and if he was actually doing any work or just typing "Gavin Longshield is number one" over and over again on a blank document.

Finally, he stopped typing and leveled a glare at her. "Tell me, Kinsey, did you take the job planning on stealing for your buddies at Beckett Cosmetics, or did you just luck into it?"

She flinched. She couldn't help it. The accusation landed like a smack across her face. "I have no idea what you're talking about."

"Really?" He scoffed. "My information is incorrect? You aren't living with Morgan Beckett in some ridiculously expensive apartment rent-free?"

Heat rushed up her body so fast, she was surprised she didn't spontaneously combust. "It's only until I can find something else."

She'd never thought about how people would view her living arrangement. She'd met Morgan as just Morgan, and they'd become friends because of their snarky sense of humor and love of journaling, stickers, and planners. It hadn't been about what Kinsey could gain from it, but that's where Gavin's brain went with it, and he'd delivered the accusation with such scathing contempt, she almost felt as if she *had* done something wrong.

"Of course it is," he said with a sneer. "It wasn't as if anyone could just accidentally find herself in such a situation. Life seldom works out that way unless it's all been planned."

"I've known Morgan for years," she said, her voice shaking with the effort to suppress the dizzying mix of her emotions that went from shock to anger to fear that this could be the universe's way of paying her back for the lies about Todd.

"And what better way for a dirt-poor girl from Podunk, South Wherever to ingratiate herself with the upper echelons of Harbor City than to do a little corporate stealing?" He placed his palms flat on his desk and leaned forward. "I've been working day and night for a year on Fontaine de Jouvence. This moisturizer will change the market and make billions. It is revolutionary, and I will not have you ruin it because Suzy Social Climber wants leverage."

She shook her head, blinking rapidly because she would not give this jerk the satisfaction of angry crying in front of him. "You're wrong about me."

"I doubt it." He turned back to his keyboard and started typing. "Just know I'm watching you. If any more of my notes in the system are accessed by unknown parties, you will be caught. Also, don't think people in the lab aren't talking about your cozy relationship with the Becketts. That's not the way you want to go if you plan to be respected around here. Everyone is already questioning your ability to do this job, what with that horrendous Southern accent—why add to the problems because of your associations in light of this leak?"

"Correlation does not equal causation," she said, falling back on her training.

Gavin let out a sarcastic *harrumph* of a chuckle. "I strongly suggest you find new living arrangements that don't include the family owners of our biggest competition. Good Lord, what would be next? Dating their head of R&D?"

There was a sharp rap on the door. Kinsey looked back over her shoulder and recognized Tanisha from HR.

"Good to see you again, Tanisha, but we're already done here." Having shot Kinsey a tight smile that was more of a snarl, he asked, "Aren't we?"

Frustration bubbled inside her, but Kinsey covered it with a cast-iron pot lid that had been seasoned with two and a half decades' worth of surviving and thriving despite patriarchal bullshit. Leigh had told her it would only be a matter of time. She'd put her trust in the woman who'd fought to create and keep the company she loved.

"Yes, absolutely," Kinsey said as she got up and then headed for the door.

Tanisha raised an eyebrow in a silent question, but Kinsey had already chosen her path. If it felt like everyone was watching her as she walked through the lab, it was because they were. No doubt Gavin had already planted the seed of doubt about her. More than likely, there wasn't a leak at all, but even the rumor of it was an awfully convenient way to push out one of Leigh's hires.

The morning went about as well as could be expected after that, but her shoulders had finally inched down from her ears and she'd stopped feeling the itch of everyone's gazes on her when one of the receptionists buzzed through on the intercom at her station.

"Kinsey, there's a Griff Beckett on line one for you."

Everyone within earshot stopped what they were doing and turned as one unit to look at her. Dread, cold and icy, crept across her skin.

Just fucking great.

Chapter Twenty-Seven

GRIFF

"Sorry again about the whole calling-at-work thing," Griff said, gripping the steering wheel tight as they headed across the Harbor Bridge to Waterbury and the Paint and Sip date Dixon and Nash had cooked up with Fiona's help.

Calling Kinsey at work had been an impulse that he probably should have ignored, but he'd gone with his gut, something he probably—no, scratch that, definitely—shouldn't have done, considering his track record with women. The stiffness in her voice when she'd picked up had told him immediately that he'd overstepped.

Some guys could get away with that shit. For example, Nash could have smoothed it over with a well-timed joke, and Dixon would have used the power of his personality to move the situation forward.

Not Griff.

He'd been all elbows and knees, everything rushing through his head at full throttle and him without the ability to catch any of it. Whatever ground he'd gained with that kiss last night had given way like quicksand. So he'd fallen back on silence and grunts after telling Kinsey he was making sure she wasn't going to ditch the date.

No denying it, he was a stone-cold charmer.

Kinsey made a little grimace face that shouldn't be cute but was. It was sorta like seeing a rainbow try to be a thunder cloud. He'd no more started to smile at the idea of her not having to pretend to be all sunshine and lollipops around him when his dad's voice roared to life in his head.

You should never offer anyone else personality advice, given you only know how to be gruff or asleep.

"Not a big deal, the timing was just messy."

Look at you, mucking it all up again, boy.

Griff shoved his dad's voice down deep, blocking it even as he knew it was only a matter of time before the old man popped up again, either in Griff's head or in real life. He had to go up to Roberts Pointe soon to see good ol' Pops, which meant his subconscious was pretty much all Dad all the time. It fucking sucked, but if he went to the family home at least once every two or three months, then Dad left Morgan alone. He could suck it up so she wouldn't have to deal with their dad's bullshit.

Kinsey put her hand on his forearm, her touch gentle. "Are you okay?"

"What do you mean?" he asked, gunning it through the intersection right as the green light he had been too distracted to notice turned yellow. "I'm fine. I'm always fine."

"Seriously, don't worry about the call." She let go of his arm and fidgeted with the strap of her purse. "Work's just tense. It was good to hear your voice."

Yanked back from the edge of complete mental fuckery with thoughts about his dad, Griff let out the breath he'd been holding and forced his grip on the steering wheel to loosen. Maybe it was being around Kinsey, maybe it was her saying she liked hearing his voice, but the right side of his mouth turned up as a warm feeling settled in his chest.

"Is that a smile?" she teased, her own grin practically ear to ear. "An actual smile from Griff Beckett?"

There was no use in trying to straighten his mouth, not that he was sure he could. "Nah, just a twitch."

"And a joke, too." Kinsey chuckled and then continued dialing up her Southern accent. "Why, Mr. Beckett, I do think you might actually have a good time tonight."

"Fun is overrated."

Is this your version of flirting?

Sadly, yes.

"Really?" She pivoted in her seat so she was practically facing him, the other cars on the parkway going by behind her.

The move pressed the seat belt tighter against her as it lay between her tits. Damn. She was wearing jean shorts and a white T-shirt with a V-neck. He couldn't stop sneaking peeks from the corner of his eye and being really fucking jealous of a piece of safety gear. He white-knuckled the steering wheel again but for a totally different reason this time.

She wet her lips and toyed with the nylon strip. "Is that why you get pummeled in the ring for a hobby?"

"I give as good as I get, and it helps me relax."

"What else do you do for fun?" she asked.

Her soft voice brushed across every nerve ending in his body. A million dirty thoughts and images of her naked, telling him with that sweet mouth of hers exactly how she wanted him to make her come slammed into his brain at once. He almost veered onto the shoulder of the road as he exited the parkway and onto the expressway that would dump them out in Waterbury's business district. Using years of practice in not saying what was going through his head, he let out a noncommittal grunt.

"Griff," she said, his name sounding like a stroke, a tug,

a squeeze to his ears. "Tell me."

It took just about everything he had not to pull over onto the side of the road and show her, but instead he shrugged, changed lanes, passed a minivan with a kid in the back flipping off every car as it went by, and grunted again.

"What do you do to relax?" she asked, her gaze intent on him as if no matter what the answer was, she'd be fascinated. "You have to have more hobbies."

He was hot, his palms were slick, and his dick was getting hard. He had a plan for this, dammit, and it didn't involve coming in his pants on the Waterbury Expressway.

"Legos," he said, grinding out the single word. "I have a whole room's worth and some more in storage."

She let out a little gasp. "You have an *entire room* devoted to Legos?"

His gut twisted. Well, there it was. He'd lost her now.

"That is so cool!" She clapped her hands together. "What's the biggest one you've ever made? Do you display them or is the room for building only? How long have you done it? How'd you get started?"

The rapid-fire questions and her enthusiasm quieted all his other thoughts, and he relaxed back against the leather seat.

"The Lego Architect Colosseum, which has more than nine thousand pieces and is based on the Roman one." He continued answering her questions in order. "Yes. Since I was a kid. And my mom got me started. She used to do them with me, and when she died, there were a bunch left over that we'd planned on doing. I did them on my own and just kept doing them."

They'd spread them out on the big dining room table that sat twenty, the one they only used when Dad was home and insisted. By the time Griff and his mom started building, he, Morgan, and Mom ate on the counter-height square table for four in the kitchen six days a week. They'd still used the crystal glasses—one filled with wine, the other two with cherry-flavored water—and the dishes came from one five-star restaurant or executive chef or another, but they got to sit close enough to one another that no one had to shout to be heard. That had all ended with the accident. After that, Dad still stayed away most nights or locked himself up in his study while he and Morgan made do with YouTube cooking tips and online grocery delivery.

Kinsey reached out and gave his shoulder a squeeze. "I'm sorry about your mom."

Of course she'd known before he'd said anything. "Morgan told you."

"Yeah." She moved her hand back into her lap and turned her body so she was facing front again, her face angled so she was looking out the passenger window. "We bonded in our group over missing moms."

He got into the far-right lane in prep for the off ramp. "Your mom's dead?"

She shook her head. "My mom is still alive, she's just out there somewhere doing whatever it is that's more important than the kids she left on her mother's doorstep. I haven't talked to her in years. Sometimes there's a Christmas card."

"Ouch."

She let out a sigh. "Pretty much."

He pulled off the expressway, and they drove the five blocks to Paint and Sip in silence.

Way to go, numb nuts. Got any other topics you want to ask her about? Maybe her last heartbreak or when she lost her first pet?

He parked in the small lot on the corner—he sucked at parallel parking—and they sat there for a second.

"Sorry for dredging up mom stuff," he said.

"It's okay. I usually don't tell people about her. It's just that with you..." She paused and then gave him a shy half smile. "Well, with you I'm just comfortable."

An unexpected warmth radiated through his chest as he tapped his fingers on the steering wheel to a chipper beat. It wasn't like him to feel like this, but around Kinsey? It was just different, better, easier.

He heard the click of her unfastening her seat belt a few beats before she leaned over and kissed him, her lips lightly touching his before she pulled back and opened her door.

"We better get in there before class starts."

Stunned from the kiss and all those 428 possibilities that involved them both naked coming at him at once, he sat there watching as she got out of the car and shut the door, ready for their date.

So maybe he hadn't fucked this up—yet.

Chapter Twenty-Eight

Kinsey's lips were still tingling, and she had no clue what she'd been thinking about with that kiss. Really, it had been barely a kiss, more of a slight brush of her lips across his. Even Webster's would have a hard time defining *that* as a kiss.

Yeah, keep telling yourself that.

She would because it was true, thank you very much.

Uh-huh, then why is your whole body tingling with anticipation and why did you scoot your chair a little closer to Griff's when you sat down?

All right. That voice in her head could just shut the fuck up now.

Work today had pretty much proven that her life had gotten complicated fast even with ditching her fake fiancé. This wasn't a date—it was just helping out her friend's older brother win a bet. All his talk last night and that kiss that had seared her right down to her toes curling in the carpet? Well, that was just the lust talking. She could understand that. She was getting off to him on a regular basis in the privacy of her bedroom. Lust was simple. Lust she understood. Lust was easy to take care of.

The plan burst to life fully formed in the time between one heartbeat and the next. There was no reason why she and Griff—two fully grown adults—couldn't get the attraction turning the air electric around them out of the way so they could go about their lives. He'd said that he'd fallen for her, but that wasn't logical. People didn't fall for her. They liked to fantasize about the idea of the big-boobed blonde in the bedroom, but there was more to her than double Ds, and that freaked people out. She was used to it. Plus, more than one ex had told her that her constant chatter and need to fix everything around her drove men away.

But if she and Griff got what was between them out of their systems, then he could go on and win his bet and she could get back to work at Archambeau without worrying that anyone would find out she was more than tangentially involved with Beckett Cosmetics's head of R&D.

She nearly blurted out her proposal before remembering where she was.

Paint and Sip was a studio crowded with tables already set up with painting supplies, a canvas with a few lines drawn on it, and small plastic cups of wine. Griff was one of the few men there, but that didn't seem to bother him. Instead, he'd just sat down on the barstool next to hers and rearranged his area so that the cup with wine of a questionable vintage and cup half filled with water to rinse his brushes were on opposite sides of his space.

Watching him get settled, the way he organized the chaos around him, was soothing and a turn-on at the same time. Then he reached over and adjusted where his paints had crossed over into her territory so that he wasn't encroaching. By the time he folded the drying paper towel in half and then set the folded strip underneath his perfectly lined-up brushes before sitting back and crossing his muscled arms over his broad chest, Kinsey's nipples were hard buds of arousal.

Fine.

There was a lot about Griff that had her catching her breath—the way his biceps curled, the rare sighting of a half smile, how the man filled out a pair of jeans—but it was the way he made a place for everything and everyone that really got her.

Letting her plan for Operation Get Naked percolate, she hooked her feet around the legs of her barstool and took another look at what they would be painting.

She leaned in close to Griff, resting her hand on his thick thigh—for balance of course— and asked, "Were you expecting a lake scene with pine trees and a few happy little birds?"

"My money was on a sunset," he said as he covered her hand with his much larger one.

Kinsey's heart missed a beat or three before restarting with a vengeance. The air crackled around them, and his gaze dipped to her mouth. She didn't mean to bite down on her lower lip, but it just sort of happened, kind of like how she'd squeezed her legs together before she gave in to the urge to slide her palm higher as she kissed him for real.

Plan? What plan? She was just winging it at this point and couldn't stop.

A pinched-faced older woman cleared her throat and then gave a meaningful glance at the girl beside her, who had to be her maybe nine-year-old granddaughter. The girl watched them with rapt attention.

Okay, Kinsey Dalton. Time to dial it back, girl. You are in public.

She slid her hand free and turned to look at the sample of tonight's painting project that was sitting on an easel at the front of the room. Larry, the man who owned Paint and Sip and led all the art classes, had told them he'd named it Unpack Your Feelings and said it was about the emotional addiction of online shopping and the negative impact it had on the environment. The painting showed a person buried under a huge pile of cardboard shipping boxes, one hand sticking out zombie-at-the-end-of-a-horror-movie-style against a backdrop of at least twenty delivery vans blowing diesel smoke into the sky.

A chorus of raucous giggles erupted from a group of four women who were obviously regulars.

"Sorry, Larry," said a lady with glasses wearing a *Get Nerdy With It* T-shirt. "We'll be good."

Larry pushed his glasses back up the bridge of his nose and smiled indulgently. "First time for everything."

The women looked at one another and all did a sort of fair-enough shoulder shrug, then started giggling again.

"Okay, we're gonna start off with a line of dismal gray across the middle of your canvas like so."

An hour and a glass of wine later, Kinsey stood up and took a step back to look at her painting. No one was ever going to mistake her for an artist anytime soon, but it wasn't half bad.

"We're not going to hang these up, are we?" Griff asked, coming to stand next to her.

"God no," she said with a chuckle. "I say we present them—framed—to Nash and Dixon, since they thought this date up."

He grinned down at her. "I like that plan."

Then he dipped his thumb in water and used it to wipe away a fleck of paint that had ended up on her cheek. His touch was gentle but firm, sending little shock waves through her that went straight to her clit. A quiet gasp escaped before she could stop it, and Griff's lips curved in a sexy smirk that said he knew exactly what he was doing.

That wasn't fair. So she grabbed his hand and turned his palm, placing a soft kiss right in the middle.

Then she gave him a wink and walked out the door with her ugly-ass painting and her very-good plan to have her wicked way with him later that night firmly in mind.

Chapter Twenty-Nine

KINSEY

The air in the car as they went over the Harbor Bridge was thick with tension. Kinsey hadn't said anything after leaving Griff to follow her at Paint and Sip. She'd waited by the car, scrolling through social media, while he strode across the parking lot, his jaw set in a hard line and his body rigid.

Someone who didn't know better might think he was pissed. She, however, did know better. She'd unwound the Griff Beckett knot, and the truth of it was the man who seemed not to have a single solitary emotion had so many of them that he had them on lockdown, unable to escape and mess with his orderly life.

All that effort expended on control had her itching to peel back the layers and see what was underneath. All that natural curiosity of hers was bound to get her into trouble one of these days, and if she had anything to say about it—and she did—then it would be today.

On the drive home from Waterbury, she sat there, quiet,

and watched him. The sinewy muscles in his forearms as he wrapped his long fingers around the steering wheel at ten and two. The tension in his jaw when he cut a glance over and accidentally on purpose caught her toying with the necklace that slipped down between her breasts. The low grumble he made, which she didn't quite catch the words of, but she understood all the same and it had her wet enough that she was a little worried about her panties.

They made it back to the city in half the time it had taken them to get to Paint and Sip. Sure, maybe the traffic gods had smiled down on them or maybe, probably, definitely it was the way he swerved around slower-moving vehicles, took several cut-through shortcuts, and treated the speed limit like a just-in-case-you-want-to suggestion. By the time they pulled into the building's parking garage, she was practically electric with want. Every nerve ending was primed, pumped, and ready for action.

She'd barely stepped out of the car before Griff was on her side, a wall of lust, determination, and promise. He glowered down at her, and her breath caught. The scientific literature had documented spontaneous orgasms in women for decades, and a Rutgers University brain scan study found that the pleasure centers of participants' brains lit up in ways indistinguishable from normal orgasm when they were enjoying the erotic fantasy of their choice. Still, Kinsey had never experienced that pulsating ache right on the edge of coming without even being touched...until now.

Griff didn't say anything. He just cupped her ass and lifted her up as his mouth came crashing down on hers.

Fuck me. Literally.

She wanted to scream the words as she wrapped her legs around his hips and ground against him, but to do so would have meant cutting off this kiss, and it was more likely she'd put six sugar packets in her grits than do that.

This was like being in the front car of a roller coaster climbing that first big peak. It was all excitement and adrenaline and scream-worthy anticipation and the knowledge that whatever was gonna happen next, it was gonna blow her hair back.

He squeezed her ass cheeks, using those big hands of his to hold her against him. The length of his cock fitting against her core was enough to make her doubt her plan. Fucking Griff out of her system so that they could go back to achieving their respective and nonconnected goals seemed like a great idea at Paint and Sip. Now, when she could feel just how hard he was, the possibility that once wouldn't be enough loomed larger—but not enough to make her change her mind.

This was too good, too much, too everything.

He broke the kiss, his hungry lips moving across her jawline and to her neck as he backed her up so she was against the car. She tightened her legs as he freed one of his hands, using it to tug her T-shirt free and slip underneath. How he managed to get a hand between them considering she was all but literally glued to him, she had no clue, but there he was, rubbing the pad of his thumb over her still-bra-covered nipple. She wasn't sure she could get any more sensitive or desperate for his touch, but she did.

He nipped at her neck, kissed the delicate skin better, and then continued on. Kinsey's fingers were tangled in his dark hair, anchoring herself before she just flew away or exploded or got a look at another dimension as she ground against him, so frantic to feel him, to get to that place where she'd find relief that dry humping him seemed a valid option.

She was close, so fucking close, and they both still had all their clothes on.

He sat her down and nudged her feet shoulder-width apart while she was still too dazed to even think to question it. One of his hands went to her hip while the other stayed under her shirt, trailing down from her rock-hard nipples and over her stomach, sending sizzles of desire in its wake.

"Kinsey, I'm gonna make you come here, and then I'm gonna take you upstairs and fuck you until neither of us can lift our heads off the pillows." He ran his fingertips across her bare skin above the waistband of her shorts. "Does that sound good to you?"

Fuck yes roared through her head, but already dick drunk without even touching it, the best she could do was nod.

He flicked his thumb across the button of her shorts, popping it open. "Words finally escaping you?" he teased.

The big, hot jerk picked this moment to tease her for being silent for once? He'd pay for that. Later. Now she just wanted—needed to get off.

"It sounds," she said, as out of breath as if she'd done laps around Meemaw's ten acres, "very, very good."

Eyes dark with lust, he slid his hands south, forcing her zipper down as he did so. Two long fingers glided over her hard, aching clit swollen with desire.

"Later, I'm gonna eat this pussy, just bury my face in it, and lick and suck and taste until you're right on the edge, and then I'm gonna back off before taking you right there again." He bracketed her clit with the length of his fingers and slid them up and down her slick slit. "My face is gonna be so wet from you and my tongue's gonna get tired and that's when I'm gonna use my fingers."

He squeezed his fingers together, increasing the pressure on her sensitive flesh. "Trace that opening. Dip inside. Stretch you, play you, make you want it so bad that it wipes out every other thought but me in your head, just like I can't think of anything else when I think of you." Up and down he stroked, gliding over her clit, demanding her response. "You take up all the space. You quiet everything else. It's just you, Kinsey."

He paused, his breath coming in nearly as fast and hard

as hers. "And when you're there, twisting on my bed, begging me not to stop, not to make you wait, I'm gonna slide my dick home, balls deep, so you come all over me and with me and we are both absolutely fucking wrecked for anyone but each other."

Her breath caught and her thighs started to shake. This was what happened when Mr. Silent started talking? Good gravy.

"Griff."

"Yeah, baby? You want more?" he asked, increasing the speed of his fingers because he obviously knew damn well the answer to that question.

"Yes," she said anyway, fighting to keep her eyes open against the onslaught of pleasure. "I want all of that."

He caught her gaze, his so intense, his eyes had gone dark with it, and then leaned forward, his breath coming in hot pants against her temple. "Fuck, Kinsey."

The yearning. The need. The bone-deep promise in those words. It was all there. All for her.

Her incoming orgasm pulled back as if someone was pulling on the strings of a slingshot. Pulling it back farther and farther until it seemed like it would break and then letting go so all of that pleasure was flying forward, through her, over her, in her, and washing over her as she climaxed hard enough that her groan of pleasure echoed in the parking garage.

Some part of her realized what she'd done and where she'd done it, but it was a small part. The rest of her felt too fucking good to care. She let out a shaky breath and opened her eyes to see Griff sucking her juices off his fingers, a possessive look on his face that should probably worry her but didn't—not even the littlest, tiniest bit.

"We're not done," she said, needing him to confirm what he'd said—that all of it had been real, that she hadn't just dreamed it up.

"Not even close." He buttoned her shorts, pulled up the zipper, and let out a groan that sounded a lot like a growl and a pledge as he patted the crotch of her shorts. "Not even a little bit."

Thank God.

Chapter Thirty

GRIFF

The elevator wasn't moving fast enough. Past Griff had been an asshole for thinking that living on the top floor was anywhere close to a good idea.

Kinsey stood in front of him, her perfect ass snug against his hard cock as he glared at the security camera in the corner of the elevator. His fingers—the same ones that had just been inside her—were resting on her hips. He still couldn't believe it. He'd never done anything close to that before. He kept his shit locked down. Words. Emotions. Wants. Needs. Complaints. Celebrations. All of it stayed folded up and shoved in a pocket to be forgotten about. The only exception was when he stepped into the ring and finally let go—until Kinsey had walked into his gym.

That moment changed everything.

It changed him.

And now here he was, in a small metal box willing it to go faster so he didn't strip her down in between the twentieth and twenty-first floors so he could drop to his knees and get a taste of her before sinking into her right up against the wall, his pants only lowered enough to get out his cock. Every inhale filled his lungs with the smell of her shampoo, of her orgasm, of *her*, and it imprinted itself on him, a sensory recall trigger he'd never forget. She may not be his, but he was hers, and fuck if he couldn't stop spinning out fantasies from the image of waking up with her asleep on his chest to one of both of them passed out naked and sweaty, exhausted, and satisfied. He wanted all of it and everything in between. He wanted *her*, and he wanted it right the fuck now.

Kinsey arched against him, watching his distorted reflection in the metal doors. "You're gonna crack a tooth if you keep grinding your teeth like that."

He let out a grunt or a growl or a groan or more than likely some sound that was a mix of all three. It was the most he could do at the moment; fighting to keep himself in check was a white-knuckle endeavor at this point.

If he let go with one thing, all the loose strands would escape his grasp. That's what had happened to his dad. The old man had been a narcissistic asshole before Griff's mom had died, and after it had only gotten worse. The scraped-up edges became cracks, became broken pieces, became jagged, rusty shards of a life busted up by his own hands and out-of-control ego. Griff couldn't—wouldn't—fall into the same trap. He couldn't stop loving Kinsey, but he'd maintain control, keep his words to himself, and bury any vulnerabilities until he could pretend they didn't exist anymore.

Kinsey twisted and wrapped her arms around his neck, a wicked smile on her face. "Guess I'll just have to try another way to convince you," she said as she raised herself on her tiptoes and kissed him.

Just like that, every thought in his head was obliterated along with his tenuous hold on his self-control right as the elevator doors opened. In one swift movement, he broke the kiss, took Kinsey by the waist, and put her over his right shoulder before striding out of the elevator like a man on a mission, because he was—to get her naked and orgasming all over his dick as soon as possible.

Not one to be undone by being mostly upside down, her hands were busy tugging his shirt free of his pants, obviously as ready as he was to get rid of all their clothes. Once inside his penthouse, though, he slid her down his front so they were face-to-face. Without taking the time to think about a plan or anything else, he wrapped his fingers around her wrists, pulling up her arms as he backed her against the wall and kissed her, putting all that need raging through him into one action. She rewarded him by wrapping her legs around his hips, tangling her fingers in his hair, and kissing him back with a focused intensity that blew him the fuck away. He could feel her heat through the layers of their clothing, and there was nothing more he wanted at the moment than to have both of them burn.

That's when he became a man facing a shitty decision: put Kinsey down so he could strip them both or hold on to her and enjoy the way she felt in his arms, the little sound she made when he did that thing with his tongue, and the way she just fit perfectly against him. Desperate beyond anything he'd ever known before to touch her bare skin again, he released her arms and took two steps back.

"Take it off," he said, breathing hard and unable to tear his gaze away from her as he toed off his shoes.

She bit her bottom lip and lifted an eyebrow. "Take what off?"

"All of it." He yanked his shirt over his head and went to work on his jeans.

"You mean these?" She undid her shorts and shimmied out of them, kicking them to the side along with her shoes.

He mentally cursed the fact that her shirt was long enough to reach the top of her thighs. The torment of seeing what was hinted at underneath was worse than no hint at all.

"More," he said, his voice low and rough.

"Greedy, aren't you?"

"Yes." He yanked his shirt over his head, then shoved down his jeans and his boxer briefs, leaving him bare to her.

The little gasp of appreciation she let out and the way her eyes went dark made his dick even harder than it had been a heartbeat ago. To be wanted by this woman was all he could hope for at this moment. She didn't love him—not yet, anyway, but by damn she was gonna want him just as badly as he craved her.

Her hands shook as she reached under the back of her shirt and performed some kind of hidden maneuver that ended with her pulling her bra out from one sleeve. But by the time it had landed on the floor, she seemed to have regained part of herself. Her hot gaze trained on him, she took in every bit of him. The muscles. The tattoos. The scar along his rib cage. Griff had been stared at a lot in his life—paparazzi after his mother died trailing after him, looking for a comment on the messy scandal that had followed; other fighters in the gym sizing him up expecting to take him down; assholes in the industry who assumed there was nothing in his head; and his own father, who only saw what was missing when he looked at his son. But Kinsey? She looked at him as if he was perfect, as if she'd been waiting her whole life for him.

"What happened to all that dirty talk downstairs?" she asked, her hands going up under her shirt, lifting it a few inches higher but not enough to reveal anything. "Hearing you say what you wanted to do to me was the hottest thing I've ever heard."

He cupped his balls, squeezing them hard to pull back from the edge of the cliff he was racing toward. "You liked that? You like it when I talk?"

She bit down on her bottom lip, looked up at him through her lashes, and nodded, then lowered her hands, taking her panties with her. He watched, anticipation a living, breathing thing inside him, as the white lace glided down her thick thighs and her strong calves before pooling at her feet.

Jesus.

He couldn't fucking take in any air. His lungs and his brain had shut down. All he could process was the lust that was kneecapping him at the sight of her in only a thin, oversize white cotton T-shirt.

"Griff," she said, yanking his attention back up to her face. "I really liked it."

Something feral raced through him, a completely uncivilized, raw lust that practically burned him from the inside out. She wanted that? She wanted that part of him that he didn't show anyone? The hard part. The rough part. The secret part. It was hers. All of it was hers, just like he was. He reached out and hooked his finger in the V of her T-shirt and pulled her in close. Desire flooded her gaze, and she let out a soft, sexy moan.

"If you liked hearing me say it," he said, "then you're gonna love actually experiencing it."

He picked her up, tossing her over his shoulder again, and then marched naked toward the bedroom, one hand on her bare ass as he worked out exactly what he was going to do to get her off next.

Chapter Thirty-One

He was so damn close to touching her *exactly* where she wanted and yet he wouldn't ease that ache between her legs. Instead, his huge hand palmed her ass as he stalked across his penthouse. Sure, she could have been pissed about the whole over-the-shoulder caveman thing, but it gave her a great view of the muscles in his butt. The man had a phenomenal ass. Somewhere Michelangelo was pissed off that he hadn't lived long enough to sculpt Griff's butt in marble. Mikey had definitely missed out.

They went through a doorway, and Kinsey went from admiring the definition of Griff's glutes to seeing the ceiling when he flipped her off his shoulder. She landed in the middle of his massive bed and had exactly zero point no seconds to acclimate herself before he grasped an ankle in each hand and dragged her so her ass was on the edge of the bed. In the next heartbeat, his hands were splayed across the insides of her inner thighs as he kneeled between her widespread legs.

Her T-shirt had gotten bunched up as he'd tugged her to him, leaving her exposed to his hungry gaze.

"Show me what you like," Griff said, his voice like rough sandpaper in the best way possible.

Heat sizzled across her skin at his demand—a little bit of embarrassed warmth mixed with a furnace blast of desire. She didn't question, just slipped her fingers down between her legs. God, she was slick and swollen. Even though she'd already had one orgasm, her body was desperate for more.

Griff let out a harsh breath the second her fingers brushed her clit. She curled that sensitive spot, letting the tips of her fingers dip lower. Just giving in to the moment, she let her head fall back against the bed and closed her eyes, imagining she was back in the parking garage again with Griff doing this to her. Circling. Teasing. Pushing her closer and closer to the edge. Then she felt his fingers on her, felt his warm breath on her sensitive folds. Her eyes snapped open and she looked down, her breath catching at the sight of his dark hair between her legs.

"So fucking pretty." He dropped a kiss high on the inside of her right thigh before moving higher and licking her as her fingers worked her clit.

Fuck.

She couldn't breathe as his fingers joined hers, tracing her opening, dipping inside, going deep and then pulling shallow. There was so much sensation at once that the intensity nearly stopped her heart. She was feeling good one moment and then she was on the edge of orgasming.

He curled his fingers inside her, rubbing against that spot that made her toes curl. "I wanna watch you come, Kinsey. Please."

That plea, that devotion, that pleasure was more than she could take, and she broke, her climax bowing her back as her entire body clenched. By the time she floated back to earth and opened her eyes, Griff was standing at the end of the bed, his mouth glistening with her pleasure and a possessive look on his face that should have worried her but didn't in the least. He didn't say anything, and she wasn't sure if she would have been able to hear him over the sound of the blood rushing in her ears as she watched him roll on a condom.

Her body was still in the process of recovering from coming, but the ache was already building inside her. This man. *This fucking man.* He was gonna kill her, but what a way to go.

She sat up enough to get her T-shirt off, and he went still, his hand around the base of his thick cock and his gaze locked on her boobs.

He let out a harsh groan, his whole body tense, so close to losing control, he practically vibrated with the effort. "Show me."

Clarification wasn't needed: her man liked a show, and she was gonna give it to him. Keeping her legs spread, she caressed her boobs, her touch soft and teasing, before rolling her hard nipples between her thumb and forefinger, tugging them. Touching herself always felt good, but doing so while Griff watched, that took it to another level. She was flying, dancing on the edge of the realization that no man had made her feel like this before, as if she wasn't an object to fulfill his desires and then dismissed from consideration of anything else but a singular being in control of an infinite amount of pleasure, knowledge, and insight that she could give, share, or keep to herself. All the power, it was hers, and Griff obviously loved watching her wield it.

She was up before the plan had even fully formed in her head, plastered against Griff, her mouth on his, her hands everywhere, desperate to feel him, taste him, be with him. She wanted to kiss every inch of him, trace the tattoos covering his arms and chest, then fall to her knees and take him deep in her mouth while holding on to his hard ass.

"Damn, baby, soon," Griff said, as if she'd said all of that out loud. "Right now, I need to be inside you."

Her whole body practically yelled *hell yes*, and her ass was on the bed again so fast, he was still standing in the same spot. It only took him half a second to catch up. God, he was so big, everywhere, but as he kissed her and then got between her legs, she could feel how hard he was working to restrain himself, to hold back. It was there in the way he touched her as if he was afraid he'd break her. The worried look in his eyes. The obvious tension in his body. It was wrong. He needed to be himself; she wanted Griff Beckett, no holds barred.

She broke the kiss. "I don't want this."

He froze.

"I need the real you. You don't have to hold back. Please, Griff," she said, cupping his face in her hands. "You don't have to be quiet."

The transformation was immediate and total. The possessive fire in his eyes sent a shiver down her spine. The rough hands holding her hips tight as he sheathed himself inside her in one long, deep stroke made her breath catch in the best way. The dirty promises that came out of his mouth as he reached between them and played her clit with his thumb like a virtuoso had her fisting the sheets as she tried to hold on from coming again so soon. It all felt so good as he pumped into her, hard and swift, filling her beyond what she thought she could take that she couldn't think. She could only feel, ride that high of being dick drunk and turned out.

"Look at me, Kinsey."

It was hard, but she managed to fight the tide of pleasure enough to open her eyes. God, he looked fierce, like a gladiator who'd been transported to the modern age. His grip on her hips tightened, and before she knew it, he was on his back now and she was on top, bracing her palms against his hard chest. She rocked against him, taking him deep as she arched her back. Then he grabbed her hair with one hand, holding her in that position as he pistoned his hips upward, each movement taking her higher and higher.

"That's it, baby, hold on and take that cock," he said, his voice strained. "So damn good."

Undulating her hips, she drove them closer and closer to the edge, unable to look away from the dark intensity in his eyes.

He flipped her onto her back and drove deep into her, once, twice, and a third time before his orgasm hit and he cried out a second before her own climax exploded like a thousand fireworks that turned everything amazingly bright.

She was still trying to catch her breath as she lay there on her back when he got up and walked to the bathroom to get rid of the condom. Her pulse had returned to normal, and she felt enough in her legs to know she was going to be sore later but was still too blissed-out to care when he came back to bed.

"I love you." He kissed her, a soft, gentle kiss that made promises, and then rolled onto his back, bringing her with him so she was snuggled against his chest, his breathing immediately falling into the slow, steady cadence of sleep.

Meanwhile, Kinsey wasn't sure she'd ever sleep again. There was too much for her to process. This was Griff, the real him, the one he kept wrapped up so tight. Untamed. Determined. Vulnerable. Protective. And he *loved* her. Her whole body tingled, an effervescent bubble sensation of hope and want and just-maybe-it's-true filling her.

Well, at least that's what he said.

She wanted to lash out at that logical thought, but she couldn't. It made too much sense. People had that reaction after sex sometimes. They forgot themselves, said things they didn't mean in the heat of the moment. After all, it wasn't like they were dating for real, no matter how much time she spent thinking about him or how much fun she had with him. By the time Griff woke up, he would have probably forgotten he'd even said it.

But Kinsey didn't think she ever would.

Chapter Thirty-Two

Kinsey woke up the next morning, her heart going a million miles an hour, thinking about it.

When she tiptoed out of Griff's bedroom while he was in the shower, worried she'd bust out with an I-could-easily-fall-in-love-you-with-too, his words were on repeat in her head.

As she set the world speed record for getting ready for work and rushing out the door, she'd moved on to analyzing each syllable and tone of his voice with the cool, critical scientific eye she brought to the lab. Okay, fine. She couldn't quite get rid of that oh-my-God bubbly feeling in her chest or the way she couldn't stop smiling. Like a fool. Like someone who was already in serious like in the beyond-fuck-buddies way.

Oh God.

Was that her? Was it already too late?

Kinsey's stomach did that tuck-and-roll thing as she walked through the distinctive doors that led into the

Archambeau lobby. She wobbled just enough to make the security guard give her a questioning look before she recovered and headed for the elevator bank on the right. By the time she was on her way up to the lab, she'd convinced herself that it had just been the postcoital bliss talking.

Fine.

"Convinced" may be a bit of hopeful exaggeration, but she was definitely getting there. Kinda. Sorta.

Ugh.

Fuck her life. She did not have the time to catch feelings right now—especially not with her best friend's older brother who was only dating her to win a bet and headed up the R&D department at Archambeau's biggest competitor when someone in the lab was leaking info about the company's next big product.

Deep breaths, girl. You got this.

It was a lie, but the kind that she was just gonna have to live with for the moment because she had a whole day of getting glowered at by Gavin to get through.

She was putting her purse in the bottom drawer of her desk when her phone buzzed.

MORGAN: *Hey, you blazed out of here before I could even give you shit for being out all night. Tell me everything.*

Her stomach knotted. Had she timed her escape from the apartment to sync with Morgan's set-your-clock-by-it shower that always lasted twenty minutes? Yes, she had. Damn, she was a bigger chicken than the fat hen that had the run of Meemaw's front porch.

KINSEY: *I had a date last night with Griff.*

It was the truth, if not the whole story.

MORGAN: *WAIT.*

Immediately, three dots popped up on the screen.

MORGAN: *WHAT?*

Another three dots appeared.

MORGAN: *YOU STAYED THE NIGHT WITH GRIFF?????*

This was followed by another question mark, one after the other, like the telltale heart beating under the floorboards warning of incoming doom. Well, it was too late to go back now. Kinsey let out a breath and typed three letters.

KINSEY: *Yes.*

The question marks stopped.
The three dots appeared and disappeared.
Kinsey gave a quick smile to a coworker, who said hello, and then tried not to give in to that gonna-throw-up feeling. Then a video arrived of Morgan dancing around in her bedroom with her arms in the air like a TikTok dance gone horribly wrong.

MORGAN: *Welcome to the family!*

A bunch of digital fireworks exploded on her screen, followed by a series of heart-eyes emojis.
Kinsey covered her smile with her hand, but a loud bark of a laugh escaped anyway. A heated blush stole across her cheeks as everyone in the lab turned and looked at her—including Gavin, who was in his glass bubble of an office with Leigh. The CEO said something to him that Kinsey couldn't hear, and a flash of anger crossed his narrow face before he smoothed it away and looked back at Leigh with a sardonic

smirk. The flip of the switch on his outward emotions was enough to make Kinsey shiver as a whisper of dread brushed across her skin.

Her phone buzzed again. Morgan had sent a gif of a Lego wedding. Kinsey watched the little block bride walk down the brick aisle a few too many times with an uncontrollable grin on her face—the kind that made her cheeks hurt, it was so big—before catching herself.

Nope. Not gonna happen. Getting married or even having a relationship wasn't on her agenda right now. She hadn't moved to Harbor City to fall in love. She'd come here for her dream job, and dating the head of R&D of their biggest competitor while company secrets were walking out the front door was a quick way to lose that job and any chance she had to be taken seriously in her field. They'd only been working out their mutual lust. That's all.

KINSEY: *It was just one time. It didn't mean anything.*

How the cute navy-blue pants she was wearing didn't burst into flames at that moment, she had no idea.

MORGAN: *Kinsey. Griff doesn't date. Ever.*

That fluttery feeling she couldn't afford to enjoy started in her chest again. Closing her eyes, she let out a breath and remembered Meemaw's warning that no lie was as bad as the ones a person told themselves. She wouldn't believe that this could actually be something more than it was.

KINSEY: *That doesn't mean he doesn't get laid.*

MORGAN: *Oh, that happens for sure, I'm just saying he doesn't date but he's dating you.*

KINSEY: *To win a bet.*

That's what she needed to remember. The rest was just a chemical reaction between two otherwise stable but suddenly combustible substances, nothing more than that.

MORGAN: *Uh-huh, sure, that's the only reason.*

Gavin's office door opened with a swiftness that had everyone in the lab looking over. Leigh walked out, her chin high and a satisfied tilt to her lips. She strutted out of the lab like the high-fashion model she'd been decades ago, leaving Kinsey and everyone else gaping a bit in her wake. The sound of a crash jerked her attention back to Gavin's office. He stood behind his desk, the contents of which were now scattered across his floor.

Oh.

Shit.

His gaze locked on Kinsey and narrowed. She'd never felt more like a neon-colored rabbit in an open field facing down a starving fox more in her entire life.

KINSEY: *I gotta go.*

Judging by how her internal danger alarm had just sent her stomach into the sub-basement, she'd just made the understatement of the year.

MORGAN: *Margaritas and enchiladas are in order because discussions must be had.*

KINSEY: *Pablo's after work?*

The restaurant had the double bonus of having the world's greatest enchiladas and being unknown to the vast majority of tourists, making it the perfect spot for locals— even new locals like her.

MORGAN: *See you there.*

Kinsey shot a covert glance back over at Gavin's office. He was still staring at her, but this time he was smiling. An icy shiver went down her spine.

Please, universe, just let me make it to the end of the day with a job and I promise I'll skip the second margarita. Although it sure is looking like a four-margarita day.

Chapter Thirty-Three

The Beckett Cosmetics boardroom was a glass fishbowl in the middle of the fifty-second floor at the crossroads of an extra-wide, north-south hallway and another going east-west. On a good day, Griff hated the exposure that had obviously been Nash's idea, but today it made his skin crawl. Everyone walking by on their way to the employee kitchen could see them sitting there like gorillas at the zoo—even worse was the paranoia that they could hear him.

Talking with his cousins had never bothered him, and communicating with the other folks in R&D wasn't a problem because the lab was full of introverts and millennials who only wanted to converse via text or email. However, that didn't mean the idea of having someone else overhear his not-thought-out-to-oblivion comments to his cousins didn't give him the cold sweats. He'd spent way too much time facing down the disappointed disgust of his father followed by a warning about showcasing all the areas he lacked proper mental acumen not to have his flight-or-fight response kick in at even the thought of talking in front of people.

Especially about what happened this morning with Kinsey.

He kept his gaze on the row of numbers on the report he was white-knuckling and gritted out, "She left."

"What do you mean, she left?" Dixon asked from his spot at the head of the conference table.

Griff concentrated harder on the row after row of typed digits until they got blurry around the edges. "She was asleep when I got in the shower, and by the time I got out, she was gone."

He'd come out of the bathroom still half wet, a towel wrapped around his hips, so he could get another peek at her sleeping in his bed. The sight of her earlier when he'd gone into the bathroom had been better than a double shot of espresso after an all-nighter. It was like getting a sneak peek at the future, and he liked that. It settled something that had always rattled around in his chest like a loose Lego brick, the extra one that was left in the clear plastic bag for step five.

"Maybe she had an early meeting," Nash said. "Or maybe she was weirded out because she had morning breath. Or maybe—"

Griff shook his head, cutting his cousin off before he could invent another ridiculous theory. "I told her I loved her."

That had to have been it. He hadn't meant to say it, but she'd taken down all his walls during sex and it just...came out. She'd stilled in his arms the second the words slipped out of his mouth, but then when she melted against him half a second later, he figured it was gonna be okay and that he hadn't fucked up everything. Again.

Dixon let out a harsh gust of breath. "For a guy with a big brain, you sure can make some dumb-ass decisions."

Well, he might as well admit to all of it.

"Then I fell asleep," he said.

Nash plopped down into his chair, laughing so hard, his whole face turned red. "Jay-sus, Griff."

"I know." He sank into his chair. *Way to go, moron.* "I fucked up."

Nash, still grinning like a complete asshole who'd just taken a massive hit of nitrous oxide, started fiddling with his pen, switching between tapping it against the table and repeatedly pressing the button on top. Anyone who didn't know him would think he was being annoying on purpose, but Griff knew this meant an idea was forming. Would it be a good one? That was a toss-up, but the odds were pretty good in his favor.

"I think you're all looking at this wrong," Nash said. "This could be the best possible thing." The tap-tapping of his pen against the edge of the walnut table went into overdrive. "It's all out there. So you don't press it, but you're cool with it being in the open." He flicked the pen so it rolled across the table to Griff. "You've told her, so now you just have to show her."

Griff ran the possibilities, everything speeding through his head like that person-doing-mental-math meme. The odds were against it working, but they were better than his chances if he sat down with Kinsey and explained to her that he'd fallen in love with her the second he heard her tell the numb nut twins the solution to their never-ending argument. It sounded laughable to him, and he *knew* it was true. Kinsey would probably back away slowly and never be alone with him again if he pushed his case now. Instead, he could do all the things to show her that he was partner material.

He looked up from the report, realization a concrete block in his stomach. "I need to learn to be a boyfriend."

"You mean you didn't figure that out from what's her name in Canada?" Dixon asked as he balled up a page of his copy of the report and tossed it at Griff.

He easily caught it before it could smack him in the face and shot it back at Dixon, hitting him square in the center of the forehead.

One time. He'd lied to his cousins *one time* when he was in high school about having a girlfriend in Canada. They'd given him shit about it ever since. "Fuck off, Dixon."

The asshole just laughed. Griff tried to keep his snarl in place, but it was impossible. It was just too fucking funny. God, he'd been an idiot—not that he'd admit that.

Nash cleared his throat, all the pen-fidgeting gone. "Maybe if you'd done less fucking around and more relationshipping, you wouldn't be so clueless right now."

A direct shot that had Griff squirming in his chair. "Relationshipping isn't even a word."

The fucking part was fun, everyone had a good time, no one got attached, and it never happened with the same woman more than a few times because everyone knew the score. All of that, though, had been nothing like what had gone down between him and Kinsey last night.

"Maybe not," Nash said. "But I notice you aren't arguing about the truth of what I'm saying—"

"Assholes, can we focus on what's important here?" Dixon interrupted before Nash could dial in his inner Aunt Celeste and get all deep and meaningful on them. "You gotta cook for her."

Of all the solutions his cousins could have offered, that was pretty much the last one he'd been expecting. "What?"

"Show that you aren't some make-me-a-sandwich Neanderthal," Dixon said, propping his forearms on the table and leaning forward the way he did when he was working the Beckett Cosmetics board of directors so they'd vote the way he wanted. "Show you have layers, that there's more to you than grunts and an ill-timed 'I love you.'"

"It's a perfect date three," Nash said, using that smooth, confident, trust-me-I-know-what-I'm-talking-about tone that either got him death glares or 100 percent trust; it never landed anywhere in between. "Plus, she's already been to your place. Did you show her your Lego room?"

"I didn't give her a tour. We were busy." It had pretty much gone hallway to bed.

Pretty much?

Fine. It *had* gone hallway to bed. He'd been too focused—bordering on obsessed in the non-stalker way—with Kinsey and the way she reacted to his touch and how he could get her to make that sexy moan again to even think of going anywhere else. Hell, it had taken all of his brainpower not to just sink down on the hard floor of the front hall and fuck her against the marble.

"Think with the big head, Griff," Dixon said, the look on his face showing he knew exactly where his cousin's thoughts had gone. "If you're gonna win her, you gotta think with the big head."

For once, Nash didn't have anything to say, which was weird enough that Griff took a closer look at his cousin, who was holding his phone under the table and grinning at it like a fool.

"What are you doing?" Griff said, already knowing in his gut whatever it was, it wouldn't be good.

Nash looked up, his eyes blank for half a second before he pulled it together. "Texting Kinsey about your dinner date tomorrow."

Yeah right. The asshole was definitely up to something.

"I can talk to her," Griff said, ready to fight off whatever shit show was about to go down.

"How do you grunt over text?" Dixon asked, chuckling at his own joke.

He flashed back to the parking garage and everything

he'd said to Kinsey in that moment when he'd forgotten the rest of the world even existed outside of the two of them. That wasn't just out of character for him to talk that much. It was out of any possible consideration. He wasn't that guy, the kind in touch with his emotions who shared his thoughts— even the dirty ones. But with her? It had just happened. He couldn't stop himself. He just talked.

His gaze dropped back to the report on the table in front of him, but he didn't see it. He was seeing her. "I can talk to Kinsey."

For a second, neither Nash nor Dixon said anything. Then Nash let out a low whistle.

"Well, shit," Dixon said. "You really are fucked."

Not that Griff would admit it out loud, but his cousin had never been more right about anything in his life.

Chapter Thirty-Four

KINSEY

Kinsey was still blissed out on cheese-and-onion enchiladas with table-side guac—a blessing upon whoever mixed cheese, onion, corn tortillas, and salsa verde for the first time—as she and Morgan walked from Pablo's to their building. Gone was the tension that had tightened her shoulders to the point of a throbbing pain that had started when Gavin called her into his office and announced without explanation that she'd be working with him on the secret new product Archambeau was developing. It sounded like the opportunity of a lifetime and felt like a trap after the in-your-face threats the day before. The man needed to decide a tactic because she had shit to do, and unwinding his no-doubt ulterior motives was taking up brain space that could be used for better things.

Like the way it had felt to wake up that morning with Griff's sheets tucked in tight around her, as if he'd made sure she was snuggled in before he'd gotten in the shower.

Okay, fine, she should have been—*and was*—working

out the possibilities of the new product, but she was also unraveling what Gavin was up to, because he sure hadn't given her this spot out of the goodness of his nonexistent heart.

By the time she walked out of the lab at the end of the day, her shoulders were up by her earlobes and her upper back was in one long, never-ending clench. Morgan had taken one look at her and ordered a pitcher of margaritas. Then, instead of interrogating Kinsey about her night with Griff, she'd cracked jokes about the awfulness of dating in Harbor City and why her one true love was her Kokuyo Jibun Techo Lite Diary in pink, which she'd bought in bulk just in case they ever stopped making them. That, of course, got them on a long-winded discussion of planner stickers, the best gel pens, and the best organizational system for it all.

Their arm-in-arm giggly walk home two hours later was the end result of that delicious mix of tequila, orange liqueur, and lime juice with the perfect amount of salt on the rim served with the best enchiladas to be had in Harbor City while diving deep into their planner nerddom.

"You know," Kinsey said as they turned onto their block. "You're pretty damn awesome."

"Right back at you, babe," Morgan said as they took a left onto Fourteenth Avenue. "But don't think that just because I took pity on you after you obviously had a shit day at work—which we do not talk about because you work for the competition, blah, blah, blah"—she rolled her eyes while swerving around a slow-walking tourist like only a Harbor City native could—"doesn't mean that now we are not going to discuss you and my big brother."

"There's nothing to discuss," Kinsey said before thanking Oswald the doorman when he swung open the large glass doors to the building for them.

She made it two steps inside the lobby before she spotted

Griff at the penthouse elevator and her feet decided to stop working.

Morgan shot her a questioning look. "Are you okay?"

"Fine," she managed to get out as she forced her right foot in front of her left as her heart hammered against her ribs.

That's when Morgan looked over and spotted her brother and a knowing grin broke out on her face. "I can't wait until we're officially sisters."

"That's not gonna happen," she said, even as her brain started rolling through the possibilities. "It's just for the bet. I'm concentrating on work. He's your brother."

Morgan chuckled and linked her arm through Kinsey's and tugged her toward the elevator. "Whatever you say, sis."

Griff still had his back to them, his broad shoulders pulling his suit jacket taut across his shoulders and his dark wavy hair brushing the top of his collar. The memory of feeling his soft hair combined with the hard bristles of his beard against her thighs as he ate her out last night sent a tidal wave of hot desire through her. She pressed her fingers to her suddenly warm cheeks and tried to remember all the reasons why she shouldn't be reacting like this to Griff Beckett and coming up with only white noise.

The elevator door opened and he walked inside, not seeing her until he turned around. His eyes widened with shock before he reached out and blocked the doors from closing with one large hand, the move tugging his shirt cuff back and revealing the tattoos on his arms. Her heart quickened. There was just something about all the different layers to Griff Beckett that made her want to peel them all back so she could work out the answer to who he really was. The science nerd? The guy who obviously loved his sister and cousins? The tatted-up boxer? The Neanderthal who grunted more than he talked? The hottest man she'd ever fucked in her life who made her come harder than she ever had, alone or with a partner? There were so many possibilities that figuring out the answer could take a lifetime.

"Oh, hey, Griff," Morgan said, as if they hadn't spotted him from across the lobby. Then she planted her hand on the small of Kinsey's back and gave her a quick shove that sent her into the elevator.

Griff released his hold on the door to catch her before she went face-first into the elevator's back wall, bringing her up tight against him, his touch sending shivers of pleasure across her skin.

"I'm taking the stairs," Morgan said. "You kids be good."

Kinsey couldn't get her brain to function well when he was touching her like this and the first thought she had just popped out. "It's thirty floors."

"Gotta love cardio day." She winked at them and gave them a jaunty little finger wave as the elevator doors closed.

Neither Griff nor Kinsey said anything for the first ten floors. Kinsey just stayed there glued to his side, his hand leaving a flaming-hot imprint on her side, as she used all of her self control not to flip the emergency stop switch and yank all of Griff's clothes off, security camera be damned. At about the eleventh floor, he did a sidestep thing that resulted in her being in front of him, her ass pressed against him, with his hands light on her hips. The harsh breath he let out was completely indecent, and she would have sold her soul to hear it again. So she took a half step back and did a little upward-wave motion with her ass against him. He didn't make a sound—she wasn't even sure if he was still breathing—but his grip tightened on her hips, holding her there against his hard length.

Anticipation licked at her skin as she watched the floor numbers light up.

Twelve.

Fourteen.

Fifteen.

Griff dipped his head down, his lips brushing the shell of her ear so softly, she questioned whether it had happened at all.

"You left this morning without saying goodbye," he said, his words barely above a whisper. He slid one hand from her hip down toward the hem of her circle skirt and tugged it higher. "That wasn't very nice."

If she could have spoken, she would have, but the light touch of his fingertips on the outside of her bare thigh had short-wired her brain. It was pleasure. It was torture. It was everything she wanted and not even close to all she wanted. She bit down on her bottom lip as lust took over, melting her against him as she watched the floors go by.

Nineteen.

Twenty.

Twenty-one.

Under her skirt, hidden from the prying eyes of the camera, his fingers skimmed across her thigh and then moved upward inch by gloriously teasing inch until he was at the edge of her panties. He didn't ask. She didn't think about it; she just spread her legs in a silent plea.

Twenty-five.

Her pulse was raging.

Twenty-six.

She was ready to straight-up beg.

Twenty-seven.

He eased underneath the elastic and slid his fingers through her slick folds. The grateful moan escaped before she could stop it.

Twenty-eight.

He dipped inside her, stretching her. She let her head fall back against his chest, not caring about the camera, about why she shouldn't be doing this again, about anything but Griff and how he was making her feel at that moment.

Twenty-nine.

Pulling out, he circled her clit once, twice, three times, so slow and controlled. She let out a gasp of pleasure, arching her hips against his soft touch.

Thirty.

He withdrew, taking his hand out from beneath her skirt, and took a step back as the elevator doors opened. While she was still trying to catch her breath and bring her brain back online, he stepped around her and out into the hallway.

"Nice talking with you, Kinsey." Pausing, he looked at her over his shoulder. "See you at my place tomorrow for dinner."

Then he walked down the hall, disappearing inside his front door before Kinsey could react. She barely made it out of the elevator before the doors closed. Turned on beyond belief and left wanting, Kinsey shook her head in disbelief.

Who was Griff Beckett?

An evil motherfucker.

Full stop.

Oh, he was going to pay for that. Big-time.

Chapter Thirty-Five

GRIFF

Griff had just pulled the pork shoulder off the smoker on his balcony and was letting it rest on the kitchen island while he wrapped ears of corn in aluminum foil when the doorbell rang.

Fuck.

He wasn't ready. He hadn't started the barbecue sauce or the boxed cornbread mix yet. This was what he got for answering a call from his dad. The old man had been at least two doubles into the good bourbon and worked up about how Griff hadn't pushed his cousins enough to take Beckett Cosmetics from luxury boutique brand—billions of dollars of revenue or not—to the top of the food chain.

"A son of mine shouldn't be working in the B league. This is what happens when you give up so easily, when you're lazy," his dad had said, slurring only the slightest bit. "If you had half my brainpower, you'd see that. You'd understand all the places where you're going wrong, but you're just too thick to see it."

Griff had nearly hung up the phone a million times during the ten-minute diatribe. But every time his thumb had gotten close to the end call button, Griff couldn't do it. It was his father, the only parent he had left, as the old man let him know every time he called. If losing his mom early had taught him anything, it was that family—even the fucked-up nuclear one he had—meant something. He was strong enough to put up with the bullshit. He could take it and then he could take some more. Plus, it distracted the old man from calling Morgan and pulling this shit on her. That, Griff wouldn't let happen.

So he'd taken his dad's call, and it had thrown him off his game.

Now here he was, standing in his open front door staring at the sex-goddess version of Kinsey in a white strappy sundress that ended a mile above her knees. It left everything and nothing to the imagination. God help him. Meanwhile, he was in a pair of jeans, a T-shirt, and a black apron Dixon had gotten him that said *Every Butt Deserves A Good Rub*.

You are such a dick, Beckett.

"You look amazing," he said as he stepped back so she could walk in.

And did he take a good look at the view behind as well when she strode into the hall? Without a fucking doubt. He may not be a genius like his dad, but he sure as hell wasn't a complete dumb-ass, either.

"This old thing?" She whirled around, the turn making the skirt of her dress flutter upward.

The move gave a peek at her plushy thighs that he'd slipped his hand between on the elevator yesterday. His cock twitched in response to the memory, having Kinsey back at his place, and just that fact that she was in this world.

"Aren't you sweet," she went on, her accent a bit thicker

than usual as she cocked her head to one side. "Nash said it was a romantic dinner for two with you making your specialty."

"I make pulled pork sandwiches." *Wow. Way to really romance her. Do you even understand the assignment here? It's not to be a complete caveman. Do you even have an inner Nash or Dixon to charm her?*

The short answer? No, he did not, never had, and never would.

Instead of being put off by the dinner announcement, though, her eyes lit up. "What kind of sauce?"

"I make my own. The latest is a mix of Memphis and Kansas City flavors with a dash of Carolina vinegar."

"Oh my." She raised herself up on her tiptoes and brushed a kiss along his jawline. "I might just marry you if you keep talking like that."

Okay, she was joking. He knew that. His brain was still zooming into mental wedding-planning Excel spreadsheets, building on everything he'd put in there since she'd shown up at his gym and wrecked him for anyone else. He was still trying to swerve from deciding between a church wedding or a ceremony out at Gable House with the lake in the background when she gave him a real kiss. This one wasn't soft. It wasn't hesitant. It was the kind that teased, promised, and tormented all at the same time.

He went from shocked receiver to giving as good as he got in a heartbeat, letting his fingers get tangled in her long hair as he angled her face upward. All of him focused in on her. The way she opened beneath him, not surrendering so much as daring him. And when she broke the kiss and took a step back, her eyes hazy with lust and a self-satisfied grin on her face, he nearly growled his frustration.

That's when it clicked. This wasn't just the kind of hello-good-to-see-you-again-can-we-get-naked-soon kiss, as much as he hated to admit it. This was straight-up revenge for the elevator.

The knock-him-on-his-ass kiss.

The extra Southern in her accent.

The view of her in that dress as she walked down the hall to the kitchen, the sway of the material across her round ass leaving absolutely no question about the fact that Miss Sweet Little Ol' Me wasn't wearing panties.

Griff shoved his hands through his hair, willed his dick to calm the fuck down, and chuckled as he shook his head. The woman was forever a few steps ahead of everyone else, and he was here for it.

It only took two steps to catch up with her. The look she gave him told him she knew he knew and that it didn't matter because she was going to make him pay for it. That was okay. He was here for that, too. He was here for whatever Kinsey wanted.

They made it a few steps into the kitchen when she pulled to a stop.

She let out a short gasp and turned to face him. "You make your own sauce, spend hours smoking the pork, and you have a box cornbread mix?"

The can of green beans and box of corn bread sat on the butcher-block island in the middle of his kitchen along with the tray holding the most gorgeous pork shoulder that he'd been smoking since early this morning. Okay, so maybe he was paying a little too much attention to the main course.

"Sides aren't really my thing," he said.

"Thank God I'm here." She grabbed the dishtowel hanging from the door of his oven and tied it around her waist. "Tell me you have a cast-iron skillet."

Griff opened up the cupboard underneath the stovetop and pulled out his seasoned cast-iron skillet that Grandma Betty had given him when he'd first started cooking.

"Bacon?" she asked.

He took out a pack of thick-cut hickory-smoked goodness. She tipped over the boxed muffin mix. "Cornmeal?"

Figuring out where she was going with this, he grabbed the cornmeal out of the pantry along with the baking soda and salt.

Kinsey clapped her hands together and did a happy shimmy with her hips. "If you have eggs, butter, and buttermilk, we are in business."

"The butter and eggs I have," he said. "Let me run to the corner market for the buttermilk."

She reached out and stopped him with her hand on his forearm before he could start for the door. "You have regular milk and lemon juice?"

He nodded.

"We can make it work." She went up on her tiptoes and gave him a quick kiss, then did a spin move accompanied by clapping again. "Oh, this is gonna be fun."

She started moving around his kitchen like she owned the place, setting him to work measuring ingredients for a recipe she knew by memory while she fried up the bacon—the bits for the green beans and the drippings for the cornbread skillet. By the time the corn bread was done, his kitchen smelled like heaven, and Kinsey's cheeks were flushed with pleasure, giving him all sorts of ideas that had absolutely nothing to do with dinner.

Chapter Thirty-Six

KINSEY

If Meemaw had known that Kinsey had used the family cornbread recipe for sin, her grandma would have gone for her flyswatter.

Sure, maybe—just maybe—she could have convinced the woman who raised her that it was a mercy not to make Griff eat the boxed corn bread that he'd been planning to cook in a sheet pan, but it wasn't likely. Meemaw knew what was what, which meant it was a damn good thing it was just Kinsey and Griff out on his balcony big enough that the studio apartment she'd looked at could fit on it, pretending to look for the Big Dipper when there was no way with all of Harbor City's lights that they would have spotted a meteor on its way down to earth.

"I think that's it," he said, stepping behind her and coming up close while pointing at absolutely nothing in the sky.

It wasn't an accident that the move put them exactly in the same position they'd been in on that elevator. Sure, she'd expected Griff to catch on to her game within five minutes of her sashaying through his front door—and he had, she was convinced of it—but he hadn't even sorta acknowledged it until now. She'd thought he'd been lucky not to play into her hand. However, feeling the press of him against her back, the almost casual touch of his fingers resting ever-so-frustratingly lightly against her hips, and the tease of his hot breath against her ear made her realize it had actually been her who'd rubbed the leprechaun's gold.

"And that has to be Venus," he said.

That whisper-soft touch of his sent a shiver down her spine, and her eyes fluttered closed. "That's Jupiter."

The big, sexy jerk face chuckled against her sensitive skin. She didn't have to guess why. At this time of year, they'd only be able to spot Venus in the morning if they were upstate, where a person could spot the stars because light pollution was minimal. Of course he'd know that. Jupiter at night. Venus in the morning, second only to the moon in brightness.

"Checking to see if I'm listening?" she asked, giving herself another few seconds to relax against him before she had to open her eyes and face reality.

He slid his hand, fingers spread wide, across her belly, holding her firmly against him. "Just wondering how far you were taking this looking-up-at-the-stars-neither-of-us-can-see thing."

Letting out a soft exhale, she forced her eyes open and took in what seemed like the whole of Harbor City spread out before them like a toy model decorated with a million fairy lights. From up here, it was easy to pretend that they were the only ones in Harbor City, that there weren't horrible bosses with huge egos looking to throw someone under the bus or tiny apartments with toilets in the kitchen or a million reasons why she shouldn't be feeling exactly the way she was right now—like all of this was more than just a fling, that

Griff had meant what he'd said the other night and had never even hinted at again. Hope for something she hadn't planned for and wasn't looking for bubbled inside her, drugging her with ideas and dreams she should ignore but couldn't.

"For someone who usually only grunts," she said, putting her hand over the one of his splayed across her belly and twining her fingers with his, "you're awful chatty tonight."

"You make me want to do things with my mouth," he said in that growly tone of his.

Her biscuits were officially buttered because her thighs had never in her life been clenched together so tight—it was either that or spin around and climb Griff like an oak tree.

She should move away, give herself some space, stick to the plan of teasing him as much as he'd teased her in that elevator. On all three counts, she failed. He smelled good. He felt good. He was fake spotting constellations as an excuse to stand close to her. Who said no to all that? Not Kinsey Anne Dalton.

"Are you gonna tease again or follow through?" she asked as she lifted herself onto her toes and stretched, a move that dragged her ass up his cock.

"That depends." He pulled her tight against him, leaving absolutely no question about how much he wanted her right now. "Are you going to sneak out when I'm in the shower?"

An embarrassed flush burned her cheeks. "I didn't sneak."

If she had been wearing panties under her dress, they would have gone up in flames at that whopper.

Still holding her against him, he toyed with the strap of her sundress before pulling it down and dropping a kiss on the top of her shoulder. The thin strap of her dress was halfway down her arm, and the only thing keeping her dress up on that side was the hard tip of her nipple. Desire whipped through her, touching every nerve before it curled tight in her belly. Griff let out a harsh hiss of breath and slipped the other strap off while he moved their hands down her front until they were cupping her hot core together.

Sweet tea and moon pies, this man was gonna melt her like butter left out in the summer sun before she was even naked. Okay. Fine. She was only wearing the white dress anyway, but she was one tug of gravity from being completely exposed. She added that to the list of things she should stop but wasn't gonna do a damn thing to hinder. It was just too damn hot.

"You're a horrible liar." Griff kissed her right behind the ear. "You did sneak out." He stroked her clit through the thin material of her dress. "Don't do it again."

"I won't." Not as long as he kept touching her like that. She'd agree to call Coke "pop," to put sugar in her grits, to wear white after Labor Day, as long as he kept touching her.

"Good." He increased the pressure of his fingers. "I like to hear that—almost as much as I like hearing you come." He moved her against him so his hard cock nestled against the cleft of her ass. The move was all it took to send her dress sliding down off her breasts. "You make the best sounds when you're squeezing my dick or my fingers or coming all over my mouth." He nipped the spot where her shoulder and her neck met, then kissed it better. "Fuck. Are you gonna make that sound again? Are you gonna let me hear it?"

"Griff." It was all she could say; everything else was gone from her mind except for him.

"I want to hear it." Harder, faster he rubbed their hands over her dress-covered folds, so slick with her own desire that it was like not having anything between them. "I want the world to know that I gave you that much pleasure. I want everyone to know you're mine."

She collapsed against him, so close to the edge, she couldn't balance on her own legs anymore and the only thing holding her up was his arm around her waist, keeping her upright and flush against him.

"That's right," he said, tormenting her with pleasure. "Here you are, legs spread with your dress around your waist, your tits bare, your nipples puckered, and your head thrown back." The words came out rough and hard and demanding. "Look at you. So wound up because you need this. So slick you're soaking through your dress. So damn close to coming all over our fingers."

God help her, she was. She wasn't in control anymore; she could only go with all of this because at the moment she needed to let go, to forcefully grab what she wanted, to send a giant middle finger to everyone who took one look at her and thought they knew who she was more than anything else. Griff knew that. He understood it. He saw that. He saw her.

"Give it to me, Kinsey," he said, speeding up their fingers, demanding everything with his touch. "Let me have that moan."

Fuck.

She couldn't hold back. She barely recognized the desperate moan as coming from her own mouth as her orgasm hit. All she could do was ride it, let the pleasure rush through her body until she was limp and her breath was coming in hard pants.

Griff shoved her dress down over her hips and left it on the stone floor of the balcony when he scooped her up and carried her to the large double chaise longue. He sat her down but didn't join her. Instead, she lay back and watched as he reached behind his head and pulled off his T-shirt in one fluid motion.

Sweet baby Jesus, the man's torso was a sight to behold. Nearly every inch of his muscular chest was covered in ink. Her body, still riding the high of her orgasm, wasn't done yet, not with the view she had. His jeans hug low on his hips, and when he flicked open the top button, she couldn't help but drop her hand between her legs again.

"Fuck yes," Griff ground out from between clenched teeth.

She spread her legs, letting him get a good look as she rounded her clit in slow, lazy circles. He rewarded her by taking off the rest of his clothes in record time and standing there, hand wrapped around his cock, stroking it as he watched. The intensity of his gaze, the way his pupils dilated with lust as he zeroed in on her fingers, God, it was enough to make her come again right then.

"One of these days," he said, starting toward her, "I'm just gonna watch you get yourself off over and over again until I can't take it and I come all over your belly."

Her core tightened at the idea, and her nipples hardened until they ached. "Not tonight?"

He shook his head. "I need inside you. Now."

Heaven help her, she'd never wanted anything more.

Chapter Thirty-Seven

Griff

PDA had never been Griff's style until Kinsey, but even if they hadn't been high enough up that only the birds flying over the park could get a view of them, he easily would have become Mr. Public Display if that meant getting to touch Kinsey right now.

His balls ached, and if his cock got any harder for her, he'd be worried about permanent damage—it would be worth it, but still. Keeping his gaze locked on her, he stopped walking toward her long enough to grab a condom out of his wallet and tried to remember a work problem—*any problem*—that he could think through in the back of his head so he wouldn't come the second he sank between her creamy thighs. For the first time in his life, he came up completely blank.

There was only Kinsey.

Not just the naked sex goddess in front of him, but all the different versions of her.

The woman who couldn't find a dance beat with a map

and a flashlight.

The one who could solve any problem—including how to fix pie display case motors.

The one whose brain worked on Autobahn speeds in a world where everyone else thought at the speed of seniors walking at the mall.

The one who joined a dating site just to save a guy the embarrassment and help him win a gift from his grandma.

The one who changed his whole life just by walking into his gym.

Whatever it took to make her happy, he'd do it.

He rolled on the condom as she watched, her gaze hot and hungry. Fuck. There was nothing in the world like having her look at him like she wanted him just as badly as he wanted her.

"So I suppose you've already worked out how this is gonna happen," she said, lifting her hand that had just been buried between her legs and holding it up to him.

"Absolutely." He wrapped his fingers around her delicate wrist and tugged her off the chaise, lifting her hand up to his mouth. Never looking away from her, he sucked her sweetness off, relishing the taste of her. "I'm going to sit back, and you're going to ride me so I can play with those perfect tits of yours while you fuck me just the way you want."

"What about what you want?"

"That is what I want. Babe, there is nothing in the world that will make me come harder than watching you get off."

He wasn't lying—not even close. Dixon wanted to rule the world. Nash wanted to manipulate it. All Griff wanted was Kinsey.

He gave his cock a hard squeeze and sat down on the chaise. Kinsey flashed him a wicked grin and swung a leg over his hip to straddle him.

"My, my, my, what do I want to do first?" She walked her

fingers down his chest and followed the line of hair from his belly button to his junk, grasping ahold of him by the base and lowering herself slowly down, enveloping him in her slick heat. "Oh yeah, that's exactly what I want."

He grabbed her hips, holding her still on his cock—even that had his vision blurring. Kinsey must have seen something on his face, the truth must have slipped through, because her gaze softened and she leaned down, cupped his cheeks, and kissed him. It wasn't like the others. It was sweet instead of demanding. It was full of promises and possibilities and forever. It was everything he wanted, and he didn't imagine it. He couldn't have, because when she broke contact and undulated her hips in a slow, steady rhythm, there was something different in how she looked at him—as if she saw what could be, too.

God, this woman, what she did to him. He wanted to yell out that he loved her, shout it loud enough that the world would hear, but she wasn't ready. Saying anything now would just freak her out. He had to show her instead.

Reaching up, he grabbed ahold of her silky hair, fisting it and tugging on it. Kinsey moaned out a "fuck yeah" and sped up her hips.

"Look at you, taking what's yours." He raised his ass off the chaise, thrusting upward to meet her downward strokes. "Damn, you look sexy as hell, babe. Does it feel good?"

She bit down on her bottom lip, her hands going to her tits, cupping them, rolling her nipples, and nodded.

"What do you want?" he asked, curling up so he could suck on her nipples.

She let out a gasp of pleasure when he did. "More."

"Then take it." He trailed kisses up her neck as she ground her core against him, undulating and rubbing herself against him. "I'm yours, babe."

"More," she said, making it sound like a plea and a

demand at the same time.

"All yours." He tweaked her nipples, then rolled the rose-pink peaks between his thumb and finger, pulling them taut. "Only yours."

She planted her hands behind her on his legs, her eyes dark with lust as she chased her orgasm. "Griff."

"Yeah, babe, that's it." He grasped her hips again, lifting her and pulling her back down, each stroke the best kind of torture because it wasn't enough—he didn't think it ever could be. Touching Kinsey. Fucking her. Being with her as she took her pleasure. He'd never get enough of it. "Ride that dick."

Pistoning his hips, he drove into her hard and sure as she dug her nails into his thighs and moaned, her core tightening around him. Whatever it took, he'd do it, just to make her happy, to give her everything she wanted. She was his. He was hers.

"Griff," she cried out, her orgasm making her core clench around him.

Her entire body went stiff as she came, and he put the mind-blowing beauty of it to memory. Her hair was going every direction, tiny tendrils near her temples damp with sweat, and her face was flush. She barely had her eyes open as her body started to loosen, but all of her focus was on him. She saw him just as much as he saw her. The realization of it punched him in the gut.

Before he could wonder if she found the real him lacking, he flipped them over, brought her legs up so her heels were on his shoulders, and thrust into her, sliding home again and again and again until he couldn't hold back any longer and he came, his orgasm slamming into him harder than an opponent's fist in the ring.

Breaths coming in harsh pants, he swung her legs down and pulled out, getting rid of the condom in a bin next to the chaise. Then he tugged her close so her ass was tucked in against him and his arms were wrapped around her. Her breathing was steady as they lay there and came back to reality, one fast heartbeat at a time.

"What are we doing, Griff?" she asked, the question coming out soft, as if she couldn't believe she hadn't unwound the riddle yet.

He had an answer for that, but it was one he couldn't share. "Whatever you want."

"Things at work are tense, and you being a Beckett definitely would jeopardize that…if we were dating for real, that is… I mean, I know this is just for a bet, just fun," she said, a slight tremble in her voice.

Because he couldn't imagine ever letting her go, he trailed a stream of soft kisses across her shoulder. "I can wait."

The second the words were out of his mouth, he caught his mistake. He couldn't scare her off, make her feel trapped, overwhelm her like a caveman intent on making his claim no matter what.

She stiffened in his arms, and he silently cursed his mistake. She'd caught his slip. Of course she had. She was Kinsey. So before she could ask for clarification on what he meant, he rolled her so they were facing each other and kissed her, putting everything he could into it so the only thing in the world there was at that moment was them and the promise of tomorrow.

Chapter Thirty-Eight

KINSEY

A week later and Kinsey's brain had been overtaken by Griff—her body, too. It was a full-on mutiny. She'd spent her days at work under the watchful glare of Gavin the Terrible as he sent her what amounted to busywork assignments on the hot new product Archambeau was going to launch and then her nights with Griff eating meals he cooked in between orgasms he helped give her. It was exhausting and exhilarating and like walking down Main Street the time the county sheriff had set an illegal pot patch to blaze only for the wind to shift and send all the smoke toward downtown, giving the entire population of their small town a contact high.

Even now, when she was tucked away in a sandwich shop six blocks from Archambeau and was supposed to be reviewing the specifications of the next task Gavin had assigned her, her thoughts kept drifting to Griff and how he'd looked this morning in bare feet and low-slung jogger shorts making her an iced coffee to drink on the walk in to work.

It was all so domestic and hot and completely and utterly dangerous.

She should cut the whole thing off right now.

Look at what being around Griff had done. Work needed to be her focus. She had to get the people at the lab to take her seriously, to understand she had a brain beneath all the blond hair and big eyes. To do that, she needed to be putting in more hours than anyone else, to see what the others didn't, to prove she deserved to be there.

And what was she doing instead? Eating a pastrami on rye with a goofy-ass grin on her face and thinking about Griff.

"Oh, fuck it," she muttered to herself and grabbed her phone.

KINSEY: *So tell me about this bet.*

GRIFF: *Nash's stupid idea.*

KINSEY: *What's on the line? What's in the present?*

It had to be something beyond amazing considering Griff, Dixon, and Nash were willing to participate in such an elaborate bet to win it.

GRIFF: *Long story.*

KINSEY: *I'm on my lunch break. I have time.*

She tucked the paperwork she'd brought with her back into a folder and dropped it into her bag.

GRIFF: *You already know. Our grandma Betty only wrapped one Christmas present before she died. We know it's for one of us because she group texted us she was putting the finishing touches on our gifts early. But sadly, we don't know which one of us she finished first.*

The possibilities rushed through her mind one after the other like thunder bolts during a summer electrical storm.

KINSEY: *Is it the deed to some fancy house or a private island?*

GRIFF: *She left Gable House, which does happen to have its own island, to all of the grandkids.*

KINSEY: *So is it a million dollars?*

GRIFF: *I already have that and more.*

Fair enough.

KINSEY: *Okay, Mr. Richie Rich, what's in the present?*

GRIFF: *No idea.*

She chewed the inside of her cheek and pondered. Not knowing was going to drive her up the wall. She hated questions without answers. It kinda went with the whole scientist thing. Okay, so maybe she could tease the answer out of him.

KINSEY: *So it could be socks? Or underwear? Or a box of hard candy that grandparents always have but no one ever eats? Or a treasure worth the GDP of a small island nation?*

GRIFF: *Yup.*

She groaned. Ugh. She should have known he wouldn't fall for it. Even worse, he'd fallen back into monosyllabic texting mode.

KINSEY: *And it would be worth all this trouble?*

GRIFF: *It could be a pile of dirty towels wrapped up by accident and it would mean something because it was from Grandma Betty.*

She scrunched up her face and sniffled because all of a sudden it was very dusty in this absolutely pristine sandwich shop. Of all the ooey-gooey answers, he had to go with the one that would hit her right in the feels. Meemaw had raised her and her siblings after their mom had dropped them off at the doorstep and never looked back. The woman could have shipped them off to state care, but she hadn't. She'd reshuffled her life for them, and there was nothing Kinsey could do to ever repay her, so the best she could do was to not fuck things up in Harbor City, to show her grandma that the completely funded retirement she'd given up to help Kinsey get through college had been worth it.

And here was Griff with so much love for his own grandma that he agreed to a bet he had absolutely no interest in being a part of. She sniffled again. Who would have thought the tattooed, muscled-up, grunting scientist and total fucking softie inside Griff would go together like peas and carrots?

KINSEY: *We'll make sure you win that bet.*

The incoming message dots appeared and disappeared about a million times as she finished up her chocolate chip cookie, all gooey from a few seconds in the corner sandwich shop's microwave, and then there was nothing. Okay, fine, they hadn't talked about the bet in weeks, but it was always there, hanging between them. The real reason they were hanging out.

And the fact that she was thinking about him pretty much twenty-four-seven? Well, that didn't matter. She was a woman starting out in her career, and she didn't have time to catch feelings—especially not for someone who headed R&D at Archambeau's biggest competitor. Nope. She wasn't gonna do it. Falling for Griff was about as smart as grabbing the unlabeled jug on the table at family reunions and taking a gulp thinking it was water and realizing too late it was Meemaw's moonshine.

Too bad you already drank it all, Kinsey girl.

Shut up, brain.

The bell above the shop's door jingled, snagging her attention away from her phone screen, which was frustratingly not displaying any new messages from Griff.

Gavin walked in with another man. Her boss spotted her as he scanned the small seating area, but instead of his usual judgmental smirk, he blushed and looked away. After a quick conversation that Kinsey was too far away to hear, he and the man walked back out and headed left down the block.

She was wondering what all that was about when her phone buzzed with a new text.

GRIFF: *Trying out a new barbecue sauce tonight. Want to come over?*

She shot back a "yes" with an embarrassing amount of exclamation points before she could stop herself. Fuck. What was she doing?

It was a rhetorical question, because she already knew. She was falling for the cinnamon roll disguised as a guy Meemaw would warn her to cross the street to avoid, who she most definitely had no business getting all cow eyes for when she had a career to establish. Plus, it was all happening way too fast.

Usually, it was her brain moving faster than the speed of light, but right now things were switched, and she didn't know how to process that beyond crossing her fingers and hoping like hell she wasn't about to have her heart ground to dust.

Chapter Thirty-Nine

A few nights later, light snuck in through Griff's bedroom window as he lay in the bed with Kinsey snuggled against him, her naked curves fitting perfectly against him as he watched the slow spin of the ceiling fan blades. There weren't a million questions in his head that he had to find the answers to or ideas bouncing off his skull like pinballs. Instead, a contented satisfaction filled him, laying like a warm blanket over Kinsey and him. All was right with the world.

Kinsey kissed the Bunsen burner tattooed on his right pec. "Only two more dates to go now, then you win."

The "and all of this stops" hung in the air above them like a sword hanging by a single hair.

Yeah, losing Kinsey sure didn't feel like winning. Every time Griff took in a breath when Kinsey wasn't with him, he heard a countdown clock in the background. This constant tick, tick, tick. He only had two more dates to make her fall in love with him, and he was fucking everything up.

"There's a really cool Lego-inspired art show at the Black Hearts Gallery next week." She traced the watercolor old-school microscope on his chest. "If Nash or Dixon haven't picked anything out yet, I thought that might be a good date."

His cousins may have picked out the last date activities already, but Griff had blocked them on his cell and was avoiding them at work as if they were covered in toxic sludge and wanted to give him a bear hug. So far, it had worked. He didn't know how much longer he could keep it up, but he'd roll with it as long as he could. In the beginning, six dates had seemed like all the time in the world, but now he knew it wasn't enough—not even close.

"It's the last Saturday of the month," she said. "We could grab a late brunch and go."

His gut cramped up at the mention of that date. "Morgan and I have our annual brunch with Dad that day." He didn't talk about this, not with his cousins or Morgan or anyone else. But all Kinsey had to do was ask, and he was opening his mouth to spill his guts. "It's the anniversary of my mom's death."

"Oh God, I'm so sorry." She flung an arm across him and squeezed him tight as she dropped a kiss on his shoulder. "You don't have to tell me. I shouldn't have pried."

Yeah, she could never do that. He had no secrets from Kinsey—well, except the one that would scare her off from seeing him again.

He kept his gaze on the ceiling fan and yanked off the Band-Aid. "She killed herself and almost killed Morgan and me with her by driving her car into a huge tree."

Kinsey let out a gasp.

"She wasn't well, and her life with my father sure didn't help," he went on, finding words for things he'd never talked about before. "I don't know why they ever got married. From what I remember, they never acted like a couple in love—not like Nash's parents or Dixon's. Instead, it was insults from him and silence from her."

His childhood home had been cold and beautiful and incredibly tense. Snide comments wrapped up in esoteric language from his dad. Silence punctuated by the sounds of wine being poured from his mom.

"The only time Mom had stood up to him was before the wedding when she'd insisted he take the Beckett name and that all the kids would be Becketts. Of course, that had probably been Grandma Betty trying to get her daughter to remember who she really was when things got tough."

It had been a Cold War waged in the hallways and over dinner on fine china. He'd spent as much of his time with Morgan as possible, distracting her from the knife-sharp bitterness that infected the house like black mold.

"Grandma knew about Dad. She always had. That's why when Morgan would go off to summer camp, she'd insisted I spend the same amount of time at Gable House with my cousins and her."

That house with its guard geese, island out in the middle of the lake, and eccentric landscaping had been a whole new world. Loud. Joyous. Competitive. Fun. It was the closest he'd ever been to happy before he'd met Kinsey.

"Everything at Gable House was a possibility. There weren't metaphorical eggshells covering the floor. I could relax. I could think when I wasn't hearing my dad take digs at me all the time." That snark still lived rent-free in his head all these years later. "His standing advice was for me to shut up so the fellow legitimate geniuses he had over at the house wouldn't realize I wasn't in their class. Better to leave them wondering rather than to prove it without a doubt."

"Griff, that's awful," Kinsey said, barely controlled fury making her voice tremble. "You have an amazing brain. You're one of the smartest people I know."

"I grew up around Nobel Prize winners, legit geniuses, and people who looked at MENSA as a gathering of average people." He shrugged, unable to look at Kinsey's face to see the disappointment that would no doubt be there. "Dad wasn't wrong; I wasn't on their level."

"Was he the same with Morgan?"

He skated his fingers up her bare back, memorizing the lines of her and the feel of her smooth skin. "No, she got a pass because she was a girl. Yeah, nothing like a healthy dose of misogyny to go with being asshole Dad of the Year."

"I'm so sorry." She pressed against him, angling her face upward to brush a kiss against the stubble on his jaw. "You both deserved a better childhood."

"One in the country with frogs in the creek and where I knew all the neighbors and everyone smiled at one another and knew the other's name?" he teased, happy to move the conversation somewhere other than his shithead father.

"Does that place even exist?" She let loose with a harsh bark of laughter. "If it does, it certainly wasn't where I grew up."

He wound a strand of her silky hair around his finger as she lay with her cheek tucked into the pocket of his shoulder. "Tell me."

She propped her chin on her hand and looked up at him. "You want the ugly story of growing up Kinsey Dalton?"

"I want to know everything about you."

"Okay, well, my mom is out there in the world somewhere, maybe, probably high if she is still around," she said, her tone light, no doubt in an effort to give the appearance that she wasn't bothered. "She dropped us off with Meemaw, saying she was going into rehab, but we never saw or heard from her again. You were right about everyone in town knowing everyone else—that part is true."

She worked her jaw back and forth before continuing.

"Everyone in town knew who my mother was—and what she was—and that no one knew who my dad was or my brother's or my sister's, but we all look different enough that the smart money is on three different dads. That shouldn't be a big deal and it shouldn't matter, but in a small town where Main Street closed down on Sunday mornings for church services, it was."

Judgmental assholes. He didn't have quite enough money to buy a town just to evict everyone who was mean to Kinsey and her family, but he was fucking close.

"So people took one look at us and decided they knew exactly who we were and dismissed us," Kinsey said, a tight quiver in her voice as she cut her gaze away and blinked several times. "Meemaw lost friends and her retirement nest egg keeping us fed and clothed. She cosigned my student loans using her land as collateral. She said she saw my potential and to hush up about worrying about paying it back. She believed in me. She was the same way with my brother and sister. She's the best human being I know. That's why I can't mess up this job. That's why this"—she dropped a kiss on his chest—"is complicated and why it needs to stay between us. It's a huge opportunity, and if I mess it up, Meemaw could lose her house when I can't make student loan payments."

"You'll do it." He dropped a kiss on her forehead, never believing anything more in his life. There wasn't a damn thing Kinsey couldn't do. "Meemaw's not wrong about you."

"And I'm not wrong about you," she said, that bright-enough-to-light-the-world smile of hers going full wattage. "Griff Beckett, you *are* amazing."

She punctuated her declaration with a kiss that blasted away everything else and, as she lowered herself down on his cock minutes later, the only thing he could think was how much he loved this woman and how he'd do whatever it took to keep her close—only two dates to go be damned.

Chapter Forty

The next morning, Kinsey was still in his bed when Griff got out of the shower. And the one after that. And the one after that for three weeks while he waged an internal battle not to give in and tell her that he'd fallen in love with her the minute he'd heard her setting the world straight at his gym. Every time he'd almost given in, he'd remember Nash's advice about showing instead of telling and Dixon's warning about scaring her off. But there she was, sprawled out on his bed, somehow managing to take up two-thirds of it even though she was a third his size.

She sat up, the T-shirt of his she was wearing covering her up a little too well for his taste. Of course, judging by the way her gaze traveled over him as he stood there fresh from the shower with his hair damp and only a towel wrapped around his hips, she was feeling the same.

"Are you smiling?" Kinsey asked.

He tried to force his mouth into a straight line and failed.

"I *do* do that."

"Hmm." She cocked her head to the side and gave him a considering look. "I've seen you snarl. I've seen the look you get right before we both end up naked. I've seen you go blank when you get knocked the fuck out."

"It was one time. I was distracted." By her.

She rolled up on the bed so she was on her knees surrounded by the rumpled sheets that always smelled like her now. "But I don't get to see you smile that often."

"You see all the smiles," he said, rubbing the back of his neck. "Well, almost all of them."

She narrowed her eyes at him. "Are you flirting with other people?"

He stilled, her jealousy, even put on as it obviously was, making his dick twitch. "Come here."

"Why?" She raised herself up on her knees and put her hands on her hips. "So you can pull up pics on your phone of all the gorgeous Beckett Cosmetics models and Insta influencers you work with?"

Like that was in his job description as head of R&D. As if he'd even noticed another woman since she'd walked into his life. She knew that. She was way too smart not to. He was ruined for anyone else but her.

He held up a finger. "One, you're a pain in my butt." He put up another finger and then pointed both of them at the ground. "Two, come here."

"And if I don't?" she asked, crossing her arms under her tits, the move pulling the T-shirt tight so that her hard nipples were more than a little apparent.

This was their game. The one they'd fallen into without ever really discussing it. She'd push his buttons. He'd let her—but only for so long—and then she'd be coming on his fingers or tongue or dick. Well, this morning was different. The Eiffel Tower had finally arrived. Usually his Lego room was off-limits, but like every other part of his life, Kinsey had changed things.

Towel wrapped around his hips, he strolled over to the bed as if the air in the room hadn't just gone thick with anticipation. Kinsey watched him out of the corner of her eye, acting as if she was paying attention to the TikToks on her phone. No doubt, she expected him to drop the towel, get in the bed, and fuck her senseless. Oh, he'd do that, but not yet. Instead, he picked her up and tossed her over his shoulder before carrying her out of the bedroom and down the hall to his Lego room.

He hesitated outside the door, one palm on Kinsey's ass and the other reaching for the handle. This wasn't a place he brought people. Sure, Dixon and Nash had seen it, as had Morgan, but that was about it.

"You don't have to show me if you don't want to," Kinsey said, her cheek resting against his back. "I know it's special and I'm just…this is…well, it's complicated."

The thing was, he did want to. Letting out a little growl—the kind that he'd learned she loved—he gave her a soft smack on the ass to let her know what he thought of that idea and then opened the door. As he put her down on her feet, he tried to look at the room through her eyes.

It was a lot. Custom display shelves took up the walls, painted white and lined with the classic green Lego base sheet so the completed kits could be held securely. In the middle, under a light that looked like it belonged in a surgery theater, was his building table, made to be compatible with a man of his size. There were drawers of blocks underneath organized by color and type. The floor was a matte white, grout-free tile because nothing sucked more than looking for a block or a mini-figure sword that had gotten knocked off the table and having it mix in with the dark floor or, even worse, get lost in the carpet.

Pulse pounding in his ears and lungs starting to ache from holding his breath over what she'd think, he kept his gaze on the individual section bags of parts for the Eiffel Tower set that were set out in order from left to right on the table.

Hand covering her mouth and her eyes round with shock, amazement, or horror—he wasn't sure—Kinsey turned and stared at him.

She dropped her hand. "This. Is. Amazing."

Griff let out the breath he'd been holding. "It's all right."

"All right? You are so full of shit. Tell me about everything. I want the full tour!"

So he took her around and showed her all of it, from the Lego Ultimate Collector's Series Millennium Falcon to the Lego Market Street that he got directly from the Lego Factory. She lifted an eyebrow when she spotted his copy of the painting they did on their date on one of the shelves. It was the only non-Lego piece in the room. But instead of asking about it, she let him continue on with the tour. He was so relieved not to have to explain his sappy self that he let her remove one of the balconies to get a great look at a spiral staircase on Market Street. Sure, he got the palm sweats and had heart palpitations while he watched, and it took everything he had not to freak out—seriously, no one touched his Legos—but it went fine.

She shot him a knowing grin. "You looked like you might pass out."

He grunted.

"Here." She led him over to the stool at his building table. "Sit down and tell me about this one. I promise not to touch any more Legos."

He sat down, making sure his towel was secure so he wasn't hanging out all over the place even though she'd seen him naked more than clothed lately, and took her through the 2007 Eiffel Tower that had more than 3,400 pieces and in its original factory-sealed box. "Now I get to build it."

"And you're good at that? Does it take a long time?"

The questions were innocent, but Kinsey had that look in her eye that meant trouble. His Spidey sense and his dick both buzzed with anticipation. "I am, and it depends."

She squeezed between the table and him, coming to a stop between his legs. "On what?"

"How often I get interrupted." Per usual with her, he was about six steps behind, working through what she was up to, even though his brain was working at full capacity.

She bit down on her bottom lip and looked at him from beneath her thick eyelashes. "Sounds like someone could use some help on developing his focus."

"Kinsey." Was it a warning? A plea? A call for help? Fuck if he knew, and he was the asshole saying it.

She sank down to her knees under the table and tugged the towel open. "Let's see how long you can go without getting distracted."

He sucked in a sharp breath.

"Kinsey." Yeah, that was definitely him begging.

"It'll be fun, I promise. Legos like you've never built them before." She circled her fingers around his cock that was already hard and stroked. "Start building, Griff."

He let out a harsh breath and grabbed the direction booklet and the clear plastic bag marked with a numeral one. He'd no more than opened it when he felt Kinsey's hot mouth around the head of his cock and then her slick lips as she took him in deeper.

Fuck.

He felt her chuckle all the way down to his balls. Oh, she was going to pay for this. And that was the last thought he had because her mouth was that good; she was that good. Her soft tongue on the head, circling it. The feel of her hands cupping his balls, rolling them, as she sucked him. It was all he could do not to fall off the damn stool or tear the bag in half, sending the bricks flying everywhere—although he knew it would be worth it even if he never found any of the pieces.

She added a hand, stroking him at the same time that her mouth slid up and down his shaft, twisting her slick palm around the base. He gave up on the damn bag, dropping it so he could wrap her silky hair around his hand, pulling it to the side so he could watch his dick disappear inside her mouth. It was mesmerizing how she took him, nearly all of him, and kept coming back for more. His whole cock was wet, his balls were already pulling up, and his entire body was tensing in anticipation of what was coming. Then she looked up at him and winked and he nearly nutted right then.

"Babe, I'm gonna come." And it felt too fucking good to be mad that it was happening this fast.

Instead of pulling back or slowing down, she amped up the suction and tugged on the springy hair above his cock, and he lost it. There was no way. It was too damn good. His vision whited out. The intensity of his orgasm forced his eyes closed as he came.

By the time he could open his eyes again, Kinsey was grinning up at him.

"I say we should definitely add focus training to our couple's time." She got out from under the table and stood up next to him, giving him a quick kiss. "That was fun, and I can't wait to do it again. You build; I'm gonna go shower."

And then she was gone, leaving him there in his most sacred of spaces, trying to process what had just happened and the fact that she wanted to do it again as couple's time. Sure, she may have been joking, but she saw a future. It wasn't just him. Maybe she was ready, finally, to hear again that he loved her, that he had since the beginning.

Chapter Forty-One

Kinsey didn't even bother to glance through Wakin' Bacon's ten-page menu on this visit to what was now her favorite brunch place in all of Harbor City. Sure, she could pretend it was because she had already memorized the menu during the past month, but the real truth was because she wouldn't have been able to concentrate enough to read it with Griff's hand on her upper thigh and moving northward under her skirt.

"Your sister is gonna be back any minute," she said, trying her best to remember they were in public and having brunch with Griff's sister—her best friend—when all she wanted was to pretend the rest of the world didn't exist right now.

He stroked the inside of her thigh, so damn close to her panties that her breath caught.

"So you're saying I have sixty seconds to get you off?" Griff asked.

"Griff!" Okay, yeah, that didn't even sound close to censure. She really had forgotten all of her home training.

The man was a bad influence, and she fucking loved it.

He dipped his head down and brushed a kiss against the shell of her ear. "Parking garages and balconies are a yes and restaurants are a no, I take it?"

"Not always, but—" She clamped her legs shut, trapping Griff's hand between her thighs. "Oh my God, here she comes."

Morgan was walking through the maze of tables packed close together into the café, her expression grim. When she made a sharp left and began beelining it to their table, Griff pulled his hand free and let loose with a string of low curses. That's when Kinsey realized there was an older man behind Morgan who was obviously following her. Kinsey had seen him before, but it took her a second to place him. He was the same guy with Gavin at the sandwich shop a few weeks ago.

"Well," the man said, not waiting for an invitation to sit down before sliding into the booth seat across from Kinsey and Griff. "Aren't I just the luckiest father in the world to run into you."

Kinsey was still trying to control her oh-shit face at the realization that Gavin had been meeting with Griff's dad the other week and all the implications that entailed when the older man stuck out his hand.

"Holden Rogers Beckett, but you already knew that, I'm sure," he said, shooting her a slick smile as he grasped her hand for a too-tight shake. "After all, my children do love to keep me front and center in their lives." He paused when Morgan sat down next to him but left as much space between them as physically possible. "I ordered a pitcher of Bloody Marys for the table."

"Our brunch isn't until next week," Griff said, his voice deceptively steady, considering how fast his knee was bouncing under the table.

"Exactly." Holden picked up his glass and inspected it

in the light, rubbing away a few water spots. "How lucky is it that you get to see me two weeks in a row?"

Griff grumbled something under his breath, and Morgan sank lower in the booth. The misery was palpable, but Holden was either oblivious or didn't care. Kinsey wasn't sure which.

Three-fourths of a pitcher of Bloody Marys by himself later and Holden was launching into another story about how he'd been the one person who saved Griff from a stupid decision by pointing out the many errors in logic that Griff had had as an eight-year-old planning out an experiment for the science fair. Kinsey's nails were basically embedded in the palms of her hands, and it was taking every fiber of her being not to Instacart rat poison to dump into the big jerk's drink.

Morgan sat next to her dad, flushed with anger as she worked her jaw back and forth as if she were chewing up every snide insult and coy dig her father issued. Griff, on the other hand, was totally relaxed next to her, buttering his toast and sprinkling cinnamon sugar onto it with bored indifference, as if his dad was talking about how nice the weather had been lately instead of being a total and complete jackass. For his part, Holden seemed completely oblivious, going on and basking in the self-assumed spotlight that all narcissists enjoyed as he barely finished one shitty story before jumping into another.

"At least Griff turned things around somewhat," Holden said with only a slight slur to his words. "Being head of research and development at a makeup company is something." He pivoted in the booth to look at his daughter, who was staring straight ahead. "Morgan, you really have to find something besides charitable fiddle-faddle."

Griff tensed, leaning forward and putting his forearms on the table, their tattooed, muscular width dwarfing his father's. "You're not gonna do that."

Holden turned his head and gave his son a look that would have translated to a bless-your-heart in the very-not-sincere way. "Do what?"

"You're not going to talk about Morgan and her life choices that way," Griff said.

"She is wasting her potential." Holden scoffed. "She has half my DNA, for God's sake. She could be doing something with her life instead of running a damn bookstore."

Morgan's face was a blank canvas, neither angry nor hurt nor murderous. Kinsey knew that look. It was the one she'd spotted on her own face when shutting down was the only way to process the level of bullshit around her. It had been her default expression when her mom had dropped her and her siblings off at Meemaw's. It had been the one she fell back into when someone patronizingly patted her on the head in the lab or spent an entire workday staring at her boobs. It wasn't being neutral. It was being armored up, being protected by layers and layers of mental shields so that nothing could reach you. It was safety when the only other option was trauma.

To keep herself from stabbing Holden in the eye with a butter knife, Kinsey reached across the table and took Morgan's hand. Her bestie's gaze flicked over to her for a second, and she gave her a brief smile before going back into lockdown mode.

Kinsey had never felt more violent in her life than when she looked at Holden and the smarmy, self-satisfied expression on his patrician face.

Griff let out an honest-to-God low growl. "Shut up, Dad."

"Why, Griff?" Morgan said, snapping back to herself, a barely leashed fury apparent in each clipped word. "We all know this is what he thinks. He's been like this since I decided against majoring in microbiology in college." She grabbed a handful of crinkle-cut fries sprinkled liberally with everything but the bagel seasoning and stuffed it in her mouth before flipping off her dad, stepping out of the booth, and walking out of the café without a single look back.

Kinsey wanted to start the slow clap for her. Fucking powerhouse. Instead, she laid her hand on Griff's thigh and gave it an encouraging squeeze, just imagining the fury he was about to unleash on his dad. His quads were tight underneath her palm, and his entire body was coiled with repressed energy.

"Not another fucking word about her again," Griff said. "Ever. Got it?"

"You two are ridiculous. You act like you know everything that's going on, but you don't have a damn clue. I can only do so much for you; don't fuck it up by getting attached." Holden tossed his napkin on the table and got up, his stance a little wavier than he had been when he'd first sat down; almost a whole pitcher of triple vodka Bloody Marys would do that to a person. "I'll see you next Saturday."

Holden turned, nearly crashed into a waiter carrying four plates at once, and stormed out of the café.

Kinsey's heart was going a million miles an hour from all the effort it took not to murder Griff's dad. Seriously. The man was worse than rancid butter slathered on a biscuit from the week-old rack at the bakery. "You're really meeting him next week?"

Griff shrugged.

Kinsey tried to wrap her brain around it. Holden Beckett was toxic as fuck, a horrible dad, and probably kicked puppies for shits and giggles. As Griff continued to eat his brunch meal of chicken and waffles with an extra cup of country gravy, she tried to imagine what could be going on. None of the options she came up with made sense.

"Is it always like that with him?" she asked, doing her damnedest to understand what in the waffle fries was going on here.

Griff kept his attention on his plate, pushing around what was left of his waffles as if he still had the stomach to eat any of it. "Pretty much."

Okay, deep breaths, Kinsey. Families can be complicated. Griff's only dating you to win a bet. Yes, you are fucking like rabbits, but that's chemistry, not a mutual connection. Just because you feel it doesn't mean he does. If he did, he would have said something by now. Treading the murky waters of family dynamics needs to be done with care. So shut your mouth. Don't say it. Stay out of it.

"And you're okay with that?" Damn. So much for listening to her smarter self.

"Not with him talking about Morgan like that," Griff said, laying his fork and knife down on his plate with exacting care, as if he couldn't trust himself not to smash it all to hell. "She doesn't deserve his shit."

"Neither do you, Griff."

That shrug of his shoulders again. "But I can take it."

Pow. Right in the heart.

Kinsey scooted closer to Griff on the bench seat, taking his hand in hers and laying her head on his shoulder. If she could have squeezed her body between him and the table's edge so she could wrap around him like a blanket, she would have. Fuck Holden Beckett.

"But do you have to? You could—"

He shook his head. "You don't understand."

"I'm trying," she said. "I really am, but I can't see it."

"My mom's gone. Grandma Betty's gone." Finally, Griff turned to look at her. Pain shone in his eyes as bright as a neon Bud Light sign at the hole-in-the-wall bar on Main Street back home. "He's all that's left."

"What about Morgan and your cousins?"

"That's different." He turned his focus back to the table.

"I watch out for them."

"And your dad watches out for you?"

Griff didn't say anything for a second, then let out a heavy sigh. "In his way."

Wow. Just capital W. O. W. Wow. She had nothing she could say to that, so instead she palmed Griff's face, his dark beard tickling her palms; turned him so he was looking at her again; and kissed him.

"You don't always have to be the one watching out for everyone," she said, her voice breaking. "You don't have to sit by the campfire in the dark alone."

He dropped a kiss on her forehead. "Is that a promise?"

"Yeah," she whispered back. "I guess it is."

And she wasn't just saying it to make him feel better. The truth of it was a warm, living thing inside her that filled her up with bubbles of hope until it was like she could float right out of the café. All of it came together the way answers always came to her in a rush of understanding that she couldn't deny. She loved Griff Beckett, and she wanted to be by his side facing off sabertooth tigers and anything else that went bump in the night—and she wanted to start now.

"Come on," she said. "We're going home."

He didn't ask. He didn't take time to think about it. He just took her hand and hauled her out of the booth with that look in his eyes that made her want to strip down in the middle of the café and have her wicked way with him right the fuck now. Since getting arrested for indecent exposure and lewd activities wasn't on her to-do list today, though, she kept it together—at least long enough to get almost all the way inside his front door.

Chapter Forty-Two

Three days later, Griff was in the shower letting the high-pressure jets set to peel-off-the-top-layer-of-skin beat against his back, working his way through two problems he couldn't find the answer to.

The first one was if it was finally the right time to tell Kinsey he loved her. She'd said she didn't want him to be alone at the campfire in the dark even after meeting his father. She wanted to protect him. He could bench-press her with one hand, but she had gone all feral on him.

He tilted his chin and let the water blast his scalp, a dumb-ass grin on his face. Thank God no one could see it. Still, he couldn't stop smiling, because Kinsey wasn't the type of person who would make that declaration if she didn't care—or, maybe, even love him back. Right? It was a question that made his balls shrink just to think about answering. The safe bet was to keep going like they were. If he didn't press the issue, she wouldn't have to answer, and he still had hope.

Dangerous fucking thing that was, an unknown variable that could make everything blow up in his face.

The second problem was what in the hell his dad was up to. There was no way he'd just happened upon them at Wakin' Bacon. Dad's idea of brunch was adding a splash of coffee to his whiskey. The man survived on spirits and spite—any actual food intake was gravy. So Griff wasn't buying the accidentally-ran-into-them excuse. His dad had been there—and on his worst behavior even for him—for a reason.

Griff took the bar of soap and scrubbed it across his chest, arms, and face, using more force than necessary as his frustration built up. Something was wrong, and it was just out of reach.

That's when it hit him—that throwaway line of his dad's about not getting attached. Holden Beckett had never given two shits about his or Morgan's love lives before. This time, though, his dad had sent out a warning.

In the next heartbeat, Griff was out of the shower and halfway across the bathroom. The water pelted the tile walls as he looked through one eye—the other one had soap in it—to text his dad.

GRIFF: *What did you mean by "don't get attached" the other day?*

DAD: *Have you sunk so low that you need a dictionary for that phrase?*

The man was never going to stop being an asshole, but that didn't mean he got to add Kinsey to his list of targets.

GRIFF: *Leave Kinsey alone.*

DAD: *I'm not the one you need to worry about.*

GRIFF: *Who?*

DAD: *She's a somewhat smart girl, but corporate secrets aren't meant to be leaked.*

And there was his dad, fucking with his head, but Griff knew Kinsey. She wasn't that person.

GRIFF: *Bullshit.*

His dad didn't bother to respond with another text, and Griff just stood there naked and dripping in the middle of his bathroom, staring at his phone screen, reading the exchange over and over again. Archambeau was on the verge of something big. Everyone in the industry knew it after their last stockholder call, but the specifics had stayed under wraps.

"Complicated."

That's how she'd described what was going on between them. She had to balance being the new person in the lab with dating the head of R&D at Beckett Cosmetics. Even if people only thought it was for a bet, there would be questions, concerns, avenues of research that would be denied to her—and that would be if it went the best way possible. Margins were tight, and even a hint of a corporate double cross or leaking company intellectual property could result in Kinsey losing her chance at the career she wanted.

But it was more than that. Kinsey's job was about more than just being her passion; it was her way of protecting her grandmother. That he could understand all too well. That's what someone did for those they loved; they protected them and those they cared about—even when it hurt, even when it was the last thing in the world the person wanted to do.

And he loved Kinsey.

He couldn't let Kinsey lose what she wanted in life if it was in his power to help protect her—and it was. The worst thing for her career if people were beginning to talk about corporate secrets being spilled was for her to be connected to a Beckett.

Griff dropped his phone onto the bathroom countertop and sat down on the edge of the tub. His big ass barely fit, but he didn't give a shit, because his legs weren't about to hold him upright at this moment. He sucked in a deep breath as his eyes watered—and it had nothing to do with the soap suds.

There was only one solution.

He slammed the heels of his palms against his eyes, trying to stop all of it, the emotions, the agony, the truth that was so obvious, he didn't need his eyes to see it.

Fuck.

This was the last thing he wanted—the very last thing— but it was the best thing for her, and that's all that mattered. After all, it wasn't like they were a real couple. This whole thing was one-sided. She was having fun. He had fallen in love. Now, all that was over.

He got up, grabbed the towel off the hook on the back of the door, and shut off the shower. The silence meant he could hear Kinsey's murder podcast, the one she listened to while doing yoga on his bedroom floor. The woman was chaotic good personified, sunshine wrapped around steel. Taking longer than necessary, he dried off and forced himself to figure out the next steps. Never in his life had his brain moved so slowly to put the pieces together.

Finally, when he had it together, he wrapped the towel around himself and walked out into his bedroom. Kinsey was laying on her back, her eyes closed, with her arms by her sides and her legs extended. If this had been the first time he'd found her like this, he would have assumed she was asleep, judging by her slow, steady breathing. He couldn't help but wish that she was, so he could delay this.

She cracked open an eye. "Well, hello there, good-looking." She opened both eyes and gave him a more considering look, her grin melting into a flat line. "Bad news?"

Griff affected a relaxed expression, forcing his mouth to curl upward as he leaned against the bathroom doorframe, and crossed his arms over his chest. "Actually, it's great news."

Kinsey sat up, her eyes wide in anticipation. "So spill."

Pain made his gut twist into a knot that nearly brought him to his knees, but he could do this—he had to—for her. "I got my cousins to agree that the dates we planned ourselves should count for the bet and so that's six dates out of the way. We're free."

She drew her knees up to her chest and wrapped her arms around them as she cocked her head to one side. "Free?"

"Yeah." He pushed through the agony squeezing his chest, determined to keep it light so she didn't feel bad.

"Griff, I can't—"

"Believe it's finally over?" he interrupted, needing to get this over with before he broke down in front of her. "I know. Don't take me wrong. It's been fun and all, but we both have regular lives to get back to."

Kinsey narrowed her gaze and stood up, placing her hands on her full hips. "That's a lot of words."

"Just excited, I guess." He shrugged, ignoring the rusty-ice-pick-worthy sharp pain in his side. "You know, there's a guy at the gym you might like; I can vouch that he's not a complete asshole." How he'd even gotten those words out, he had no idea. There was no one at his gym good enough for her. She was amazing. Smart. Funny. Ambitious. She deserved everything that she had coming to her, and he wasn't about to stand in the way of that. "Can I give him your number?"

"Sure," she said as her expression changed, going from concerned to utterly and completely neutral.

There. The confirmation he needed to see that all of this was just fun for her, that none of it mattered. She was just being a friend, helping him win a bet. He'd known it all along; he'd just been foolish enough to think he could change that.

Somewhere, his dad was laughing his ass off.

"Cool." It was anything fucking but. God, his whole body hurt; every inch of skin was on fire and his joints blazed. It was like he was only seconds from combusting.

She let out a long, shaky sigh and grabbed her phone and keys. "Congrats on winning the bet."

This fucking bet. He didn't give a shit about it and hadn't since he'd first heard her voice, but he had to play along for her. All of this had to be convincing. She wasn't the type of person who would leave someone who needed help, which was why she'd agreed to help him in the first place. She'd sat by him at the campfire, but now he had to let her go—for her own good.

"I haven't yet. Nash still has to fall in love, but I have ideas." God, he sounded like the biggest douche even to himself. "Thanks for doing this. I can't imagine it working with anyone else but you."

She shot him a tight smile. "I'll get out of your hair, then."

He kept his arms bolted to his sides so he wouldn't reach for her. "Let me know when I can return the favor."

Kinsey nodded, her lips smashed together, and then walked out of his front door and his life—exactly what he wanted to happen. Just like he wanted his legs to finally give out, because his heart had cracked wide open.

Chapter Forty-Three

Kinsey made it to her front door before everything clicked into place.

The bet.

The breakup.

The bullshit.

That. Fucker.

Whole body practically vibrating, she spun around and marched back into Griff's, throwing open the door without even knocking first, and marched into his bedroom.

He was sitting on the edge of the bed, still in just a towel, looking out the windows overlooking the city. He scrubbed at his cheek with the back of his hand, trying to be all smooth about it like no one would be able to guess he was upset. All the what-the-fuck annoyance left her body like a demon after an exorcism. Dammit. Why was she so frickin' soft when it came to this man? She closed her eyes and let out a breath, nearly giving in to that gooey feeling before yanking herself back to reality.

By the time she opened her eyes again, Griff was standing in the middle of his room, his whole demeanor changed. Gone was any hint of softness, replaced with that gruff exterior he wore like a shield. Well, too bad, because she knew better. Still, her gaze dipped down to the towel barely hanging onto his hips.

Focus, Kinsey!

Damn, that was hard when Griff was basically naked. He was all muscles, tattoos, and a really fucking bad attempt at a snarl. Ha! Like that was going to work on her—especially when he had the one piece of information she needed to figure out what in the hell had just happened.

"No," she said, looking him square in the face. "I don't accept that breakup."

"Too bad." He shrugged his broad shoulders and dialed up the intensity to four billion. "That's just the way it is."

Oh yeah, she was not buying this casual performance at all—not when he was holding on to one of her bright pink hair ties like a talisman. Nope. She had not gotten through one of the hardest pharmaceutical science programs in the country and landed a job at Archambeau because she gave up easily.

"You're more full of shit than my little brother when he said he had no idea how the weasel had ended up wearing our sister's favorite doll's clothes."

"I don't even know what that means," he said, shaking his head and looking down, as if to hide the beginning of a grin that she most definitely spotted.

"Doesn't matter," she said, determined to get to the bottom of this. "Tell me everything right now."

When he didn't, Kinsey stalked over to him, putting every bit of don't-fuck-with-me she had in the tank in each step. By the time she got to him, she was nearly to Avengers-level badassery—an effect that was ruined by being this close to him. One inhale and she was surrounded by the smell of him while being close enough to see the water droplets clinging to his chest. Her skin tingled with awareness that made her stomach dip, as if she was out driving and crested a hill going at just the right speed to give it the roller-coaster effect.

Griff let out a sigh that sounded like it came from the depths of his soul. "Something's going on at your work."

"Gavin's setting me up." The urge to touch Griff was too much to ignore. She brushed her fingers along the molecular-formula tattoo across his left pec, relishing his harsh intake of breath as he closed the distance between them. "I knew that giant donkey's behind was up to something."

Griff cupped her face, tilting her chin upward. "You're not surprised he's leaking and setting you up to take the fall?"

She snorted. No, it wasn't the sexiest sound she could make when she was this close to Griff, but it couldn't be helped. Gavin was about as opaque as handwoven lace and, while she didn't have proof yet, her gut didn't lie.

"The man has been on me like bees on a wildflower patch since I started at Archambeau, then all of a sudden he gives me this great opportunity to work with him on a top secret project that had a leak?" She took in a deep inhale of Griff's soap, the crisp scent unwinding the tension in her shoulders because it smelled like safety and home and love and acceptance. He didn't look at her and see Elle Woods on her first day at Harvard. He saw *her*, and it was the courtroom scene when Elle broke the whole case because she knew a person who'd just gotten a perm couldn't get their hair wet within twenty-four hours. He saw what she could do, not only what she looked like. He saw her. "But what does that have to do with dumping me?"

That's when Griff wrapped his arms around her, pulling her close so her cheek was against his chest, his arms around her like a protective shield. She started to relax against him when the reality of the situation hit, slamming her hard enough to knock her brain sideways. There was only one reason why he wouldn't tell her this before, why he'd make a decision for her without even giving her the opportunity to weigh in on something that impacted her life.

"You aren't serious. This is a shitty joke, right?" She pressed her hands against the steel wall of his chest and shoved, backing away from him. "You broke up with me because you didn't think I could handle the truth of the situation?" Heat sizzled across every nerve in her body, and her heart raced in her chest. "That you needed to protect little ol' me? You didn't think I deserved to know what was actually going on but instead went all caveman on me?" She ran through the scenarios at lightning speed, searching for that one option that would provide a different result, but every single one came back the same. "You big, tough man make all the decisions, save silly Southern blonde from the reality of the situation."

"Kinsey." He started toward her but stopped when she held up her hand. "That's not what I did."

"Fine. Then what's the real reason you broke up with me?"

There was a chance, a small one, that she'd missed something, that there was a logical explanation.

He shoved his fingers through his damp hair, enough barely contained frustration in the movement that she wouldn't be surprised if it tore out a good chunk of it. "Technically, we weren't really going out."

If she'd just gotten pecked in the eye by Meemaw's rooster, it wouldn't have hurt as much. She went from fire to ice in an instant, the shock of it numbing her, but she knew from experience that the sweet feeling of nothing wouldn't last long.

"Are you trying to gaslight me?" she asked, pressing a hand to her chest to make sure her heart was still beating, because it felt like the whole world had stopped. "We weren't going out? Are you still trying to pretend that all of this was about some bet? Do you really think I am that dumb?" The pain started, rushing over her like a wave of rusty spikes. "That I am three cups of flour short of a pan of drop biscuits away from understanding that we were falling in love?"

That she already had.

Best to keep that to yourself.

No shit, brain. I've had enough humiliation for one day, thank you very fucking much.

"It's for the best," he said, his words barely above a whisper. "Can't you see I'm doing this because I care about you?"

She laughed, because it was better than breaking down and crying in front of the man who she'd thought she'd known, who she still loved because life was a shit show. "That's bullshit. All of this is bullshit, patronizing bullshit. You don't get to make my decisions for me. You don't get to protect me by keeping me in the dark. You don't get to act like you know what's best for me and then wrap it in a cheap blanket called 'caring.' Really, Griff, if that's your definition of love, no wonder you're so certain you're going to win that bet."

"Kinsey," he roared, his voice like a thunderclap. "You don't understand."

"That's where you're wrong." Her voice broke on the last word as she fought to keep it together. "This dumb blonde understands it all too fucking well."

She stormed out of Griff's apartment and didn't stop until she was back in her bedroom. That was when she figured she'd start crying, but none of the expected tears fell.

Letting out a deep breath, she took a look around and

knew what needed to happen next. She went to the closet and got her suitcase. The clock was ticking on her job. There was no way she could stay with Morgan after what had just happened. Everything had gone to shit, and she was going to have to find a way—somehow—to explain to Meemaw that she'd ruined everything.

Chapter Forty-Four

Her room had gone dark, but Kinsey didn't bother to turn on the lights. The switch was way across the room, and she didn't have the energy or spirit to take the ten steps to get there. Damn. She was droopier than an overwatered house plant dripping water and turning yellow. Every part of her body was exhausted or ached or was both at the same time. She'd already tried to escape into the mother of all naps, but as soon as she closed her eyes, all she could see was Griff's face as he admitted what he'd done.

Nothing had hurt as much as the realization that he believed all the way down to the core of his being that what he'd done was right, that making decisions for her was the right thing to do, that he was protecting her by taking away her agency over her own life. She spun the scenarios of what could happen next in her head over and over and over like some kind of internet doomsday generator and couldn't come up with a single instance in which this had a happy ending.

Her phone, which was squished between her cheek and the mattress because that's how she'd landed when she'd all but melted onto the bed earlier, vibrated with an incoming call. It took more oomph than she thought she had in her to sit up enough to look at the screen. All the breath whooshed out of her as her stomach dropped to the building's sub-basement and landed with a splat by the huge furnace. Even presuming why the call was coming didn't make it any easier to answer, but Meemaw hadn't raised a wimp.

She swiped the screen to answer the call. "Hi, Gavin."

"You sound like you already know what I'm going to say."

She closed her eyes and let out a tired sigh. "I have a pretty good idea."

"I'm sure you do." He paused dramatically like some superhero-movie villain expecting her to break down and beg for mercy. When she didn't, he went on. "I just spoke with Jeannie from HR."

"On a Sunday?" The smarmy asshole had no consideration for other people. No wonder he'd made a connection with Holden Beckett.

"When something is this important, yes." Another dramatic and completely unnecessary pause. "Jeannie found your emails."

She started, surprise at his sheer audacity yanking her upright. "My what?"

"Your emails to Holden Beckett, offering up insider information on the Le Chardonneret serum."

This motherfucker. Bless his heart, she was gonna run him over with her brother's four-wheeler. "I never sent those."

"I know it's what you'd like everyone to believe, but Jeannie obtained the proof here in black and white."

"If it was me, why would I send the emails from my work account? That doesn't make sense." Because if she was doing that, it would be about the most boneheaded move she could make.

But getting into her emails would be child's play for her supervisor, who had all of her login information. A few choice key words in the emails that had supposedly come from her would make it simple for IT to do a search and report the findings to HR.

"I would have thought you'd be smarter than that, too—after all, I was really rooting for you to succeed here, which is why I picked you to be a part of the Le Chardonneret team," he said, almost making the lies sound like the truth. "Obviously, I made a mistake in trusting you. You're fired. I've spoken with Jeannie and while the final decision isn't mine, I've recommended that they not press criminal charges for industrial espionage against you. All of that ugliness will only hurt Archambeau's reputation when the gossip has finally started to die down because of Leigh's messy divorce—Jeannie agrees and so does Leigh."

And there it was. The key part of this whole play. He'd set her up as the patsy and had managed to get everything swept under the rug so no one looked too closely at what had gone down. It was brilliant in its evil simplicity.

"Really, it's a gift to you. Even a hint of this type of thing in the public sphere will sink any hope you have of finding employment in another lab," he went on, sinking the shiv a little deeper. "And to show how sorry I am about the error of my ways concerning your involvement in the product that was going to help Archambeau regain its position in the market, I'm turning in my resignation."

"Already have a place lined up in a country without an extradition treaty?" He may be acting the martyr by resigning, but it really was his only move.

"Please don't project your troubles on me, young lady," he said, his usual patronizing snippiness thick in his voice. "You're in it deep enough as it is."

While it was unlikely he'd get twenty years for industrial espionage, that was part of the sentencing guidelines, along with a ten-million-dollar fine. Considering that Le Chardonneret was likely to revolutionize the pharmaceutical cosmetics industry, he'd probably gotten at least that much for the information and would still be getting all the licensing fees from the other Archambeau patents he'd managed to get during Leigh's wreck of a divorce. The man was setting himself up to live out the rest of his days on a beach somewhere.

He was still talking when she hung up. Really, what was the point?

She was lying flat on her back on her bed staring at the ceiling, her brain so smooth and blank, it might as well have been pore-blurring primer, when Morgan came home an hour later.

Her best friend paused just inside Kinsey's bedroom door. "Who do I need to kill?"

Kinsey started to chuckle, but it came out as more of a groan. "Did you bring a pen and paper so you could make a list?"

"No," Morgan said, walking over to the bed and then flopping down onto it so she was laying on her back beside Kinsey. "I've binged *The Wire*; I know better than to take notes about a criminal conspiracy."

Despite everything, this time she really did laugh. It was a little too long and definitely too loud, but it emptied some of the weight pressing down on her. She rolled onto her side and flung her arms around Morgan, squeezing her tight. "I'm gonna miss you."

"Why?" Morgan asked, her words muffled by the death grip Kinsey had on her. "Where am I going?"

"You're not." Kinsey unwound herself from her best friend until she was staring back up at the ceiling. "I'm moving back home."

"Tell me everything," Morgan said in a tone that allowed for absolutely no dissention.

So Kinsey did. She shared all the work details, from the antagonism that had started on day one to the bullshit phone conversation. Then she explained all the stuff with Griff that Morgan already had a good idea about and then the big-Neanderthal-energy move he'd pulled.

"My brother is clueless, and that Gavin dude needs to be pushed out of a window," Morgan said once Kinsey was done.

"I can't disagree with any of that."

Are you sure? He fucked up, yes, but still—

Shut up, brain.

"So what will you do?" Morgan asked.

"Go home. Find another job somewhere and pay off my student loans so Meemaw doesn't lose her house when the bill comes due. Eat enough chocolate to forget your brother."

"There has to be something we can do," Morgan said. "You didn't do anything wrong."

Yeah, but life wasn't fair. If it was, her mom would have stayed. People wouldn't immediately decide after she opened her mouth that she was just a dumb Southern redneck because of her accent. And Griff would have never had the balls to make her decisions for her in the name of protecting her.

"I've barely worked at Archambeau for a month," Kinsey said. "I have no history. He made up the emails. What's the point? If I go quietly, then there's no publicity and I have a chance to stay in the industry. If I fight this, I won't stand a chance of getting another job in cosmetics."

"I don't want you to go."

Kinsey sighed, the world coming back and sitting on the middle of her chest again. "Me either, but there's not a way around it."

"I can talk to Griff, fix this."

Kinsey shook her head. Like brother, like sister—except that in her own way, Morgan was asking if it was okay instead of just assuming she knew best.

"There's nothing to fix," Kinsey said. "Sometimes you can love someone and it doesn't matter because it'll never work out. The whole thing was just a bet for him anyway. He didn't love me, because if he had, he never would have done this."

She'd run the scenarios. There was no happily ever after, and it hurt like getting run over by the zero-turn lawn mower. Clamping her jaw tight, she inhaled a sharp breath as she tried to keep the emotion clogging her throat from breaking free.

"I don't believe that," Morgan said.

"That's because the world wouldn't dare disappoint you."

"If that was true, you wouldn't be leaving," Morgan said with a frustrated growl that reminded Kinsey more than a little of Griff. "I'm gonna throw them both out the window."

Kinsey took her friend's hand and squeezed it as a tear slid free. "I love you, too."

Chapter Forty-Five

Griff's penthouse was booby-trapped.

Everywhere he looked were reminders of Kinsey. Her towel still on the hook on the back of his bathroom door. The cast-iron skillet sitting in the middle of his island because he couldn't stop making corn bread now. The painting they'd done on their date hanging up in his Lego room. Each one was a little pipe bomb waiting to go off. Desperate to get the fuck out of there, he packed a bag and headed out to Grandma Betty's house.

Gable House was a few hours outside of Harbor City and had a flock of attack geese guarding it. Grandma had been almost as much good chaos as Kinsey, knowing what she wanted and then just going for it. They would have loved each other.

Sitting out on the dock overlooking the lake and the island where he, Nash, and Dixon had spent summers competing to be the ultimate Beckett cousin, Griff took another swig off the bottle he'd grabbed from Grandma's collection.

The Old Pulteney single-malt scotch with its spicy sweetness wasn't his first choice, but it was getting the job done. Another few hours and his brain would be too scrambled to think about Kinsey.

Maybe.

Hopefully.

If he got fucking lucky.

"Aha," Morgan shouted, her triumphant squawk bouncing off the lake like a skipping rock. "I should have looked for you here first."

He sank down lower in the hot-pink Adirondack chair as if he could hide from his sister, the woman who'd been his shadow pretty much since she could walk. When their parents had fought, the two of them had gone down to the wine cellar to block out as much of the screaming as possible. After Mom died, he'd found Morgan down there asleep, wrapped up in a quilt Grandma Betty had given her. Eventually, it happened so often that he kept an extra sweatshirt down there to ward off the chill while he kept guard.

"What are you doing here?" he asked after another swig of scotch.

Morgan flopped down onto the deck and swiped the bottle from him. "Stopping you from making the biggest mistake of your life."

It was far too late for that. If only Mac had thrown that punch thirty seconds earlier, Griff never would have heard Kinsey giving the "what for" to half the gym. He wouldn't have fallen in love at first sound. He wouldn't be sitting here like an asshole getting drunk like his old man to block out the fact that the only way to take care of the woman he loved was to let her go.

"Did Kinsey send you?" He tried—and failed—to squash the note of hope in his voice.

"No." Morgan took a swig off the bottle and spent the next

thirty seconds coughing while waving off Griff's attempts to whack her on the back so she could catch her breath. "She's as stubborn as you are."

"Not stubborn." He snagged the bottle back. "Right."

Morgan rolled her eyes. "Now you sound like Dad."

"Fuck you." That was about as far from the truth as possible. He was nothing like his dad—current lack of sobriety aside.

They stared out at the lake in silence as the sky went from blue to a reddish orange and the moon became visible. The water lapped at the shore, a constant promise of change and a reminder that life kept moving no matter what, as Grandma Betty had told them when they were little. Gable House had been a refuge for all the Beckett kids when Grandma was around, a welcome respite from the complications at home. Here, things were simple, fun, peaceful. Even now, he felt at home here like he never had at the penthouse in Harbor City.

"Do you love her?" Morgan asked as the stars started twinkling above them.

Griff took a long drink, letting the scotch burn its way down his throat, wishing like hell it was enough to drown out the hurt in his chest. "I wouldn't have broken up with her if I didn't."

"You are the dumbest smart man I know," she said as she smacked his shin.

"Love you, too." He flicked her on the back of the head as the solar lights ringing the dock came to life, washing them in a soft glow.

"Does she know?"

He shrugged. "I agreed with Nash and Dixon that the important part was to show, not to tell."

"What in the world are you doing listening to those two about women?" Morgan tossed back her head and groaned, then shook her fist at the sky for good measure. "I mean, Dixon somehow miraculously found Fiona, but that really was a shock to the system. And Nash? Whew. I love the man, but if he keeps 'well actually-ing' women, he's gonna end up with one less ball."

"Is there a point you're trying to make?"

"Hello." She jumped up from the deck and whirled around to glare at him. "You have me! Your sister. Who is a woman and understands women."

"You aren't part of the bet," he grumbled.

"Withering" didn't begin to describe the look his sister gave him. Somehow she managed to express annoyance, disappointment, and disbelief all with one lift of an eyebrow and tilt of her head. "Again, because I am not Nash or Dixon. Oh my God, what were you guys thinking with that ridiculous bet?"

"Nash is up to something." There was a reason why he'd suggested the bet. Beyond everything else, Nash never did anything without a very specific end goal in mind. That Griff still hadn't figured out what it was just went to show the impact Kinsey coming into his life had had. "Why are you here, Morgan?"

She crossed her arms and stuck out her hip, dialing up the withering to ten. "To smack some sense into you before you go down the Holden Beckett path of lubricated assholery."

He flinched. "I'm nothing like our dad."

"Are you shitting me?" She laughed so hard, she had to wipe away tears after she got ahold of herself. "You're not a narcissist, but you sure did play the testosterone control-freak He-Man like Dad does with Kinsey, making decisions for her life without her input."

That was utter bullshit. He was nothing like his dad. The old man was controlling, snide, and telling everyone that he knew exactly what they were doing wrong and how to fix it. The perfect example of which popped into Griff's head without him even having to think about it.

"Like when he picked your college major for you and

scheduled all your classes your freshman year?" he asked.

"Or when you decided that you'd break up with Kinsey to fix things at her work rather than ask her how you guys could handle it together?" she shot back without hesitation.

He ground his molars together, pulverizing the enamel. No. That wasn't fair. "Her job makes her happy, and I just want her to be happy."

"No. You thought you knew what was best for her without asking," Morgan said, the sympathy in her tone doing nothing to lessen the one-two punch of her words that made a roundhouse from Mac in the ring seem like a love tap. "You're just as bad as the assholes who take one look at her, see a cute blonde with big boobs, and decide she's gotta have a box of rocks in her head."

Griff curled his hands around the ends of the arm of the Adirondack chair, his frustration making his grip tight enough that the wood bit into his palms. "I'm nothing like them."

"Yeah, well, maybe she should be the one to decide what makes her happy. And if you're lucky enough to have that be you in her life, don't fuck it up again by trying to make her decisions for her."

"I did what I did because Dad gave me a heads up what was going to happen to her at work if I didn't let her go."

"Oh my God, Griff. Why do you ever listen to that bitter old man?" She sighed and looked up at the stars that were so much brighter out here than in Harbor City. "Kinsey was wrongly accused of industrial espionage and fired, and it had absolutely nothing to do with you. Her boss was shady as fuck all on his own. Regardless, though, you broke up with her to prevent her from being fired and she got fired anyway, so how smart was that plan?"

Griff froze, his heart pounding in his chest. Kinsey must be devastated to lose her dream job. And then another thought slammed into him. "That asshole isn't threatening to have her arrested, is he?"

"No, he told her if she went away quietly, he would 'spare her the embarrassment.'" She added air quotes around the last bit with sarcasm, but Griff's mind was already running through possible scenarios.

If her boss had any real proof, he would most assuredly press charges. Which meant there was nothing irrefutable connecting her to the leak. Her boss was likely counting on Kinsey tucking her tail and running. Well, the guy didn't know his Kinsey if he thought that woman would ever back down from a fight. "I hope Kinsey gives him hell and sues him for wrongful termination and slander."

"Griff, I love you. I will always love you and be here for you, but I will never forgive you if you let my best friend go through all of this alone. You made matters worse, not better, when you decided to break it off with her. You left her to fight this trumped-up accusation alone, her support from you gone, and dealing with a broken heart on top of this shitty job. And now she feels she has no choice but to go back home, surround herself with people who love her and believe in her." She laid her hand on his shoulder and squeezed. "Believe me, all of this hurts now, but it's going to be so much worse when you wake up one morning and realize it's too late to fix any of it."

Morgan dropped a kiss on the top of his head, then turned and walked back toward Gable House, the motion-sensor lights turning on as she made her way back to their grandmother's home. Griff watched until the light closest to the back door went on and then clicked off, letting out the breath he always held until he knew someone he loved was safe.

Morgan was wrong. His dad hadn't given him bad advice. What had happened with Kinsey was for the best for her.

It had to be, or he'd made the worst mistake of his life by making her go.

Chapter Forty-Six

The next day, Griff was back home, shut up in his Lego room, looking at the three-thousand-plus individual bricks that would come together to make the Eiffel Tower, but he wasn't building. The one thing that had always kept one side of his brain busy while the other side worked out the six or seven problems he was dealing with at the moment wasn't working this time.

He looked over his shoulder at the painting of a man buried under a pile of online shopping delivery boxes from his date night across the harbor. The stupid thing was called *Unpack Your Feelings*, but despite the Paint and Sip guy's talk about excessive consumerism in place of actual connections, it would always be *The Kiss* to Griff.

One glance at that painting and all he could think about was the taste of cheap wine on Kinsey's lips when she'd kissed him silly. The drive home when it had taken everything he'd had to stop from pulling over in the lot of the outlet mall they'd passed, finding a dark corner to park in, and fucking her until they could both breathe again. He'd made it home to their building's garage instead, and Jesus, the way she'd looked when she'd come all over his hand. It was imprinted on his brain forever—as was the sound of her laugh, the way she loved to tease him, and the absolutely fucking impressive way her brain worked. She wasn't perfect, but damn, she was perfect for him.

Doesn't matter, asshole. She's gone, and that's the best thing for her, for her career, for her hopes and dreams and all the things that will make her happy.

He did what had to be done.

The buzzer on his front door went off. Dixon and Fiona were out at brunch with Nash and his little sister and brother, Bristol and Macon. Like him, Morgan had turned down the invite. No doubt she saw it as the perfect opportunity to come for round two of why Griff is an asshole—as if he didn't already know that.

"It's open," he hollered.

Griff spent the time it took her to get from the front door to his Lego room to put a few bricks together—that click was satisfying even when everything had gone to shit—so she wouldn't realize just how fucked in the head he was at the moment. She didn't need to see that. She was his little sister. He had to be the strong one for her.

"Good, you're alone," said someone who definitely wasn't Morgan.

Griff's head snapped up at the sound of his father's only slightly slurred words, and his shoulders tensed up as if waiting for a blow.

"What are you doing here?" Whatever it was, it wasn't good. It never was.

His dad smirked. "Saving your ass per usual."

He resisted the urge to throw the old man out of his place

because the rejection would mean he'd start focusing his bile on Morgan. Griff let out a deep breath and reminded himself he could take it.

"How's that?" Griff asked, forcing himself to sound as if his entire body wasn't on high alert and an adrenaline rush wasn't blasting through him.

"With this." His dad pulled out a thick nine-by-twelve tan envelope with Archambeau's logo in one corner and tossed it onto the table, sending Lego bricks flying. "Take it."

Griff's stomach clenched and his hands stilled. He knew exactly what was in that envelope without having to open it. This fucker. This absolute motherfucker.

He fisted his hands to stop from throwing the envelope at his dad. "Get that away from me."

"Don't go all high and mighty on me." Holden scoffed. "If you think all companies don't do this, then you're wrong."

"I don't need it."

"Oh, your little department has come up with its own product that is going to revolutionize the pharmaceutical cosmetics space?" his dad asked with enough snark in his tone to send Griff back to middle school when he'd brought home an A minus. "One that will take Beckett Cosmetics from a luxury boutique line to the most important cosmetics company in the world?"

"We're doing fine." They had their niche, and the company was wildly successful by any benchmark his dad wanted to cite.

"No. You're not." Holden started pacing the building room, his gait just the slightest bit wobbly, as he poked and prodded the completed Lego sets on display. "God, why are you like this? I spoiled you growing up; that's why you aren't hungry. This is for the best. You need to understand that, stop your whining, and take the damn formula. It's for your own good."

What. The. Absolute. Fuck.

And that's when it hit him. *Really* hit him.

He'd always known his father considered him a disappointment, but Griff had clung to some childish idea, he realized now, some fragile hope, that his mom hadn't left him all alone, that his dad loved him, he just had the absolute shittiest way of showing it.

Every single one of the horrible things his dad had ever said to him, Griff had just absorbed them all—and kept each spiteful thing inside, building a wall around himself so his doubts never escaped. So his fears and anger and frustration and heartache didn't ever leak through. Because the alternative was too scary to face.

It was the real reason he'd pushed Kinsey away.

If he hadn't, he would have had to admit once and for all that his dad had never loved him. Only a father who doesn't care about his son's happiness would tell him to lose the woman he loved. That was it, plain and simple. And his father hadn't hesitated.

His mind was whirring now, everything sliding into place like a puzzle it had taken him literally a lifetime to figure out. Griff loved Kinsey—and she loved him back. He was certain of it, even though she'd never said the words. All he had to do was imagine the look of joy on her face as she walked around his Lego room that was his happy space, the curve of her mouth as they teased each other over who made the best scratch biscuits, the tilt of her chin when she told his sister about his latest barbecue sauce creation. All things he'd never once witnessed with his father. Acceptance. Pride. Understanding.

All he had to do was look at that envelope sitting on his build table to know with absolute clarity that his father was incapable of any of those things with Griff.

And not because Griff wasn't perfect. Hell, Kinsey was

the first one to call him on his shit when he deserved it. But even then, even when her heart had to have been shattering after he'd broken things off with her, she'd told him some hard truths about his dad, but she'd not torn him down to do it.

His hands started to shake as he realized he might never get the chance to fight with Kinsey ever again. And he wanted a lifetime of anything with her. Good times or bad times, he'd love her through all of them—if she let him.

He was so focused on running through various scenarios of how to beg her forgiveness and get her back that he almost forgot his dad was still standing there.

"If you had an ounce of sense in you, you'd take that envelope and make something of your life, son," his dad repeated. "I only want what's best for you."

"Since when do you care about anyone's good beyond your own?" Griff asked, his voice barely above a whisper because he was holding on so tight to his emotions. If he let the volume go up, that could be the trigger that would set off everything else and a lifetime of anger and frustration and bitterness would roll out like hot lava.

"Don't talk to me like that, boy," Holden said, spinning around to try to stare down his son as if he were still a scared, vulnerable kid trying to deal with the loss of his mom. "I am your father, and everything I do, every push I give you, every hand up like this is to make you better."

"I'm good enough for Kinsey, and that's good enough for me," Griff replied, shaking his head. "Monthly brunch with Morgan and me is permanently canceled. You'll have to find someone else desperate for your approval you can tear down from now on." He looked his dad dead in the eyes before he could object. "Don't let the door hit your Nobel ass on the way out."

His father bristled, but Griff had already wasted too

much time listening to this man speak, so he got up and walked out of the room. Eventually, the old man would find his way to the door.

Right now, Griff had to win back the woman he loved, and that focus would require every last ounce of his attention.

He grabbed his phone from his pocket and opened up the Beckett cousin group chat.

GRIFF: *SOS MY PLACE ASAP*

Chapter Forty-Seven

KINSEY

Kinsey was packing up what was supposed to be her life in Harbor City two days later—alone, since Morgan had run out of the apartment a minute ago, saying she'd explain soon—when Meemaw's face popped up on her phone. Taking a deep breath and wiping away the tracks of the latest bout of tears—there was nothing she could do for her red nose and puffy eyes—she swiped the screen, accepting the FaceTime call.

Meemaw brought the phone close enough to her face that Kinsey got a good look up her grandma's nose. If she'd been in Meemaw's living room right now, no doubt she'd wrap her fleshy arms around her oldest grandchild and pull her in tight until all Kinsey could smell was Dove soap and warm butter. Home was the last place Kinsey wanted to go right now, but at least she'd be surrounded by family who loved her and believed in her.

"Bless your heart," Meemaw said before clicking her tongue against the roof of her mouth. "You need sweet potato pecan pie."

"I do." She hadn't been lying when she'd told Griff that first time at Wakin' Bacon that it fixed everything.

Meemaw peered around Kinsey. "So you were serious in that text that you were coming home."

Kinsey flipped her camera so Meemaw could see the half-filled suitcases open on her bed. "I can't wait to see y'all again."

Meemaw's bark of laugher bounced around the otherwise quiet room, followed by a series of coughs. "Don't try lying to me; I've been able to spot you out on fibs since you were a kid."

Kinsey swapped the camera back and did her best to look like she hadn't just been caught in a whopper. "It's not a lie. I do miss you."

"I miss you, too, but that's not the same as saying you can't wait to come home. You have your dream job in your dream city. That's a lot to walk away from just because. What's the real reason?"

She tried to obfuscate, but Meemaw wasn't having it. She interrupted each time she tried to sugarcoat her humiliation at work and with Griff until Kinsey gave in and just fessed up to it all.

"So the woman who owns the company knows what a slimy toad this boss of yours is," Meemaw said. "But you don't want to take this up the chain and fight it?"

"I can't." Shouldn't. Wouldn't. Whatever. It wouldn't lead to anything beyond her being labeled an industry pariah because Gavin was right, no one would believe her. "I'm the new person in the lab. I'm younger than everyone else. I sound like I sound and people assume I'm dumb because of it."

Meemaw snorted in that dismissive way only grandmas could do that said both that the person was full of it and still loved. "That doesn't make a bit of difference here or there; people are gonna think what they're gonna think. You can't control that. All you can do is live your life and fight for your dreams."

"I already sent in my resignation to HR." And then she'd cried into her pillow that somehow managed to smell like Griff even though he'd never used it.

Her grandma shrugged. "So unsend it."

"It doesn't work that way."

"Not if you don't try, it doesn't. I've never known you to not go one hundred percent toward what you wanted. Why are you stopping now?"

Kinsey sank down onto her bed in the middle of a pile of folded T-shirts that tumbled over.

Hello, symbolism of my life right now.

She let out a sniffly sigh and said, "It's just easier."

"And you've always liked the easy way out. Yep. That sounds like the Kinsey Dalton I know," Meemaw said in that tone that every Southern woman knew sounded sugary sweet but carried an underlying dose of sass. "Graduating from high school at fifteen was easy."

Meemaw had stayed up late with Kinsey, helping her study for tests and making flashcards. Kinsey had worked her ass off, not so much because she loved learning about Jane Austen and macroeconomics but because she knew what she'd wanted and nothing was going to stand in her way.

"Getting your degree and being at the top of your class in undergrad, that was easy," her grandma went on.

Kinsey blinked back tears, remembering how many calls she'd had with Meemaw about being in the dorm rooms when she was barely old enough to drive, telling her that everything was fine, even though she was lonely and isolated while everyone in her classes was going out. She'd studied so much because it was the only thing she could do, especially when her Pell Grant barely covered the essentials.

"Going on to grad school, finding your dream job, doing what you love despite the odds stacked against you as a poor kid from rural Virginia with no connections, that was all easy," Meemaw said. "Yep. When I think Kinsey Dalton, I definitely think of someone who takes the easy route."

No one could tell a person to pull their head out of their ass quite like a grandma, but that didn't mean Kinsey was ready to give in quite yet. Anyway, all of this was different. "You don't understand."

"Young lady," Meemaw said in *that* tone, "I understand exactly. You got so caught up in trying to prove everything to everyone that you forgot to just live your damn life already. Plus, you got your heart broken by a man who is a jerk."

Kinsey's chest tightened, and it was all she could do to talk past the emotion clogging her throat. "Griff is not a jerk."

"Really? He sure sounds like one. Who wants someone who occasionally messes up by trying to protect those he loves?"

She looked up at the ceiling and let out a shaky breath because her grandma wasn't wrong and part of her knew that. Of course, that didn't make the fact that Meemaw was going at it with both barrels today any easier to hear.

"What he did was wrong," Kinsey managed to croak out.

"Sometimes people do the wrong thing for the right reasons, and God knows none of us are perfect." Meemaw gave her a gap-toothed smile. "Sounds to me like he could have made a mistake out of desperation. Some people think it's their mission in life to take care of those they love, and sometimes they do that in ridiculous ways. Sometimes they think it's their mission in life to prove to the whole world they're not the person everyone thinks they are even if in the end, the only opinion that matters is their own." Meemaw shot her a don't-miss-the-goodness-of-the-words-being-said look. "He loves you and he messed up. Do you really want to walk away without giving him the chance to fix it—if he deserves it, that is?"

But that was the catch. "He doesn't love me."

Meemaw straight-up cackled. "Are you sure about that?"

Sure, he'd said it once, but that was in the heat of the moment, and he'd never mentioned it since. All he'd done was let her touch his Legos—not a euphemism—cook for her, drop what he had going on to see her, taken her dancing even though she was horrible, and made her feel like she was the only person in the world. And he listened to her. Really listened. Asked questions like her answers were the most important thing he'd hear that day, too.

She gulped as the truth smacked her right in the jaw harder than that guy who'd knocked Griff on his ass when they'd met. "Shit."

"Watch your mouth, young lady," Meemaw said with more than a little bit of warning in her tone, "but yes, shit."

She sat straight up, her heart racing as possible ways this could work out ran through her head at light speed. "I can't believe I missed that."

"No one's a genius about everything. Not even you, sugar," Meemaw said with a wink. "Now you've got to figure out what you're gonna do about it. Do you love him?"

Kinsey nodded, too excited and panicked and oh-my-God-what-happens-next freaked out to use actual words.

"You'll figure it out; you always do," her grandma said. "Love you."

She was still processing all of what Meemaw said ten minutes after they'd ended the call when the doorbell rang. No doubt Morgan must have forgotten her keys when she'd run out of the penthouse so fast.

The last person Kinsey expected to see was the duo outside the door when she flung it open: Leigh, looking every inch the CEO of a cosmetics company, and Billie, with her always present iPad, stylus at the ready, stood in the hall.

"Hi there," Leigh said. "I'm so sorry for just arriving on your doorstep without notice."

"What she means," Billie said with a grin, "is that you didn't think you could get away from us that easily, did you?"

Kinsey pressed a hand to her belly, which had flipped, flopped, and sank down to her toes. "I know how it looks, but there's no way I would have sold secrets."

"Honey, we know," Billie said with an eyeroll. "Gavin's sitting in a dingy room talking to a detective as we speak. How delicious is that?"

Leigh looked like she could barely hold in a triumphant "hell yeah," but she managed to keep it together. "Could we come inside? We have a lot to discuss, including the fact that I expect to see you back in the lab tomorrow. We have a lot of work to do before launching Le Chardonneret."

Chapter Forty-Eight

GRIFF

There was no other explanation than that the Beckett DNA had ridiculous ideas written into it. First, the bizarre Last Man Standing bet, and now the completely random cringe ideas for how to show Kinsey that he was a reformed Neanderthal.

"I've got it." Nash stopped pacing across the living room and turned to face the attendees of the emergency Beckett family meeting. "Bring her to an Ice Knights game and then propose while you're both being shown on the Jumbotron."

Griff let his head thunk against the wall he was leaning on. And to think he'd asked everyone here to help because he'd thought *his* ideas to win Kinsey back were bad. At this rate, she was going to be back in Virginia before he even got a sliver of a plan put together.

"You shouldn't be left alone unsupervised," Morgan said.

Nash flipped her off. "Market research shows that women love dramatic results."

"Yeah," Morgan shot back. "From their moisturizer, not

their personal life."

"She's right—that was a shit idea, Nash," Dixon said.

"Well, what's your plan?" Nash asked.

Dixon straightened up on the couch, a confident smile on his face. "She didn't run screaming when you showed her your Lego room, right?"

Yeah, considering she'd given him the blow job of a lifetime in the Lego room, the only screaming had been from him in his head as he came.

"I'll take your silence as a no," Dixon said, waiting until Griff nodded in the affirmative to go on. "What you need to do is build a Lego sculpture of her and present it as a token of your love."

Everyone in the room was silent as they all stared slack-jawed at Dixon.

Fucking A, Griff was so screwed. Why in the hell had he called together these knuckleheads? Oh yeah, because he was even worse at it than they were. Hell, maybe Kinsey really should stay away from his ass.

"And you're the one running the billion-dollar cosmetics company?" Morgan asked, the question so rhetorical that if she were to text it, it wouldn't have a question mark at the end.

"What?" Dixon shrugged. "It's unique and meaningful."

Morgan crossed her arms and stared down at Dixon on the couch, a mix of disappointment and disgust on her face. "So you're gonna do that for Fiona's next birthday gift?"

The tips of Dixon's ears went red. "We don't have that kind of relationship connection to Legos."

"And you're not entirely an idiot," Griff said.

"That too," Dixon agreed.

After that, the only sound was Nash's footsteps on the hardwood floor as he paced from one end of the living room to the other. It sounded like a countdown to Griff, each step another tick of the clock marking the moments until it was too late.

Morgan let out an exhausted sigh and looked from Nash to Dixon to Griff. "You three do realize that Kinsey is just across the hall, right?"

Griff nodded. "Yeah."

"And the best way to fix this is to actually talk to her. You know, communicate? With words?" Morgan sounded like a woman who had been trapped in a car with small children for twelve hours and was at her breaking point. "That's when you tell her what needs to be said." She held up a finger, shockingly not the middle one. "First, that you love her." Another finger. "Second, that you fucked it all up and are sincerely sorry." Now she raised her middle finger. "Third, that you want to spend the rest of your life with her maybe making little makeup scientist babies."

"I'm quitting," Griff said, the words coming out even faster than he could think them up.

Morgan's face dropped and she flopped down, defeated, onto the couch next to Dixon. "Just like that? You're not even going to try to fix things with Kinsey?"

"Beckett Cosmetics," he clarified. "I never really wanted to work as a chemist. That's Kinsey's passion. It just seemed easier to follow that path than to fight what Dad had planned for me and have him turn his attention to Morgan." He pushed off the wall, his shoulders feeling lighter than they had in a decade. "I quit, effective immediately. Sheva is a phenomenal number two, and she'll be even better when she's in charge of everything."

She would. The woman was smart, innovative, and had a passion for her job that Griff had never had.

He started toward the door, words already partnering up to form sentences and then paragraphs and then a speech for Kinsey, explaining everything he'd done, everything he was gonna do, and everything he hoped could be in their future together.

"Where are you going?" Nash asked, a deep V of worry forming between his eyes.

He grunted and shot them all a where-do-you-think look and pointed in the general direction of Morgan's apartment. Really, his cousins were incredibly dense sometimes.

On the way, he grabbed the folder with Archambeau's logo on it. Even if she didn't give him a second chance, she deserved proof to share with her boss's boss that she hadn't stolen anything.

No one said anything as he marched to his front door, more than ready for the rest of his life to start right now. They came back to themselves when he opened the door, and by the time he was closing it, the decibels in his living room were at true Beckett levels.

He was almost to Kinsey's front door when it swung open and she walked out with Archambeau's CEO and another woman. They were all smiles and excited chatter. At the same moment, his own front door blasted open and Morgan, Nash, and Dixon all came rushing out, still hollering about the fact that he was quitting the family business.

Kinsey jerked to a stop in the middle of the hall, her blue eyes wide. "You're quitting?"

This was when all those words and sentences and paragraphs and the whole damn speech was supposed to come out of his mouth, but old habits died hard, and all he could do was grunt. The light in Kinsey's eyes dimmed, and she sighed, her attention dropping to the floor as she turned and stepped toward the elevator.

Way to go, fucknuts. Get out the words before she's gone.

"I love you," he said, his voice booming in the hall.

Okay, that's what it had sounded like in his head. To his ears, it all came out in one loud growl of "Iloveyou," each word squished together.

"All right then," Morgan said, putting a hand on Dixon's and Nash's backs and shoving them toward the elevator. "Everyone get in the elevator. Come on." She hit the Down button once, twice, and a third time as she yanked Nash closer to her side. "No, Nash, you cannot stay and watch." She used her free hand to swipe Dixon's phone. "No, you are not allowed to record this." In a motion so fast, it should have scared Griff if it hadn't been done on his behalf, Morgan's glare at their cousins turned into a friendly expression as she smiled at the women beside them in front of the elevator. "Hi, you must be Leigh and Billie. Kinsey told me all about you and you both sound like the kind of women I'd love to go have a glass of wine with *right now*."

"That sounds marvelous," Leigh said. "It's been a helluva week."

"Lots of drama," the other woman said. "I agree."

"Excuse me, Leigh." Griff's words stopped her, and she turned to face him. He shoved the envelope into her hands. "Proof my shit father conspired with Kinsey's boss to sell your new formula. I did not open the envelope and want no part in stealing our way to bigger profits."

Both ladies' eyes narrowed on the envelope as Leigh reached to take it. "Thank you. I know a police officer who would be delighted to receive this information."

Griff nodded. His father dug that bed; he could damn well sleep in it now.

"We need a bottle of rosé stat." Morgan hooked an arm through the crook of Nash's and Dixon's arms in a move that gave the appearance of there's-no-escape-trust-me. "I know the best wine bar, has this great PB&J rosé from a winery owned by one of the Ice Knights, so we'll have to dodge some of the puck bunnies, but it will be worth it."

Finally, the elevator dinged its arrival. Morgan started

shoving people inside as soon as the doors opened, then she planted herself in the front of the bay, blocking anyone from exiting.

"Now kiss and make up," she hollered as the doors closed.

Now *that* was his sister. And he'd thought he had to watch out for her? It sure looked like the tables had turned.

"You love me?" Kinsey asked, her attention still on the floor. "Since when?"

He crossed over to her in two strides but lost his nerve to reveal everything at the last second. He shoved his fists deep in his pockets and considered his next words. It wasn't that he didn't want to tell her everything, beg her forgiveness, but he had bottled up his words for decades. He was worried if he ever truly let all his emotions out—neither he nor Kinsey were prepared for that.

"Since when?" he repeated, his chest aching with hope and fear and love, so much love. "Forever. I've loved you forever."

There, that summed it up nicely. Forever was a long time.

But Kinsey didn't seem impressed, the corners of her mouth turning down farther.

He rushed on to add, "Since you showed up at the gym."

There, that had to be enough. But she seemed even less excited by this revelation.

"Okay. Well, thank you for sharing," she said and turned to go back into the apartment.

Griff's pulse was hammering so fast, he thought he might vomit. Or pass out. Or both.

Jaysus, this was going badly. And it was all his fault. He knew what he wanted to say, but he'd never been good with words. He was terrified he was going to screw things up, although he had no idea what would be worse than losing Kinsey. What if he told her everything and she couldn't respect a man who let his father twist him up so much that he dumped her? If only he could find the right words to tell her how he felt.

Wait, why was he standing here worrying about how he could talk to Kinsey? He never had a problem talking to this woman. He just had to open up and let her in.

And like a tsunami, the words came to him.

"I've loved you since I heard you at the gym solving everyone's problems and putting Eggsy's friend Wade in his place without breaking a sweat. I loved you when you tried to dance and I realized that there were people in this world with negative rhythm—really, it was impressive."

It was like he'd turned on a faucet that had been rusted shut for years but when it came to Kinsey, he wasn't sure there was such a thing as too many words. "I loved you when you told me everything I never realized I wanted to know about maple syrup, shared your meemaw's secret biscuit with a *slab* of butter recipe with me, and explained to my neighbor why everyone has a green thumb, they just have to find plants that need their kind of loving. I've loved you since the first time I touched you, since the first time I saw you bite down on your bottom lip, and since the first time you looked at me and asked for more."

He dropped his hands when her bottom lip started trembling, and his gut dropped. He was fucking this up, but he couldn't stop now. "I've loved you since you suggested I should spend a night with my Legos instead of you just because you knew how excited I was to win that eBay bid." Now his eyes were getting watery. *Shut up, numb nuts. Shut. Your. Mouth.* "I've loved you since you convinced me to watch *Glow Up* with you and then didn't stop saying 'ding dong' for the next two hours straight. I've loved you since we lost three hours we could have spent making love debating the pros and cons of cotton versus linen sheets." He sucked in a breath, trying to replace all the oxygen from that rush of words, a desperate sense of dread sinking into him as her first tear fell and then another and another. "I've loved you since that moment just before I got knocked out in the gym—and I've spent the past months scared to death I'd never be able to find the words to convince you to give me a chance and love me back even a fraction of as much as I love you. So yeah, I've loved you forever and I always will."

She wiped her cheek with the back of her hand. "You can stop now."

"I can't yet. Please." She deserved to know everything and honestly, he couldn't stop the words from coming even if he'd wanted to. They were pressing against his chest, begging to be let loose and freed. He took a deep breath and rushed on. "I fucked it up. I am fucked up. You were right—my daddy issues are bigger than Harbor City. I see that now. And I tried to show you I love you the way I thought my dad showed he loved me—by making decisions about our relationship that I had no business making on my own in the name of caring. But now I see it all. That man has never loved me, and nothing I do is ever going to change that. I know because that's not how you treat people you love. You understand their needs and accept their limitations and take pride in their accomplishments. You lift them up; you don't tear them down. All things you've taught me. When my mom died—"

His voice cracked with emotion, and the tears in his eyes started rolling down his cheeks, but Griff wasn't going to stop; he would never stop giving this amazing woman all of his words. He took her hands, lifting them up and pressing them against his chest where his heart was beating a million miles an hour.

"When my mom died, I couldn't deal with the prospect that she'd left me all alone. So I've spent the last two decades convincing myself that my dad's hateful words were hiding his love. He pushed me because he cared. But I was wrong, and I'm ready to deal with that now. I'm ready to really love someone, learn to love the right way—if that person is you, Kinsey. I can't promise I won't fuck up again, but I'm a fast learner and I know I can learn how love is really supposed to look, if you'll just give me a chance. Please tell me I haven't fucked things up too much and you'll forgive me. I swear I'll keep talking until I find the right words to convince you—"

God, her tears were free-flowing now. He'd ruined it, ruined it all with all these words. But he couldn't stop now. He was just rusty at sharing his feelings, that's all, because he refused to accept he was too late. He just needed to find the right words. "Please don't give—"

"Shut up, Griff," she said, her voice breaking as she pulled her hands free and took a step back away from him. "That's more than enough words."

And that's when he knew with the sense of certainty that only comes with disaster that he was too late.

Chapter Forty-Nine

Kinsey never thought she'd want to have Griff stop talking. He had a great voice, all low and rough, that sent shivers of anticipation down her spine. This time, however, she'd heard enough.

She sniffled, annoyed that she was still crying, but there was just too much emotion for her to be able to put it away. It had to get out. "We only met because of a toilet in the kitchen."

He blinked a few times. She couldn't blame him. It was a weird start to their story, but that's what it was. Their story.

"And Morgan offered up her apartment," she went on, trying to wrap her brain around how one random decision had changed her life so significantly. "Then I met you and you called me a disaster."

"I meant that I was the disaster," Griff rushed in. "I was already in love with you, and you were engaged—or so I thought."

"Stupid Todd," she muttered, taking his hand because she just couldn't go another second without skin-to-skin contact with the man she loved.

"Exactly." He nodded, rubbing the pad of his thumb across her knuckles while looking down at their hands as if he couldn't believe he was touching her again. "Stupid Todd."

"And then there was the bet and the dates and the best sex of my life." Honestly, her toes were about to curl in her shoes at the memory of what he could do with those big hands of his, not to mention everything else. "I thought you'd seen me and respected me."

He stepped closer until there was no space between them, curling his other arm around her and resting his chin on the top of her head, wrapping her in him. "I did and I do."

"Then why did you decide that you had to break up with me?" she asked, barely getting the words out past the raw hurt and undeniable hope clogging her throat.

His chest vibrated under her cheek with the power of his frustrated growl. "My dad said that I should let you go so you didn't get arrested. Without someone to sell the formula you stole in your bed, it would be harder to prove the theft. It was a mistake. But if I admitted his words weren't meant to help me, I'd have to face the fact that none of his words were ever meant to help, Kinsey. And I wasn't ready to face that. I'm sorry. Can you give me another chance?"

It was all she needed to hear. The truth of it settled over her, warm and sure and as comfortable as a hand-knit blanket on a cold night. Her heart ached for the little boy who just wanted his dad's love. God, she hoped that man got stuck in a dark alley with her someday. Still, she wasn't about to let Griff off without a stern warning.

She pushed against his chest, enough so that while they were still pressed together, she could look up at him, let him see on her face the seriousness of her words. "If you break my heart again, I'm going to go find Mac and slip him a twenty to knock you on your ass in the ring again."

"Knowing Mac, he'd do it for free." He dipped his head down and brushed his lips across hers, teasing her and making promises she knew he could deliver on. "No heartbreaks. No acting like a Neanderthal and taking your agency. No being a dick—well, at least not often."

One of the things she'd always loved about science was the certainty, at least on one level. If a person mixed vinegar and peroxide, they'd get parachutic acid. Blend bleach with rubbing alcohol and the result would be chloroform that could kill a person if they inhaled too much. Combine Griff Beckett and Kinsey Dalton and there were fireworks that would last a lifetime.

She raised herself up on her tiptoes, bringing her lips within inches of his earlobe. "Will you still be communicating in the form of grunts and growls?" The low rumble of his answer turned her knees to jelly. "Thank God." She kissed and nipped her way down the corded column of his thick, tattooed neck. "So did you really quit your job?"

He nodded, his hands moving to cup her ass. "Yeah."

"What are you going to do?"

"Start a line of barbecue sauces," he answered without hesitation. "Don't suppose you know of anyone who will help me taste test?"

"I might." She kissed the exposed skin at the neck of his T-shirt. "She will expect payment, however."

"I *am* a billionaire." He grabbed her ass with both hands and pulled her close enough that there was no missing *all* of the assets he had.

"Oh, she doesn't want cash," she said, anticipation and lust licking every inch of her skin as Griff was no doubt about to do very soon. "Do you remember that thing you did the first time we had sex in your shower?"

She didn't have to say anything else. Griff picked her up, and she wrapped her legs around his waist as his mouth crashed down on hers in a kiss that knocked her brain sideways and took all the air out of her lungs. Yeah, it was that good. They were halfway down the hall to his door before she had gathered her wits.

"Griff Beckett, you're so bad."

"Babe, you are about to find out exactly how bad I can be."

Then he started whispering in her ear all the things he was going to do as soon as they got in the shower, and she'd never been more glad in her life that she'd skipped panties under her leggings. The less that was between them, the better. Oh hell, who was she kidding. She was about to be as naked as the time she'd agreed to a dare to streak down Main Street back home, and Kinsey couldn't be more excited.

"I love you, Griff."

"Kinsey, I will love you forever."

She'd run the scenarios in her head at lightning speed, and she had absolutely no doubt that he would—that they both would.

Acknowledgments

Thinking up a book is the easy part. The hard part is yanking it word by word out of your head and onto the page. It would be pretty unbearable if I wasn't surrounded by amazing people who make that process seem like fun. A huge thank you to the entire Entangled team, my editor Liz, Stacy the copyediting genius and a million other folks who make this all happen (special shout outs to Jessica, Rikki, Amy and Bree). Thank you!!! Another huge thank you goes to my family who are used to me mumbling to myself and speed typing while holding conversations with people who don't exist off the page. I'm sure they'll have lots of "you think your mom is weird" stories to tell their friends at parties. And, of course, none of this would happen if it wasn't for the readers who have fallen in love with the people of Harbor City right there with me. Thank you for reading. Thank you for leaving your honest reviews. Thank you for being a part of Romancelandia where happy endings are guaranteed.

Xoxo,
Avery

About the Author

USA Today and *Wall Street Journal* bestselling romance author Avery Flynn has three slightly wild children, loves a hockey-addicted husband, and is desperately hoping someone invents the coffee IV drip. She lives with her family (including the dogs Gravy, Pepper, Tater Tot, and Eggnog, who are either sleeping or guarding the house from squirrels as well as the cat, Dwight, who is totally plotting world domination) outside of Washington, D.C. She loves to chat with readers. You can email her at avery@averyflynn.com and join her reader group, The Flynnbots, on Facebook!

averyflynn.com

Discover more Amara titles...

THERE'S SOMETHING ABOUT MOLLY
a novel by Christina Hovland

Molly Princeton is a dating coach who's great at making matches for others, but she hasn't met her Mr. Right. When a matchmaking competition requires couples to compete, Molly turns to Gavin Frank, her nemesis, to help her out. She gets a partner for the competition, and he gets his nagging mother off his back. As things heat up between them, Molly is unsure of her next move. And Gavin finds Molly difficult to resist.

WILD IN CAPTIVITY
a Captivity, Alaska novel by Samanthe Beck

If big city lawyer Isabelle Marcano has to be marooned in Alaska to close a major deal, she's going to take full advantage of the seemingly unending supply of hunky men. Or that's the plan until her client, sexy bush pilot Trace Shanahan, introduces her as his fiancée to hide the fact he's selling his stake in the small-town airfreight business. Now her fantasies of hot lumberjack sex are out...or are they?

IT'S RAINING MEN
a novel by Julie Hammerle

After my single best friend got engaged, I decided to drown my loneliness in booze. Several Old Fashioneds later, I woke up to thirty-nine text messages. I had apparently offered myself up in marriage to every guy in my phone... Thirty-seven rejections later, two guys have actually said yes, and I'm left to choose between Rob, my old high school crush, and Darius, a flashy news reporter. Let's see if happily ever after is meant for me...

Made in the USA
Middletown, DE
17 October 2021

50231006R00169